Demons, Dolls, & Milkshakes

NELSON W. PYLES

Burning Bulb
PUBLISHING

Demons, Dolls, & Milkshakes
By **Nelson W. Pyles**

Burning Bulb Publishing
P.O. Box 4721
Bridgeport, WV 26330-4721
United States of America
www.BurningBulbPublishing.com

Cover designed by Jeanette Andromeda.

Second Edition.

Paperback Edition ISBN: 978-1-948278-09-6

Printed in the United States of America

smoking goth gal with a black belt in armchair psychology, severed limbs (and nipples), random possessions, a smoking hot red-head, and buckets and buckets of blood. I have done nothing but chuckle, right to the last page."

–Myk Pilgrim-author/co-host of Deadflicks

"DEMONS, DOLLS, & MILKSHAKES is a satisfying blend of comedy and horror, as original and mesmerizing as its title."

–Lou Tambone, writer/editor of THE CYBERPUNK NEXUS

"Nelson W. Pyles's DEMONS, DOLLS, & MILKSHAKES is a big 'ol barrel of screams and laughs, shaken together to create an absurd stew you could imagine James Gunn directing. Watching Kat extricate herself from the messes Stitch created was an exciting, propulsive activity that had me tearing through pages to see what happened next."

–Paul Michael Anderson,
author of BONES ARE MADE TO BE BROKEN

FOREWORD
By Daniel Foytik

My friend Nelson W. Pyles is a talented storyteller whose stories often focus on longing - one of the most powerful motivations in our lives.

Whether it's longing for power, to impress the one we fancy, to fix a mistake, or just for simple acceptance, it makes us do things we might otherwise not. Longing is often the driving force behind our creative endeavors, but just as often, it leads us down dark paths and makes us compromise our principles in ways we later regret.

Stories about longing and the pursuit of power certainly aren't uncommon. However, the magic required to create an engaging tale that both entertains and subconsciously examines the reasons we make the choices we do - why our humanity and our desires come into conflict - is a rarer thing. This magic is what you'll find in the book you hold.

This new edition of Demons, Dolls, and Milkshakes (how can you not love that title, by the way), is a finely-tuned story machine. Out of respect to fans of the original novel, it remains largely unchanged — staying faithful to the first edition as a powerful tale of longing and desire gone wrong - but it's just honed and updated enough to make it a really fun revisit. And if you're coming to this tale for the first time, you're in for a real treat.

This is a horror story with a surprising amount of heart, something that will actually come as no surprise to fans of Nelson's work. He loves his characters, and that shows in the way he delves deep into their motivations, allowing them to become relatable in a way many others cannot. True to life, we're presented with flawed characters who struggle to make the right choices and more often make the wrong ones - and face the consequences. Nelson has the courage to show there sometimes isn't a way back from choosing poorly, while many other authors don't.

While there are truly terrifying and disturbing moments in Demons, Dolls and Milkshakes, it isn't just a dark ride into the shadows; you'll find substance, and thought-provoking situations that will make you examine your own decisions and motivations.

The story presents us with a slice of life in modern America, where society and peer pressure make a young teen boy named Martin unleash a powerful demon – one who seems to be in his thrall. We also meet Kat, a self-reliant woman with style and spunk who manages to handle amazing events with strength and wit. She's relatable, real, and truly jumps off the page.

And, of course, there's Stitch. But I'll stop short of giving away anymore of who and what Nelson has in store for you, and just say you can expect to have a soft spot for this sighing, frustrated demon by the end of the book. Nelson never forgets that we're dealing with a demon, though, and despite how charming and likeable that demon may be, he's still, well, a demon.

So make a milkshake or conjure up your own demon, and prepare to be entertained, moved, changed, and of course, scared by this wickedly entertaining, dark, and very funny story.

Daniel Foytik
Producer of the PARSEC Award-winning podcast
The Wicked Library
Producer/ Creator:
The Lift and The Private Collector

AUTHOR'S INTRODUCTION

This version of Demons Dolls and Milkshakes is nearly identical to the original version with a few exceptions. The most obvious is the new cover, which I absolutely love. It was designed by the extraordinarily talented Jeanette Andromeda who also did the cover for SPIDERS IN THE DAFFODILS as well as amazing art for The Wicked Library and The Lift podcasts.

Another difference is a much tighter edit. The book was originally released in two thousand thirteen, but was completed in two thousand eleven. A lot of things have been written since then and frankly, I'm not the same writer I was; I'd like to think I'm better. In rereading the book to see what if anything could use some polish, I decided to send it out to some writer friends of mine to give it a fresh set of eyes.

And thus began the overhaul!

I got lots of great feedback as well as some hard truth about my first novel.

So as the feedback and suggestions came in, I tried to be careful to remain as true to the book as much as possible and as far as I can tell, it seems to have done nothing except make this version a lot tighter and *meaner*. The biggest help came from four wonderful people. First, brother and cohort Dan Foytik, who bravely took over and currently runs The Wicked Library. (For that alone he deserves the Universe.) He is a trusted friend and ally and he gave excellent insight into this book. A million ongoing thanks to you my friend!

Pippa Bailey and Myk Pilgrim gave absolutely fantastic feedback that was invaluable to this edition. I put them both together because they have become quite a duo and they do amazing work together. They're amazing writers on their own, but they are a super couple in every sense. They are also wonderful and generous friends and I can't believe my good fortune in knowing them both-Cheers, my dears!

Gary Vincent may be the last true risk taking publisher. He's a good guy, and part of that is he's an honest guy. He's the most transparent and honest publisher I've worked with. This isn't to say I have worked with crooks, but of the group, he's always been very up front and honest to a fault. He's also great to work with; a great motivator with a talent to make you excited about your own book. He has endless energy and enthusiasm. He keeps taking chances on my work and I keep letting him. I proudly carry the Burning Bulb Publishing flag! Thanks, my friend.

If this is your first time reading this book, or if you're reading it again, I truly hope you enjoy it even more this time around; the often teased sequel is well under way.

Nelson W Pyles
November 2018

For "Mighty" Matt Storey and all the important time on the porch.

And also to my aunts Lee Popovich and Patricia Caras. I wouldn't be here without you.

CHAPTER 1

Katrina Dougherty slowly inched her 1977 Buick Century to the edge of her snow covered driveway. She looked both ways before stomping her boot on the accelerator. The car lurched forward as she yanked the car to the left and onto the busy Shadyside street in Pittsburgh. The green monster, as she lovingly called it, was greeted with the usual volley of horns honking and bad language. She smiled and gave the finger to all of them.

The radio had claimed it would snow in Pittsburgh all day.

"*If you don't need to go out, don't.*" said the cheesy radio disc jockey.

Kat was pretty sure she didn't *need* to go out, but she also knew that cigarettes and milkshakes wouldn't just magically appear at her door.

It was nine o'clock in the morning.

She and the green monster began to pick up speed as she traveled past the hospital. If she played her cards right and got her unnecessary chores done with quickly, there might even be time to stop by the comic shop and rummage through the bargain bins of used DVD's for under a buck. Since she was going to be snowed in alone, a little cheap entertainment would be needed.

She could have all of this done in forty-five minutes. This thought made her smile for a moment then she frowned. She was twenty-nine years old and this was the total sum of her ambition; cheap DVD's, cigarettes and a Neapolitan milkshake from the Circle K on a snow day. She didn't even have a job. She shook her head and reached for her cigarettes. Without looking, she found the pack, shook out a smoke and stuck it in her mouth. She pushed in the cigarette lighter and waited. She wanted to quit smoking, but not so much today. The lighter popped out and she lit up. Inhaling deeply and exhaling, she drove on to the first stop.

There was a surprisingly busy scene at the Circle K when Kat slid into an empty parking space. The store's location was already dubious; it was on the edge of the bad part of the North Side of Pittsburgh. She didn't like the location, but the store had a few things no other stop and shop stores had and the main one was the Neapolitan milkshake.

It also was filled with hoodlums at any given time during the day or night. She frowned and stepped out of her car.

She walked through the shady teenagers standing outside. Of course, there were some catcalls thrown her way. These were all stopped by a singular icy look that shot from her eyes. As pretty as she was, her stare was one of the rare ones that stopped you dead in your tracks because of how serious it looked. This throng of teenagers was no exception and they actually parted to let her through. She flung her cigarette onto the sidewalk in front of them and let the smoke trail out of her mouth.

She kicked the door open with one of her boots and heard the terrible electronic bell resound through the store. Judging from the line of people clutching gallons of milk and sidewalk salt, folks were really thinking this snow storm was going to be something. She shook her head and went to the empty self-serve milkshake machine.

Ten long minutes later, she kicked the door open again and marched to her car, glaring again at the teenagers who, once again stopped talking as soon as they saw her.

She put the shake on top of the green monster and opened the door. She saw the teenagers staring at her in silence. She looked directly at them and lit a cigarette. Through a puff of smoke, she cocked her head to one side.

"Quit eyeballin' me, jagoffs."

The teenagers, all five of them suddenly looked away and shuffled toward the other side of the parking lot, where them saw another woman walking into the store.

Kat got into the car, started it and drove away, smirking.

Another ten minutes later, she walked into Bruce's Comix Empire. She waited for the reaction of Bruce, who stood at the front of the store. She wouldn't have to wait long.

Bruce, with his long curly red hair and beard to match heard the bell on the door as Kat entered. Without looking at her, he looked instead, up and sniffed the air.

"Ah..." he said, elated. "I know that lovely smell. It is my queen, my unrequited sweetheart." He slowly looked in Kat's direction. She shook her head and smiled.

"Never ends with you does it?"

"Never ever." He replied and smiled. "What's shaking?"

She walked into the main room of the store. It was a massive room, with every square inch covered with either merchandise or pictures of merchandise. Comic books, album covers, toys from the 70's, horror movie posters and mirrors. Kat could see herself from nearly every angle and so could Bruce.

"Just checking out the bins before the snow starts to suck."

"Oh, it already sucks darling." Bruce said. "But, my discount bins do not. Have at it."

"Thanks," she said and walked over to the three wire bins of used DVD's. She started to poke through them, methodically.

Soon, she had three DVD's in hand-each according to the sign, for 99 cents and 'dirty rotten stinkin' cheap.' As she walked up to Bruce and the front cash register, she saw another display with small odd stuffed animals. One was a puppy holding a sword. Another was a kitten wearing a hockey mask. Cute, she thought.

And then saw something that struck her as genuinely creepy.

It was some kind of doll that seemed like it wasn't sewn together as much as it was *sutchered*. It was brown with a crude stitched line for a mouth and two button eyes. She looked at it and frowned.

"Hey, what's this?" She called over to Bruce.

Bruce, ever the paramour, was next to her in a second.

"Is it the kitten? I see you as a kitten kind of girl," He said.

She chuckled.

"I'm allergic to everything. Kittens included, but especially bullshit. What is *this* thing?" She pointed at the crude doll.

Bruce picked it up and examined it. He seemed to regard it with hesitation and squinted as he looked at it.

"Hmmm..." he said. "As I thought. Its three bucks, just like the sign says. That's what it is."

He casually tossed the doll back into the bin.

"Asshole," Kat said, laughing and picking it back up. It felt rough and heavier than it looked. "I didn't ask how much. What is it supposed to be?"

Bruce turned and started to walk back to the register.

"I really don't know," He said. "To be honest, some homeless person probably dropped it in there. Could be like a baby doll for whack-o's. Know what I mean?"

"Oh, so then it's free?" Kat asked smirking.

Bruce turned slowly to her.

"I have *never* acknowledged that word inside of this store," He replied.

She laughed and threw the doll back into the bin.

"Okay, then just these," she said, walking up to the register with the DVD's. Bruce took them and rang them up. He held the last one up to her, frowning.

"You're going to actually watch this? Seriously?" he asked.

"That is the idea, yeah."

Bruce shook his head.

"It's awful."

"I'd like to see for myself."

"Trust me, you don't want to."

"Oh, but I do."

"What? Trust me?"

Kat snorted.

"Hell no. I just want to see the movie."

Bruce frowned.

"If there is one thing I know, it is movies and this," he said, holding the DVD up as a talking point, "is *not* a movie. It's a stain on your soul. I can't in good conscience sell this to you."

"Sweet!" Kat exclaimed and grabbed the DVD. "A freebie. You're a sweetheart, Bru."

Bruce wanted to protest and actually opened his mouth to do so, but stopped. He frowned again and then smirked.

"You will be destroyer of my business, Katrina. Go ahead and take it."

Kat hugged the DVD and went to put it down on the counter while Bruce rang up the other 2 items. Instead, she looked down, because it seemed that there was something else on the counter she hadn't seen.

It was the creepy doll.

'Oh, *shit*!" Kat said and actually took a step back.

Bruce looked at Kat and then down at the doll.

"Want that too I suppose," he grumbled. "Go ahead and take it along with my retirement."

Kat would have been thrilled, except the doll was really scary. She didn't remember picking it back up and did not remember bringing it to the counter. She looked at the hideous thing and then at Bruce.

"That's okay. I don't really-"

"On the house Kat. Get that fucking homeless baby doll out of my store." He smiled. "You don't come in like you used to. Kinda miss you."

Kat melted slightly. Bruce was miles away from her type, but he was a sweet guy. It always feels good even when someone you don't like likes you, her Mom used to say.

"Thanks, Bru," She said. "Once I get some real money, I'll be back more often. Promise."

Bruce beamed as he bagged the 2 DVD's. He grabbed the third one and the doll and put them in the bag as well.

"You know, I might be hiring."

"That a fact?"

"Absolute fact. Just give me your resume and we'll talk."

"You'd be my boss."

"Well, yeah. I'm a good boss."

"You've never had anyone work for you that I've seen. How do you know you're a good boss?"

Bruce grinned.

"I'd love to work with me."

"You already do, Bru. You're biased."

His grin faded slightly.

"Seriously, Kat. If you need a job, you have one here. Anytime. No resume needed."

She smiled.

"You are a good man, Bruce. Thank you."

The comment made him blush.

"You're gonna regret that movie," he said, handing her the bag.

She took it and smiled sweetly at Bruce.

"I probably will, but sometimes, you have to find things out for yourself. It's part of the adventure."

"Life is just one big adventure with different assholes." Bruce smiled the widest smile she'd ever seen.

Kat chuckled as she walked out of the door. The snow looked like it meant business. The wind started to pick up making the snow whip into her face. She swore as she crossed the street to the parked green monster. She had left the windows opened a crack to keep her milkshake cold, but now she didn't think she wanted it. She opened the door, threw her bag, then herself inside. She slammed the door and started the car, then franticly began rolling all four windows up. When she was done, she sat upright and closed her eyes for a moment. The effort had made her a little out of breath. She felt the car humming loudly. She smiled.

It took a lot of energy to roll up four windows by hand, but she didn't really miss automatic windows. This lack of technology had saved her quite a few times and never grumbled about it to anyone. For one thing, the driver side window could be opened from the outside by hand, simply by getting your fingers in through the insulation and gently pushing it down. Helpful if you locked your keys in the car.

Of course, she didn't need keys either. The ignition lock had been destroyed ages ago-before she'd even bought the car. These things she looked upon as perks.

The heater took a minute, but was pumping hot air. She opened her eyes and turned her wipers on, then threw the car into gear and launched into the street.

Thirty minutes later, Kat was home; a miracle or luck she hadn't been killed by potholes, other drivers or her own awful driving. She knew this as she knew her own face. She had changed into pajamas and her fuzzy monster slippers. She walked downstairs from her bedroom and into the small kitchen to get her snacks. She still had half a milkshake and a new pack of smokes. There was a new bag of lemon crème cookies and she had half of a pot of coffee. The news had said the city was now requesting all drivers to stay put, and had begun closing schools and all city offices.

She grabbed her snacks and walked into the living room. Her used faux leather couch was waiting patiently for her as was her blanket, pillow and her trusty giant glass ashtray. She put her stuff on the coffee table and sat down.

Grabbing the bag and the remote, she flicked on the TV for background noise as she decided which DVD to watch first. She pulled out the DVD's and the creepy doll. She took the DVD Bruce had suggested not watching and put it on the coffee table, followed by the other two. Then she put the doll on top of them.

She looked at, studying it carefully.

Who would make something like this, she thought. It was ugly. It had stains on the front and on the little crude hands. She shuddered. Maybe Bruce was right. Maybe it was some surrogate baby for some poor soul.

Still, there was something she seemed to like about the doll, although she couldn't put her finger on it. She picked it up and looked into its button eyes. Up close it looked kind of sad.

She smiled and tossed him on the couch next to her.

"Alright, Pooky. You can stay." She said, and got up to put the DVD in the player. "We're gonna watch the shitty one first, just to get it out of the way." She laughed. "Great. Talking to myself."

She jumped back to the couch, and grabbed her smokes. Lighting one up, she looked at her doll.

"Been a long time since I had a doll friend," she said. She looked at the television and blew a thin line of blue smoke into the air. "And if you're gonna be my doll friend, we watch lots of crappy horror movies here."

She reached over and grabbed her milk shake. She kicked off her slippers and got comfortable on the couch for the long 90-minute haul. She felt oddly good. She looked over at the doll.

It was gone.

Kat blinked a few times and stood up. She pulled the blanket off and checked under the cushions. Her cigarette dangled and she put her shake down.

She stood up straight and looked blankly at the couch, as if by some stupid mistake, she just didn't see it. It was a brown couch, she thought. The movie started on the television. A loud fake explosion followed by bad dramatic music began to play and the even worse narration began.

"The events you are about to witness," the voice said in an almost threatening manner, "may one day be TRUE!"

It was of course, the indicator for trailers of other crap movies before the main feature. This registered with Katrina, but she didn't hear it at the same time.

"Where the *fuck*..." she nearly whispered.

The television shut off. Kat whirled around and saw nothing out of the ordinary.

"*Here*, the fuck," the doll said. Kat looked down and saw the doll in front of the television.

Kat's cigarette fell out of her mouth.

She stared at the doll and the doll stared back for nearly a full minute.

"Isn't that going to light your house on fire?" the doll asked, pointing at the still active smoke on the floor.

Kat blinked hard and looked down.

"Whoa, shit!" She said and picked it up and before stabbing it out in the ashtray, she took a double hit from it. She stood back up and looked at the doll.

"Thanks," she said without thinking. And then, "Wait, how are you talking?" She sat down. "Wait, *why* are you talking? Holy shit, this is insane. Have I lost my shit?"

The doll just stood there, not saying anything. It looked like it was watching her carefully.

"This is so nuts, know what I mean?" Kat continued. She grabbed her cigarettes and lit another one up.

"You just put one of those out," the doll said.

"Yeah, well I don't drink or get high, so it's either this or I shit my pants," Kat said.

"That's refreshing," the doll said.

"I get that a lot," she said. "Wait, how...*are* you?"

"I'm not doing well," he replied.

"No, I don't mean *how* are you doing, I mean how *are* you? *What* are you?"

"I'm a demon. I am trapped inside of this doll. Can you help me get a body?"

"You're a demon and you're stuck in that doll?"

"That's almost exactly what I said, yes."

"And you need help getting a body."

The doll sighed.

Kat took a large drag from her cigarette.

"Let's say that I'm not asleep and making this shit up in my head," Kat began. "If you're a demon, why would I help you?"

"What?" he asked.

"If you're a demon," Kat continued, "And we all know demons are *bad*, then why would I help one?"

The little doll went to reply and couldn't.

"Are you like a *new* demon or something? Because the whole demon as a bad thing is fairly obvious I would think." Kat said, taking another drag.

"Tell me, when was the last time *you* were trapped inside of a sewn up football?"

Kat actually opened her mouth to say something but was cut off.

"That's right, you *haven't* been." He said. "I didn't ask to come here. I'm just stuck here and while I'm stuck here I'd rather not do it in *this body*. Is that so wrong?"

"But, you're asking for a new body, not a sweater. I imagine there are some messy things that come with getting a body, am I right?" Kat took another drag. The room was filling with smoke. "I mean, shit. I guess it's not like I can just knit you a body, know what I mean?"

The little doll stared at her and said nothing. The blank stare was unnerving, but Kat pressed on with her questioning.

"Are you offering up some kind of reward?" Kat asked. "You haven't offered me anything, so you're not out for my soul I guess."

"I don't *want* your soul," he said. "I just don't want to be *six fucking inches* tall anymore."

Kat looked at him again. She took a drag from the smoke again, and saw it was almost done. She put it in the ashtray and grabbed her milk shake.

"I'm taking this really well," she said to the doll and herself.

He nodded his head.

"Well, you aren't screaming."

"Are you going to hurt me or possess me?"

"Possess, no. If I could do that, I wouldn't need you."

Kat let this sink in for a moment and swallowed.

"So are you going to hurt me?"

"I don't know. Are you going to help me?"

"I haven't decided." She said.

"How about I won't hurt you if you help me?"

"Sorry, I don't respond well to threats. You could hurt me, but you'll still be a doll."

He seemed to consider this for a moment.

"Okay. What do you want?"

Kat stood up.

"A shower. This is a lot to take in. Can you wait here and not destroy anything?"

The doll nodded and then added, almost unnecessarily,

"Are you going to run away? Sneak out of the back door? Because I'll kill you."

"Look Pooky," Kat said, "There's a blizzard going on outside. I'm not going anywhere. I just need a shower. Where I come from, ugly ass little dolls filled with demons don't actually exist. Be right back."

Kat backed carefully out of the living room. Once she was out, she ran up the stairs.

She ran into her bathroom and locked the door. She quickly turned on the shower and stripped. When the water was tolerable, she got in and began to cry. She shook and sobbed hard in disbelief. She tried hard not to make a single noise that could be heard over the water and she felt that she'd been successful.

Eventually, she turned the shower off and got out. The mirror was steamed up and she was still crying a little. The worst, was over. She wiped a hand across the mirror and saw a distorted version of herself. Her short black hair was starting to look all spiky on its own. Normally even by her own standards, she was a pretty girl, but now she just looked spent. Grabbing a towel she started to dry herself off. She was trying to pull herself together and surprising herself that she was starting to succeed. Which of course, began to freak her out a little more. She looked at herself in the mirror. Her eyes were red, but they were clearing up since she had stopped crying.

At least that's what she *hoped* she saw.

She left the bathroom wrapped in a towel and walked quietly to her bedroom down the hall. She kicked open the door and stepped over the huge pile of clothes on the floor. "Mountain climbing" she sometimes called it, when the clothes from the month were so big it nearly came up as high as the bed. She made it to the large oak dresser opposite the door and yanked a drawer open. Clothes were crammed into every square inch of it, but they were clean.

She dressed quickly-almost entirely in black except for the splash of pink skull on her t-shirt. She had considered finding something else, but the only other shirt had a devil's head on it, so she opted for the most human thing she found. She grabbed a pair of black and pink socks and climbed out of the room.

She carefully came back down the stairs. The creepy doll was nowhere to be seen just yet. She stopped on the stairs.

"Where are you?" she called. No reply. "Look, you need to not scare the shit out of me like this, okay?"

She heard a sigh from her living room.

"Still here," the doll replied.

"'Kay," she said and came down the stairs into the living room. There it was, sitting on her couch, television off. She stopped and stared at it, then sat in the large worn out recliner opposite the couch to put her socks on.

"There was a point I was hoping that I had invented you in my imagination," Kat said, smirking a little.

"No, you were crying." Stitch said back. "I'm surprised your neighbors didn't call the police."

Kat frowned.

"You got some nerve for a hunk of rawhide," she said. "I thought you needed help."

"I'm not helpless,"

"No, but you *are* little prick." She said. "Maybe where you're from, little jagoffs like you are running around all over, but not here." She finished putting her socks on and then tucked her legs underneath her in the chair.

"So, you little jagoff," she started. "Now that I'm clean and not crying anymore, why don't you tell me exactly what you'd like me to do for you?"

"What's a jagoff?"

"It's like a jerkoff, except it's *you*. Spit it out already."

"What else do you need to know? I'm a demon, I need a new body and you're going to help me."

"How did you get stuck in the body for one thing?" Kat asked. "You need to give a girl a little background, Pooky."

"Why do you keep calling me Pooky?" he asked.

"I can keep calling you jagoff, or Pooky until you tell me your name if that's good for you."

"Just call me Stitch," he said finally.

"Stitch," Kat said, trying the word out. "Really? That's it? That's the best you could come up with? Stitch?"

"What do you mean?" he asked.

"Just sounds cheesy that's all. Did a kid name you?"

The demon stomped a little foot and said, "Just call me Stitch."

Kat chuckled.

"Sensitive aren't we?" she asked smirking. "Is it a complex 'cause you're so teeny tiny?"

"I could kill you right now, you know," Stitch said.

Kat was a resilient girl in that, once she had finished freaking out, or crying or being scared of something, she was done with it, period. You could scare her, but not for very long. Maybe it was the large volume of horror movies she loved, or something in her psychological make up, but the things that truly scared her were *not* talking demon dolls.

At least, not right at that moment.

"You're not killing anyone, Pooky." she said. "And I'm still waiting for my story."

Stitch looked at her.

"Why do you need to hear my story? Can't you just do it for the sake of doing it?"

"Nope." Kat replied. "And as if it really needed repeating, the helping of demons, is kind of a *bad* thing."

Stitch said nothing.

"You aren't very good at selling me on this idea of yours. How do you get people's souls and stuff?"

"I *don't* take people's souls!" Stitch said.

"So, tell me your story. We have all the time in the world since we're getting snowed in pretty good here. How does a demon get stuck inside a stupid looking doll?"

He sighed.

"You might want to sit," Stitch said.

CHAPTER 2

It was a warm autumn evening when three teenage boys went to the Eternal Rest Cemetery in the Pine Barrens. No one noticed them at all-it was an old cemetery and often teenagers came there to sit, make out, drink or smoke, but not do much else. There hadn't been any vandalism in the cemetery in close to a decade, and even that was almost laughable. Pete Wysonski had staggered drunk into the cemetery and had tripped over a headstone. His long coat had somehow gotten trapped under it as he fell, and he had been trapped for two hours, crying for someone to help him. The police finally showed and lifted the stone up enough for him to get free.

When they were done, they put the stone back down. The family had to be notified of the stone falling, if there were anyone from that family left to notify; the date of death on the stone was 1952.

The three boys however hadn't come to sit, make out, drink or smoke. They were doing something different.

Kneeling in front of the gravestone, Martin began to squint at the book. He was dressed in a grey hoodie and jeans. He had considered maybe wearing a facemask, or even black make up, or head to toe black clothes, but the idea had been mercilessly made fun of and shot down. He ran a hand through his mop of curly black hair and squinted.

"Mal...um...fi...fi...eri sine..." He recited, sounding unsure. "I really can't read it." He looked at his two friends for support.

James and Stu looked puzzled and simply shrugged.

"Whatever," James grumbled.

"Is there a flashlight?" Martin asked.

The three teens had been at this ritual for an hour. At first, the fading daylight was okay to read by, but the increasing darkness and the pronunciation of certain words were proving difficult by the second. Not that that was any surprise; the words weren't in any language Martin recognized. Most of the words were spelled in impossible configurations, like a small child had just started tapping randomly on a typewriter.

"You said we wouldn't need flashlights. You said it would be done before it got dark, genius, so go and read your shit again." Stu said in a flat heavy tone.

Stu was a menacing kid. At seventeen, he was already six foot four, and 240 pounds. He looked like an angry drill sergeant complete with a buzz cut. All he needed were tattoos. He crossed his arms defiantly and stared at Martin.

Martin shook his head.

"How is this supposed to work if I can't read the words?"

"I thought you *knew* how this stuff worked, Marty." James said. James was also a big kid, but not as tall as Stu. With a shock of nearly white hair, he looked like a teenaged James Bond villain.

"But, I can't *see* the words."

He didn't bother telling James not to call him "Marty."

Masters of demons weren't called Marty.

The three teens sighed. It was useless.

"Well, let's pack up an' go, I guess," James said, resigned. "I knew this was gonna be bullshit."

Martin's face grew stern. He looked at the small altar they had made. They had done everything right. They had the mandrake root, the book, ("*Raising Demons For Dummies-Millennium Edition*") the stitched figurine made of flesh, the blood-

Blood!

"We forgot the blood," Martin said. "We're supposed to sprinkle it on the totem."

"Seriously?" James asked. He sounded disgusted. Stu stomped a foot, disgusted.

"James, lemmie see your hand." Stu said sharply.

James stuck his hand out near the candle. Stu looked at it and nodded.

"Thanks," he said, pulling out his small penknife. In one swift motion, he opened the knife and stabbed James' hand with the sharp blade. James made a tight hissing noise and pulled his hand away, penknife still stuck in.

"Damn!" he cried, looking at his bleeding hand.

Stu grabbed James' hand and held it over the stitched figurine. Blood dripped steadily onto the thing (*a "totem" the book had called it.*) James glared at Stu and angrily pulled his hand back.

"You could've asked," he whimpered.

"Shut up, fucktard," Stu said. "Try it again, Marty."

Martin strained at the book again with new resolve. Surprisingly, it seemed to be easier to read. He began the chant slowly. He found and pronounced the words, impossible to read minutes ago and he nearly whispered them over and over, slowly becoming louder each time.

"I still think this is *bullshit*," whispered James to Stu, who didn't even bother looking at him when he slapped him, hissing, "Shush."

Martin continued, speaking faster and louder now. He moved onto the section that had been giving him the most difficulty. He knew some of the language was Latin, but it changed to something different halfway through. It seemed to be much older than Latin and now, he was speaking it fluently.

Stu looked at James and then at Martin. Martin wasn't reading from the book anymore. His eyes were closed as impossible words flew from his lips. There seemed to be a low rumble, like the steady sound of high-tension power lines coming from all around them. The air grew stale, as Martin's voice became a loud monotone.

Martin abruptly stopped.

James, his hand throbbing, looked at Martin, who was covered in sweat, his eyes still closed.

"Well?' James finally asked.

Martin's eyelids fluttered.

"Huh?"

"What the hell was that?" Stu asked.

"I don't know," Martin said quietly.

"Come on," James said standing up. "Didn't work. Grab the shit and let's go. I need fucking stitches."

Martin remained kneeling, stunned. He barely remembered reading the words in the book, but he had done it. He had felt the power of...something. It felt like electricity had flowed not into him, but *from* him.

Stu grabbed the candle and the mandrake. He reached for the blood-covered totem.

It wasn't there.

"Marty, you got the little guy?" He asked.

Martin blinked a few times. He looked down and saw an outline from where the totem had been and what looked like scorch marks, but it was gone.

"Um, no." Martin said, still a little dizzy. "Maybe James took it,"

"Fuck you man. I didn't take *shit*." James spat. "And I need a fuckin' doctor." He clutched his still bleeding hand. Stuart at least had the courtesy to laugh.

Martin looked puzzled. *Where did it go?*

"We should get going," Stu said, turning to leave.

"Stay where you are," said a voice from behind the headstone.

"Fuck this Marty, I'm gone." Stu said, and then stopped walking. "Wait. Was that you Marty?"

"No, it wasn't Marty," the voice spoke again. The three teens looked around, but saw no one else.

"I'm down here, *boys*."

They looked at the headstone, and the totem appeared from behind. It was a totally scary looking totem when James had crudely stitched it together. Seeing it move made it worse.

And of course, now it was talking.

It looked like a third grade leatherworking project, which is exactly where James had learned to sew.

"Now then," the totem said quietly, it's crudely sewn mouth moving. "Which one of you made this body? That's the *very* first thing I want to know."

James, clutching his hand, stared at the small, mobile totem. He was in mild shock, but since he had been proud of the sewing job he had done, he spoke up.

"Me dude. That was me. Holy shit, you're real?"

"Oh, I'm real." the totem said.

"So, you gotta do our bidding, right? Hey, fix my hand."

The little totem looked up at James. Its eyes were two different sized buttons torn off of James' mother's winter coat. Odd, that they seemed to narrow. A small leathery arm pointed to James.

"Why did you make the body so small?"

"Well," James said, excited that his creativity had paid off, "I figured it wouldn't work anyway, right? So I figured what the hell? Besides, where were we gonna get a full body of flesh, right?"

For a moment, no one said anything until the totem moved.

"For starters," the totem said, moving towards James, "You could've actually believed it would have worked."

He stopped abruptly and picked up the small penknife that had been dropped.

"And then, you could have realized that a demon might not be too happy about being put into a body of...what is *this*?"

The totem was inches away from James' feet. It looked up at him, waiting for an answer.

"A football." James said, "You know, pig skin? I used my grandpa's old football."

"A body made from a pig skin football," The totem said, almost to itself. "I've been cast into the flesh of a pig. This is almost hilarious."

The totem sighed.

James smiled. He had found the football in his grandfather's garage. A genuine pig skin football. *Perfect*, he had thought. The football had been popped and all the stitches pulled out so it was flat. Then it was just a matter of making it look like a little guy. After he had sewn the eyes-buttons of course and the mouth, it looked like a brown voodoo doll. Initially it had scared the crap out of him, but it was outweighed by the sense of accomplishment. James looked at the totem now; his creation and felt very proud. He smiled.

"Yeah, little dude. I made you. So to thank me, you can fix my-"

The totem drove the three-inch penknife into the top of James' shoe and into his foot all the way up to the hilt. James howled in pain. Martin and Stuart watched in shock, as James bent down to pull the knife from his foot.

The totem had the courtesy to pull it out for him. As James' head came within reach, the totem stabbed James in the eye. Fresh pain exploded in a scream from James. He collapsed face first, driving the knife in further. He walked up to James, who was clutching his eye with both hands now and crying. He noticed the hand that had been stabbed was still bleeding. The totem waved a small hand and the wound healed.

The totem walked over to James' ear.

"Your hand's fine now, my little *seamstress*," It said. "But the rest of you is pretty well fucked."   Then, the thing reached up to James' ear and ripped it off of his head. James screamed again.

The totem turned around and walked towards Martin and Stuart, who had backed up a considerable distance. James howled in agony. The totem stopped and casually tossed the ear to one side. Then he raised an arm.

"Are you boys cold?."

James' body exploded into flames. The totem began to walk towards Martin and Stuart.

"Nothing like a little fire on a brisk night, am I right?"

The totem stopped directly in front of the two terrified teens and looked up. James' screams were turning into whimpers, as the fire seemed to be burning brighter than it should have been.

"So, now that I'm through *thanking* him for my body which, by the way, is supposed to be much fucking bigger than *this*," the totem snarled, "What exactly do I have *you two* to thank for?"

Stu fainted and fell down backwards while Martin stood there with his jaw hanging open. James had stopped thrashing; the fire still burned, but most of what could have been James was nearly burned away. Martin couldn't believe his eyes.

He looked down at what he had done. A six-inch tall thing made out of an old football, with a sewn mouth, and button eyes. Tears began to streak his face.

"Are you really *real?*" Martin heard himself ask the totem.

"What do *you* think?"

Martin sank to his knees.

"It worked," Martin said softly, more to himself than to anyone else.

The totem moved closer to Martin, who was now crying.

And smiling.

"I wouldn't be smiling, boy." The totem said, angrily.

Martin ignored this and said, "It really *really* worked!"

An hour later, Martin quietly opened the back door to his house with his backpack full of all the materials from the night's activities. Except for the totem, which he had shoved into his pocket. He was nearly hyperventilating from running and the release of adrenaline. The totem squirmed in his pants pocket. Martin couldn't make out what it was saying, but he thought he could make out some vulgarities. Unthinkingly, he slapped his pocket to quiet the totem. It worked.

For exactly five seconds.

As Martin crept though the kitchen as quietly as possible, he noticed a note from his mother. He read the first five words of the note, which read; "Martin, We'll Be Out, So" when a very sharp pain exploded in his leg.

Martin screamed as he dug into his pocket. He grabbed the totem, which still had the pen knife gripped in its little hands.

"You tried to stab me!" Martin cried, holding the totem up to his face.

"You slapped me!" the totem yelled back.

"You have to be quiet. Someone could've heard you, and that hurt."

The totem threw the knife down and glared at Martin.

"Your parents are gone. Didn't you see the note?"

Martin stared at the totem and then at the note.

"How did you-"he started.

"Do we have to go through the whole 'I'm a supernatural being' thing again?" the totem asked. "And put me down already. It's embarrassing enough."

Martin let go, dropping the totem to the floor with a thud.

"Damn you," the totem said from the floor.

Martin gasped.

"Oh dude, I'm so sorry."

The totem looked up at Martin.

"Don't call me *man*. We have a lot of work to do. Well, actually, *you* have a lot of work to do. We need to get a new body and transfer me into it. We need to do it as soon as possible."

Martin nodded.

"Because if we don't, you'll be stuck in the football doll forever, like in 'Child's Play?'"

"No," it replied. "No, we need to do it quickly because I'm only six fucking inches tall! Do you have any idea how ridiculous I look like this?"

Martin nodded again in agreement.

"I guess you're right. But, why can't you just, you know, take over another body? I mean, you are supernatural and stuff."

"Because it doesn't *work* that way," The totem replied. "If I could do that, what the hell would I need you for?"

Martin hesitated in replying. He looked at the demon he had just brought into the world. That *he* had brought into the world. The one thing the book had mentioned was that if the ritual worked, you had to establish your authority right away, or the demon would try to trick its way out of your service. And if that happened, the demon would be likely to kill its former Master. He cleared his throat.

"Well," Martin began, "For starters, you needed me to exist, right? In a physical form I mean."

"Yes?" It asked. It didn't like where this was going.

Martin nodded.

"So, you need me for a lot of things."

"What's your point?"

Martin leaned down to the totem.

"We need to clear a few things up. I took a big chance that the book would work and so far it has."

"You actually believed the book would work, didn't you?"

"Yes I did." Martin said. "But I didn't know it would work like *this*."

"Well, since you have two dead friends who helped you out this evening, how accurate do you think it's been so far?"

"Pretty accurate." Martin replied. He was trying desperately to not sound like a sixteen year old. "I mean they were just helping me. They weren't actually *friends* either. The book did call for a sacrifice or two. So, done. That means you're in my 'thrall.' Right?" Martin actually made quotation marks in the air with his fingers when he said 'thrall.'

The demon seemed to consider this for a moment. Martin continued.

"In other words, you can't kill me like you did them."

"You're right," the totem said, nodding. "I can't kill you. But remember there are worse things than being killed."

Martin nodded.

"Hey, don't worry. I'll help you get a new body, but I need to know how. But just remember who's in charge. I raised you up for a reason."

"I wouldn't exactly call this 'raised up,' Master." The totem said.

Martin stood there.

Master.

He could have floated.

He was a *Master*.

He took a deep breath. He was about to tell the totem what he had agonized over for more than a year. The reason he wanted...*needed* a demon.

Martin opened his mouth to speak, when Barky, the family sheepdog barreled through the kitchen door, panting and wagging his tail.

Barky saw Martin first and then he saw the totem, which whirled around to see what just came in through the door. Barky growled and darted toward the totem.

Barky picked it up in his teeth and ran out of the kitchen at full speed. Martin's eyes grew wide with horror as he heard the dog pound his way up the staircase.

"Oh shit," Martin mumbled as he took off after the dog.

CHAPTER 3

Stu felt the cold earth beneath him and tried to focus his eyes. He tried to speak, but he found he couldn't. He decided to lay there for a bit and collect himself.

Jesus, he thought, *that little ugly assed doll knocked me out.* Anger rose in his mind and he tried to move.

He couldn't.

So he tried to look around to see who was left in the graveyard.

He couldn't do that either.

After a few minutes, he discovered he couldn't do anything *except* think. He managed to realize he was lying on his back and that it was still night, but that was it. He couldn't focus his eyes, but he could make out some lights in the sky. And he could at least hear. However, the one thing he couldn't hear, among the distant barking dogs, the passing cars, and the occasional airplane was something that finally began to scare him.

He couldn't hear his breathing. Or his heartbeat, which he imagined should be pounding.

He tried to speak again. Then he tried to scream. He just looked up at the night sky with his dead eyes and wondered how long he would be this way. He wondered that over and over until he heard something coming toward him from his left.

And it was growling.

Something began nibbling on Stu's right thigh and the pain was amplified by the fact that he could no longer move. It was also worse in that he couldn't see that it was a small stray dog. He wished he'd worn jeans.

In the distance, he heard voices and allowed himself hope that they would find him and save him. Stuart lay there silently, dead for the whole world to see. But, his mind, still very much active, was screaming louder than he ever could have hoped for.

CHAPTER 4

"Hold still," Marty said, trying to sew a small arm to the torso of the totem. Barky, was cowering in the corner of Marty's room.

"I am going to kill your dog. You hear me? You're *dead*!" the totem said to Barky. Barky emitted a high-pitched whine as if he understood what might happen to him.

"Yeah, you go on and whine. It won't save you. You'll suffer for-"

"Shut up." Marty said and held the one armed totem in his hand. The second arm, not quite sewn back on, dangled limply from its socket.

"Don't threaten my dog. Ever. He's a good boy. Right, Barky?"

Barky, hearing Marty's voice let his tail wag and thump the floor twice, before returning to his cowering state.

The totem glared at Marty.

"Look what he did to me!"

"He didn't mean it. He was playing."

"Oh, he was *playing*. That's different. So if I choke him to death with his own tongue, that would that be considered playing too?"

Martin glared at the totem and held him up to his eyes.

"I'm tired of how you've been talking to me. You're under *my* control and don't forget it. Touch Barky and you'll be trapped in this little body of yours forever."

The totem sighed and nodded.

"Just fix me."

Martin continued to stare.

The totem added,

"Please, Master."

Martin dropped the totem and grabbed the sewing kit.

"Glad that's all cleared up. Now, let's get the arm back on."

Barky, still whining, let loose a low growl, but from a distance.

"That's right, Barky. *Bad*, ugly football chew toy!" Martin laughed.

"So, what do I call you?" Martin asked suddenly. "You have a name, right?"

"Oh, you mean you don't wish to refer to me as 'bad ugly football chew toy?'"

Martin ignored this.

"The book said what you do and how powerful you are, but it only referred to you as "the merciless one.' Still, I have to call you something."

"I like 'the merciless one.'"

Martin snickered.

"I'm not calling you 'merciless one.' Ouch!"

Martin had stabbed himself in the finger with the stitching needle. A bright red drop of blood bubbled to his index finger as the totem watched intently.

"I wish you weren't so damn hard to stitch," He said through gritted teeth.

After some time and some effort, Martin had finished with the arm. He took him time looking at the totem up close and wondered how it was able to pick things up without any actual fingers. He thought of asking, but decided against it.

"So, is that good for you then?" Martin asked. The totem was extending his sewn arm and bending it slowly.

"I suppose it'll work," the totem replied. He picked a pencil up from the floor and threw it at the bedroom door. It slammed into the doorframe and stuck, point in.

"Yes, it'll work." He said. Martin walked over to the doorframe and pulled the pencil out.

"No, the name. Stitch. You like it?"

The totem waddled over to Martin, who still stood in the doorway. Barky, still shaking in a corner whined again as he watched the ugly thing move.

"It doesn't matter what I like, does it? I am in your thrall. You want to call me Stitch, than I guess my name is Stitch."

"Don't say it like that," Martin said. "Since I don't know what your real name is, I have to call you something."

"Rules, Marty. Can't have my real name." Stitch said.

"Okay. And don't call me 'Marty.' That's a boy's name."

Stitch cocked his head to one side.

"But, you are a boy."

Martin moved back into the room and sat on his bed. He slumped down like the boy he was, but had a vicious look in his eye.

"I am a master of demons," he said softly. "I am *not* a boy."

Stitch padded over to the bed and jumped on it. He sighed.

"And yet, you want us to be 'Martin and Stitch?' That's a *boy's* thought. It sounds like a vaudville show."

"I don't know what that means. I just want to be..." Martin struggled for the right word.

"More than you are?" Stitch offered.

Martin nodded.

"Yeah, more. More than I am. More than people think. I want..."

"Everything?" Stitch finished for him. Martin smiled.

"Yeah."

"That's still a boy's line of thought, Master." Stitch said. "But, I understand."

"How?" Martin asked a bit angrily.

"I've been there. Did you think I was always a chew toy?"

"You've always been a demon."

"I wasn't *always* a demonic chew toy." He said. "I was one of the true princes of hell. I was everything evil is supposed to be. I was a god."

Martin considered this for a moment.

"What happened?"

"I came to New Jersey."

Barky whined.

"I was conjured by a witch in 1735. A common practice back then, you know not like now where conjuring only happens when fat ugly people want to fuck." Stitch said, and then looked at Martin. "You didn't conjure me for *that*, did you?"

Martin shook his head 'no.'

"Good," Stitch said. "Anyway, this witch wanted a demon for revenge on her fellow townsfolk for killing her girlfriend. You think there's no tolerance these days? Should've seen *that* stuff go down. I'll tell you something, when two evil lesbians like them get together-"

"Just get on with the story, if you don't mind."

"What, two lesbian witches aren't interesting?"

Now it was Martin's turn to sigh.

"Fine," Stitch spat. "So this witch conjures me and says, 'I need to destroy this town for what they have done.' I ask what my end of the deal is, which means usually, what sacrifice I get. Tit for tat, as you well know."

Martin nodded. The first rule of simple conjuring, according to the book, was to have something to offer as a sacrifice, usually involving blood. He thought of Stuart and James, both dead and didn't bother to stifle a nervous smile.

"So, after I ate the baby, I started to-"

"After you ate the *what*??" Martin asked.

"Baby. Babies are for the really big favors."

Martin was repulsed. A short wave of nausea ran though him as he tried to imagine it. It wouldn't go away when he tried to stop thinking of it.

"That's so fucked up! How *could* you?"

Stitch cocked his head to one side.

"You sacrificed your two friends for me didn't you? They were young, like you."

"But they weren't babies."

"Weren't they?" Stitch asked. "What's the difference between what you just did and what the witch did?"

"Eating babies is..." Martin couldn't finish.

"Evil? Were you going to say evil?"

Martin didn't say anything.

"Well, I am evil." Stitch said. "Evil begets evil. What do you think that makes *you*?"

Martin sat there with his mouth open. He closed it and shook his head. He then said, "Go on with the story."

"I took over a pregnant woman's body and allowed myself to be 'born' I guess you could say. It was a legend around here."

Martin frowned.

"Wait. What was this woman's name?" He asked.

"Leeds," Stitch said. "I was the thirteenth child of Mother Leeds. Ring a bell yet?"

Martin seemed to recall the name Leeds. He thought about it for a moment and suddenly remembered where he had heard the name.

"*You're* the Jersey Devil?"

Martin sat up in his chair. He smiled.

"That's so cool! I mean, shit, that's *awesome!*"

Stitch stamped a little foot.

"No it *isn't*." He said. "For two weeks, I got some really good terror in; eating livestock, children...yes, *babies*. But the woman I came out of, Leeds? She wasn't just some local yokel. When she found out she was pregnant, she proclaimed 'Let this one be a devil!' I thought that would have been perfect. Well, guess what? Her family- all twelve kids and the town got real *un*-scared of me. The town found out that the witch who conjured me was also a cousin of Leeds."

"They used her to track you down?" Martin asked.

"She led them right to me." Stitch said, and started sounding angrier as he continued. "I was sleeping in a cave hip deep in children's bones, when they caught me, and staked me, and lit me on fire. As a demon in true form, I can't be killed, but a conjured demon can be driven out of its occupying form - like the Jersey Devil form – if the body is destroyed. It was humiliating. Not unlike now, actually."

Martin looked puzzled.

"Why?"

Stitch jumped off of the bed and over to "Raising Demons-Millennium Edition" and kicked it with his small pigskin foot.

"This book is a 'Who's No One' in the demon world, Master. The rituals aren't supposed to work. You get put into this book, and you're done. I've been in the sand and dirt of the Pine Barrens for 200 years. And now?" He spread his small arms out to show Martin what he already knew.

Stitch was an ugly little chew toy.

"But," Martin started, standing up. "You're out. I did the ritual right. The body is only temporary."

Stitch looked up.

"Is it?"

Martin picked up Stitch and held him up to his face. He smiled.

"What kind of demon master would I be if I left you like this?" He asked.

Stitch just looked at him.

"Are you going to kiss me now?"

CHAPTER 5

Stuart lay on a gurney at the hospital morgue. He only knew this because that's where the two cops who had found him said he was. He was still zipped up in the bag they had shoved him into, roughly. He didn't understand. He was alive. He had to be. He could still hear, and feel everything. His eyes were blurry (when not in the zip lock bag) but he was alive.

Alive! He screamed inside his head. His only hope would be the doctor. Doctors knew that kind of stuff. Once a doctor showed up, he'd be okay.

He wished someone would unzip the bag.

CHAPTER 6

"So, what do you say we begin tomorrow?" Martin said to Stitch. Martin was in his bed, under the covers. Stitch, was in a shoebox half under the bed.

"Great," Stitch said flatly. "Wonderful."

"Don't you want to know what it is?"

Stitch said nothing.

"Good night, Stitch."

Stitch sighed.

He could just imagine what it would be. Some insipid revenge plan by a sixteen year old. How far he had fallen. In the thrall of a child: a boy who had no idea what he had his hands on or what he was doing. The boy was smart, but he wasn't evil. Not yet. When that happened, he could be free. He just had to be patient.

Which would be nearly impossible for him.

Hours later, Martin snored lightly in his bed. Barky lay curled at the foot of the bed. And Stitch stared up at the bedsprings from inside of the shoebox.

He tried to close his eyes, but couldn't. Damn buttons, he thought. I have buttons for eyes. Humiliating. Still, he tried to think of a way to change his situation sooner than later and realized he would need more than patience. Patience was not an option. He needed to find a new body before word of his embarrassing resurrection was discovered.

He didn't have to wait long.

"If I hadn't seen this, I would not have believed it," Stitch heard the words and shuddered. Barky emitted a low growl, but stayed asleep.

Stitch pulled himself and the shoebox from under the bed and looked. He saw her and felt a mix of relief and fear.

Lilith.

She smiled her terrible smile, full of fangs and malice. She stood in the room, cowering so she could fit. Her long black wings folded into her back and she stood, terrible and magnificent before Stitch. She was almost human to see, but the claws on her hands and feet and the black/red of her skin kept that resemblance to a minimum. For a demon, she was both beautiful and terrifying.

"Um," Stitch began, but couldn't say anything else. He was humiliated.

Lilith's face contorted into one of almost pity.

"Poor little Benny."

"What are you doing here?" Stitch said in a whisper.

"I came as soon as I heard." She said. "I just *had* to see what became of you." She bent down closer to him. "You're so small."

"I didn't think word would be out yet."

"Oh, simply *everyone* knows, Benial. Everyone."

"Don't say my name!" He hissed. "If he hears my name, I'm done."

Lilith nodded. Names were power. Once a human learned a demon's true name, the demon would forever be in the thrall of that human. It would also render it helpless against any attacks from other demons; the one time a demon could actually be destroyed. Considering the dire consequences, it was an event that rarely occurred and which caused more demons to 'convince' their masters to either kill themselves, or release the demon altogether.

"Relax, he's asleep," Lilith replied and waved a hand over Martin. He stirred a moment and then there was silence. Barky growled again, but remained asleep as well. "There, we can speak freely."

Stitch moved away from the bed and closer to Lilith.

"Lil, you have to help me." He said. "I need a new body."

Lilith picked him up and brought him close to her face. She clicked her fangs.

"But you're so *cute* like this," She teased.

"Knock it off, Lil. This is a real problem, especially since-"

Lilith licked his face with a long, forked tongue.

"Pig skin," she said and dropped him on the floor. "Appalling, lover. Simply appalling."

Stitch rose to his feet and glared up at Lilith.

"You've come to mock me?" He snarled.

She smiled again.

"We're demons, Benny. Torment is what we do."

"Lil it's *me*,"

Lilith again bent down close to Stitch's face. This time she wasn't smiling. She was listening.

Stitch sighed and told her everything. When he was finished, he asked a question.

"Who created that fucking Raising Demons book?"

Lilith straightened a little.

"That would be Azaziel," She said, voice full of contempt. "You know, you're actually lucky you were freed."

"Do you call *this* lucky?" He snarled. "You call this freed?"

"Yes, I do," She snapped. "Do you know who else is in that book that may never be released? Do you have any idea?"

Stitch looked at her.

"Who?"

"Cabal." She said. "You and Cabal were not supposed to get free of the book."

"Impossible," Stitch muttered, and then said, "*Cabal?*"

Lilith nodded and stifled a growl. She glared at Stitch.

"Yes, Cabal, so yes, you're *lucky*. But perhaps, you were luckier in the book after all. Azaziel is looking for you right now to finish you off. And if I found you…"

Stitch turned and walked towards Martin's bed. Then he whirled around.

"Why are you here, Lil?"

She sighed.

"To see you. Warn you. All I know is how it became after you and Cabal were sent into the book. How it *is*. It's…awful. Azaziel is…"

Stitch stared at Lilith and said nothing for a long time.

"Damn," Lilith said, breaking the silence. "At least you made it back."

"This is not *back*," Stitch snapped. "And if it's true about Cabal, you have to help me get him out."

Lilith straightened up.

"I can't do that, Benny. Not for you, not even for Cabal. It's too dangerous."

"Dangerous for whom? From what you've told me, *I'm* the one who needs help."

"For me. Do you know what he'd do if he found out I was even here?"

"Maybe Azaziel will give you your own chapter in 'Raising Demons'," he replied dismissively. "You didn't have to come here to patronize me."

Now it was Lilith's turn to sigh.

"I can't help you, Benny. And I'm *not* patronizing you. I'm just warning you. He's looking for you."

"Fat lot of good a warning is at this point. I can't do anything in this skin."

"There is one thing," Lilith said quietly.

Stitch said nothing.

"Get the boy to get you a new body."

"Seriously, Lilith." Stitch said. "Thanks. That had *never* occurred to me."

Lilith looked down.

"I just wanted to warn you."

And then she was gone. Stitch stood in silence for a long time taking in what had just happened. He was in worse trouble than he had ever thought possible, but he was free to do something. But what, he had no idea.

From downstairs, he heard the front door of the house open. Martin's parents had come home at last. He looked at the boy's alarm clock-it was a child's clock; Snoopy and Woodstock on a doghouse, with the display announcing in green light 3:10 AM.

And then he had an idea that would have made him smile if he had been able to smile.

CHAPTER 7

Stuart heard the bag unzip and if he had been able to breathe, he would have sighed in relief. They would see him and see that he was still alive and he'd be okay. As the bag was unzipped, he found himself staring up at a very bright light. Then he heard a voice he recognized.

"Oh, Jesus, no." he heard his mother say. "Oh *please* God..."

He couldn't move his head to see her. He could only hear her, inches from his face, weeping. He heard another voice.

"I'm so sorry, folks," said the voice. "This is your son, Stuart?"

He then heard his father speak.

"Yes," his father said weakly. "That's our boy."

"What happened?" His mother moaned. "What happened to him?"

"We're not sure yet, ma'am. We need to perform an autopsy, but we'll need your permission first."

"Whatever it takes," His father said, angrily. "Whatever it takes to find out who killed my boy."

"We'll begin the autopsy in the morning. My condolences Mr. and Mrs. Fender. I do need to have you both fill out some paperwork."

I'm not dead! Stuart screamed in his head. I'm still alive!!

Stuart stared blankly at the light over his head as the body bag was zipped back up. He heard muffled voices and footsteps walking away from the bag. Again, he was alone in the darkness of the bag. He knew the next time the bag would be opened, he would also be opened. In his mind, he screamed again and again.

CHAPTER 8

Martin dreamed he was burning. He was ablaze; engulfed entirely in flames, but he wasn't in pain. Far from it. He felt alive and powerful. He looked out in front of him and saw thousands and thousands of people, bowing to him. The looks of terror and awe were on everyone's faces, and Martin drank it in deeply. This was power, he thought. This was control. He spread his arm out and a great roar came forth. But the roar was strange, almost melodic. It sounded like...

... a rock song blasted out and Martin opened his eyes. He looked at the Snoopy and Woodstock alarm clock radio face and saw that it was 6:45 AM. He rubbed his eyes and sat up. Barky was still asleep at the foot of his bed and snoring. Martin looked down and saw the shoebox he had placed Stitch. The box was there, but Stitch was missing.

"Oh no," he muttered and swung his feet over the side of his bed.

CHAPTER 9

Stuart waited. The coroner had said the autopsy would take place first thing in the morning, and he was certain that it was morning. He lay there, trying to convince himself that this was just a bad dream for the hundredth time. He was trying to be resigned to the fact that he was doomed.

He was not succeeding. The worst part, he thought, was that he couldn't even cry, or shake, or anything. There was no release. He was going to be sliced open and feel everything.

Please, he screamed in his head. Don't let this happen to me!

"Well, what do we have here?" Said a voice that seemed to come from all around him. "A poor, lost soul. And so young too."

Please, oh please don't hurt me, Stuart thought.

"I'm not here to hurt you, Stuart." The voice replied.

Stuart ran out of thoughts for a moment, because he didn't believe he had heard correctly.

"I *know* you can hear me, Stuart. I can hear you thinking. You should say hello or something."

Instead, Stuart screamed in his head a single word.

Help!

"Well, that's why I'm here." The voice said pleasantly enough. "We've got to get you out of here before the medical examiner comes bouncing along. Any minute now, in fact."

Oh God, thank you! I'm not dead and they all think I'm dead.

"Oh, but you *are* dead, Stuart. Make no mistake about that. You're quite in fact, dead."

How can I be?

"That demon you and your stupid friends raised? *He* killed you. He just left your consciousness in your body so you could watch and feel it rot. Had I not come along, you'd be spending eternity in a hole, never seeing or hearing anything but the bugs digesting you. Unless, you were going to be cremated. Good heavens! We wouldn't want that, would we?"

I'm...*dead?*

"I'm afraid so."

Stuart whimpered in his head.

"Easy, son. We have little time." The voice said quietly. "I will need a favor if I help you though. You want help, right?"

God, yes. Anything.

"Good." The voice let off a little chuckle. "*Very* good. Now, listen. To get you out of here, I need to reanimate your body. You'll still be dead, but you'll be able to move. With me so far?"

Yes, Stuart thought loudly. Whoever this person was, he had his attention.

"Okay. To get that rolling, I need you to say something."

I can't talk.

The voice chuckled again.

"I know that, silly pants. Just *think* it hard."

Okay. What is it?

"You need to say-'posside cum tua quoniam.' And you should be able to leap right off of the table."

What does it mean?

"I'm sorry; did you *want* to stay here?" The voice asked. "Because I can go if I'm not wanted. I *did* say we needed to hurry this up"

No! Stuart screamed. What do I need to say again?

"Repeat after me." The voice said coolly. "Posside."

Posside.

"Cum tua."

Cum tua

"Quoniam."

Quoniam.

"And, presto!" The voice exclaimed. Upon the last word thought, Stuart's eyes, which had been diminishing after hours of non-blinking and drying out, suddenly could focus again. He blinked several times to clear them, but it didn't work. He slowly sat up.

He tried to swallow several times. His mouth was bone dry.

"Wadur," He croaked.

"What?" The voice asked. The voice was still coming from everywhere. "Oh, *water*. Five feet, right in front of you. Have a drink. Pour some over your eyes as well."

Stuart carefully hopped off of the gurney and walked to the water cooler. He drank fifteen small cups and periodically dumped water on his eyes. The water helped his throat and vision. He looked around.

"Where are you?" Stuart asked.

"We need to talk a little bit, you and I," the voice said. "But we need to be quick about it. I know who did this to you and I can help you get him, but we must leave right now."

Stuart was still looking around when a sharp pain in his stomach doubled him over. He grunted. His head shot back up, looking desperately around.

"Shut up and stop looking for me!" The voice said irritated. "I'm in your *head*, okay? Can we go please?"

The pain subsided and Stuart looked for the door. He shuffled towards it.

Suddenly, he felt himself running to the door. His hand shot out and opened it. He darted through and looked for the exit.

Except, Stuart wasn't doing any of this at all.

He tried to talk, but couldn't. His head began to buzz.

"Sorry, Stuart, but you're taking too damn long to get it together. Let me drive you for a while, okay?"

Stuart ran to the door on his left. He felt like he did a few minutes ago, except now he couldn't stop moving. Well, he thought, at least I'm okay.

The voice in his head began to laugh.

CHAPTER 10

"Mom? Dad?" Martin called as he rushed into the kitchen.

"Well, look who's up early this morning." His father said over a newspaper. "Mom's got your breakfast on the way."

Martin's mother stood over the stove, cooking what looked to be some eggs.

"Have a seat Marty. Breakfast is almost ready." Mom said cheerily enough.

Martin's eyes darted around the room.

There was no sign of Stitch.

He pulled out a chair and sat down. He wondered if he hadn't dreamed the whole thing. This thought filled him with an odd mix of relief and disappointment. Maybe his friends weren't dead after all.

They weren't your friends, he told himself. And if it was all a dream, you're back to being plain old Marty.

He gritted his teeth.

"Didn't you know this kid?" His father said, breaking Martin's train of thought.

His father folded the newspaper and showed Martin the article he was reading. It was a small article with a headline that read, 'TEEN FOUND DEAD AT CEMETERY'

Martin blinked and read the piece.

"The body of seventeen year old Stuart Fender was found in the Pine Barren Cemetery late last evening. The cause of death is at this time unknown according to police. An autopsy is scheduled for later this morning. The parents of the deceased refused to comment. No other information was available at the time of this report-"

It happened, the little voice in his head bellowed. Martin was still uncertain of how to feel.

"Wow," was all he could manage to say.

"Did you know him, Marty?" his father repeated.

"Um, kind of, yeah." He replied. "We had some classes together, but...wow."

"You okay?" His mother asked, delivering a plate of hot scrambled eggs in front of him.

Martin stared into the eggs.

"I think so." He said flatly. Where the hell is Stitch, he thought.

Barky, padded slowly into the kitchen and went right to his food dish. He ate quietly but hungrily. Martin watched him. Something didn't feel right. Barky, usually up at the crack of dawn and insane to be let outside was never this quiet.

"Barky's kinda quiet." His father said. "So are you, Marty. Are you sure you're okay?"

Martin just looked at him. He had seen his friends killed the night before and it didn't bother him. It was beginning to bother him that it didn't bother him, but he couldn't tell his father that.

"Can I stay home today?" he asked. "I don't think I want to go to school."

His mother didn't turn around, but instead said,

"Well, that might be a problem if the police show up."

Martin blinked.

"Huh?"

"Leave him alone, Polly." His father said, winking.

Martin hadn't noticed until just then that his father's eyes were bloodshot. You couldn't really tell unless you looked hard through his glasses, but they were beyond bloodshot.

"What's wrong with your eyes Dad?"

His father winked again, but this time a thin line of drool escaped from his mouth. He brushed it away absently and began to read his newspaper again.

Martin frowned and looked at his mother. Her back was to him, but he noticed she was shaking, just a little, but shaking nonetheless. Almost vibrating.

"You can stay home," She said, "But the police will probably stop by here if you do."

Martin's jaw dropped.

"You'd be better off going to school." His father added from behind the paper.

Martin pushed himself up from the table and looked around the kitchen. He saw something on top of the freezer out of the corner of his eye.

It was Stitch.

He was sitting on a box marked COUPONS and looking around the room.

"Morning, Master." He said. "You should eat your breakfast. It's going to be a very long day."

Martin shot a look at his parents, who appeared to not hear Stitch, until his mother said,

"He's right, hon."

"Drink your juice," His father chimed in.

Martin looked angrily at Stitch.

"What did you do?"

He stood, reached up and grabbed Stitch, squeezing him tightly.

"What did you *do*?" He repeated.

"My role is to serve you, Master. The pages of history drip with the blood of plans being fouled by the parents of young rulers."

Martin continued to glare at him.

"This was preventative. Your parents would only stand to betray you eventually."

"What are you talking about? How do you know that?"

"I'm an eternal being. I've seen it happen thousands of times."

"What did you *do* to them?"

"Put me down, and I'll tell you." Stitch said. Martin threw him to the floor with a thud. Barky stopped eating long enough to turn, look and whine.

Stitch sighed and stood up.

"You've really got to stop doing that, Master." He said. He walked over to his mother, who bent down and picked him up. She held him affectionately. Like a little doll.

"What he did was open our minds," She said. Her eyes, Martin could see, were just as bloodshot as his fathers. "He told us who he was and what you had become. We're just so...*proud,* Marty."

His father said chiming in, "And we want you to know that whatever you decide to do with me and Mom is more than okay with us."

"What the hell did you do to them?" Martin yelled directly at Stitch.

Stitch ignored him and said,

"You're going to be late for school, Master. The police will be there, waiting to question you about your two dead lackeys. They are also going to show up here to question your parents about where you were last night. I thought it would be nice if they could vouch for your story."

Martin considered this and went from angry to nervous.

"What's my story?"

"Let's start walking to the bus. I'll explain everything." Stitch said adding "Master."

"Tell me *now!*" Martin said through his teeth. "What did you do to my parents?"

Stitch sighed.

"How much of the book did you read?"

"What book?"

"You know what book." Stitch snapped. "Raising Demons. Did you read the whole thing?"

"What does that have to do with anything?"

"Let me *enlighten* you, Master. I am your thrall, which means I must obey you at all times." He said. "It also means it falls on *me* to ensure your safety and well being at all times, no matter what that may be."

Martin heard this and didn't hear it at the same time. He understood what he was saying, but couldn't really believe it.

"What did you do already?"

"They are in my thrall. They fall under the same circumstances as I do with you. They only exist to ensure your well-being. Their will is mine. And of course, yours."

"They're my *parents*!"

"They were dangerous to you. They were a threat and I took care of it."

Martin sat down. He looked at his parents, who were looking at him, smiling. Smiling, but their eyes were bloodshot and...something else.

"Reverse it." Martin said flatly.

Stitch walked towards the kitchen door.

"If I do that, then they'll be more dead than they are now. It's better this way."

"More...*dead*?" Martin felt like crying as the import of it started to sink in slowly. This wasn't going well at all. This was not what he wanted.

His mother, or what was his mother, put a shaky hand on his shoulder.

"He's right, Marty. You should go to school. Don't worry about us. We're...*fine*."

Martin stood up.

"You killed my parents," Martin said through his teeth.

"They would've had to die sooner or later, Master. You knew that would have to happen eventually."

"Did I?" Martin asked. "Did I *really*?"

Martin grabbed Stitch and held him in front of his face.

"You are a Master of Demons." Stitch said plainly. "Whatever you were before you summoned me is gone. *Dead* and gone. You wanted to be more than you were? You *are*. Your old life is gone and the sooner you accept what you are now, the sooner we can go about doing *your will*."

Stitch squirmed in Martin's grip.

"And what is *my* will?" Martin asked.

"Your will is *your* will. You've chosen not to tell me anything specific, so I improvised."

Martin closed his eyes.

"Oh my God,"

Stitch sighed.

"*That* door is closed." Stitch said, almost too quietly. Martin said nothing, but nodded. He was beginning to get it, Stitch thought.

Suddenly, the kitchen floor rose up quickly to meet Stitch as he was dropped again. When he righted himself, he saw Martin grabbing his backpack. Martin wiped his eyes with his hand. He walked over to Barky and patted him on the head and then looked at Stitch.

"Barky's fine, right?"

Stitch waited a moment to answer him. Something seemed to have switched on inside of the boy.

"I'm not allowed to touch him, remember?"

"We'll be going over some other things you're *not* allowed to touch later. I have to get to school. Can one of them drive me?"

Stitch turned to Martin's father.

"Sure Marty. I can do it." His father said, happily.

He stood up, folding the newspaper.

"Are we all ready?" He asked, smiling that terrible smile.

CHAPTER 11

"Is this a crack house?" Stuart asked.

"You bet!" said the voice in his head. "Let's go inside."

Stuart had been walked all over town in the early morning until stopping in front of the dilapidated six-story hovel. There was a pile of garbage blocking the front door. And the place, even outside, reeked of human feces.

"I don't think it'll be safe," Stuart said.

"Well, not for whoever's inside, certainly. Let's go already, or should I take over again?"

Stuart did not want that. Being controlled like that was scarier than being dead. He climbed the stairs and then over the garbage.

The lobby was dark and smoky. He heard people inside coughing and moaning.

"Upstairs, my boy. No time to waste!" Said the voice in his head. Stuart had no idea what the voice in his head looked like, but he sure sounded like a game show host.

"Do you have a name?"

After a quick pause, the voice came back and said,

"Call me Lord."

Stuart stepped over a man who may or may not have been dead, lying halfway across the steps.

"Lord? That's kind of a cool name."

"More of a title really."

"Oh,"

"Don't worry, my boy. Not a big deal. I have many names anyway. What would you be comfortable with?"

"Um," Stuart thought about this as he cleared the first floor. "I don't know. I guess Lord is okay."

"Okay then!" Lord said happily. "Let's get those legs pumping, Stu. Lots of work to do."

Stuart moved up the stairs a little faster. He started to think about Marty. Marty, that little fucktard, let me die, Stuart thought. Lord laughed.

"Fucktard. That's funny."

"No, it isn't," Stuart said.

"Easy. He'll get his sooner than later. The first part of our problem is the demon. Benial is his name. He's the one who did this to you."

"Benial. Stupid name."

"I'm sure he has a new one by now." Lord said. "But yes, stupid name indeed."

Finally, Stuart reached the top floor. He walked to the end of a hallway and found a room with the door opened. He looked inside and saw a young woman curled up in a ball by an open window.

"Perfect!" Lord said. "We can use her."

Stuart was confused.

"For what?"

Stuart felt Lord smile in his head.

"Breakfast."

"What, you're gonna eat her?" Stuart snickered.

"No, silly." Lord said quietly. "*You* are."

Stuart was repulsed only for a moment, but the mention of something to eat made him hungry.

"Um," Stuart started.

"Just go over there and dig in."

"But,"

"Time you realized that you're not the same guy you used to be anymore. You're a different species altogether. You're dead, but you still have to take care of yourself. One of the things you have to do is eat. So, eat."

"But, she's still alive. And besides, isn't that cannibalism?"

Lord sighed.

"When a human eats a human, its cannibalism. When *you* eat a human, its survival. More importantly, it's *breakfast.*"

"Breakfast?" Stuart was getting hungrier the more he looked at the sleeping young woman.

"Most important meal of the day!" Lord said.

Stuart swallowed. To his surprise, he was having less of a problem with what he was about to do than he thought.

"Do I just...go and start eating, or do I have to kill her first?"

"It's your breakfast, Stu." Lord said. "However you like it is *fine.*"

Stuart began to smile as the young woman began to stir.

CHAPTER 12

One thing about human thralls, Stitch observed, is that they drove like shit. Stitch had never been in a car before, but he was pretty sure you weren't supposed to weave all over the road. Martin was clutching the dashboard in fear and anger. Stitch had fallen onto the front seat floor about ten minutes previous and Martin was in no hurry to pick him back up. Not that it bothered him so much; he was better off not looking out of a window.

Stitch could see Martin's father from the floor. He was drooling again with that stupid smile on his face.

He sighed.

"What's your problem?" Martin asked, glaring down at the demon.

"Nada," Stitch replied.

"Why do you talk like that? You've been in the ground for two hundred years."

This had been bothering Martin since resurrecting the demon the night previous, but it hadn't bothered him enough to ask until now.

"What do you mean?"

"You talk like you've been in the twenty first century your whole existence. You knew the reference to that horror movie,' Child's Play.' You swear. You know what I mean."

"Would you like the short explanation or the long one?"

"The short one."

"Because."

Martin waited for more.

"That's it? Because?"

"Yes."

"Okay, how about the long version before I stomp on you?"

Stitch nearly laughed, but held it in.

"Just because I was stuck in the ground, doesn't mean I couldn't get around. I could go anywhere I wanted. I watched, I listened and listened some more. I just couldn't *do* anything. I'm eternal if I have a physical form or not."

Martin nodded his head.

"Any other questions?" Stitch asked, trying not to sound condescending.

Martin lifted his shoe and brought it down on Stitch as hard as he could. He lifted it back up and looked at the squirming little thing.

"That'll do for now." Martin said.

Stitch sighed.

"Here we are!" Martin's father said through clenched teeth.

Martin could see several police cars in the front of the school. Policemen were lining up the students in front and talking to them as they each went inside. There were two policemen by the curb, talking to parents as they dropped their sons and daughters off.

"You should hide me, Master." Stitch said.

"Well, what do I say to the cop before I shove you into my bag?"

"Your father knows what to say. You just be sullen. Do you know what that means, Master?"

Martin picked up Stitch and shoved him into his backpack. He thought he heard Stitch swear, so he punched the bag. The noise stopped.

"Here we go," Martin said as the car approached the curb.

The policeman made a motion for Martin's father to roll his window down.

"Good morning sir," The cop said. "I'm sure you heard there's been some trouble."

"Oh, yes sir." Martin's father said. "Poor Marty knew him I'm afraid. Not real well, but he knew him."

The cop looked at Martin, who was slumped down in the front seat. He certainly looks pretty shook up, the cop thought.

"What we're doing is asking the kids to see if anybody knew what trouble those boys might have gotten themselves into."

"Boys?" Martin heard himself ask. Then he remembered James. He swallowed hard.

"Yes, son. There was another body at the scene." The cop said sympathetically.

Martin's father put a shaky hand on his knee as if to comfort him. Martin tried not to freak out.

"This is just awful, officer. Awful. Do you think the kids will be sent home early?"

The cop shook his head.

"That's up to the principal sir." The cop shifted his attention back to Martin.

"You gonna be okay, son?"

Martin nodded, but didn't look at the cop. He was beginning to panic. As if the creepiness of his dead father's hand on his knee weren't enough, he felt a sharp pain in his head that made him wince.

Sorry, Master, Stitch's voice said, exploding in his head, *but crying is a really good idea right now.*

Martin burst into tears brought on by the pain. He felt humiliated, but angrier than anything. He'd already spent the morning crying over his parents, so he was pretty exhausted by it at this point.

"Easy, son." The cop said reassuringly. "I think your principal is bringing in someone to talk to you kids."

"That's very smart," Martin's dad said, squeezing Martin's knee again.

"You ready?" The cop asked Martin.

He nodded and opened the car door. He looked at his father, who just sat there, stupidly smiling and drooling.

"Love you," Martin muttered. The pain was excruciating, but it was beginning to ebb.

"Love you back!" His father replied, but there wasn't any love behind it. It was an automated response, like a recording from an actor who couldn't mean what it was he was saying. Martin started to fight tears again. He climbed out of the car and walked toward the school. He heard his father pull away from the curb.

Martin put the backpack over one shoulder.

What now? He thought to himself.

We go in, Stitch replied in his head. Martin got on the long line to enter the school. He looked around at the other students. They all had that same look of dull shock on their faces.

The same look on my face, he thought.

That's a good thing, Stitch replied.

Are you going to keep answering my thoughts?

I thought you were talking to me. Stitch replied. *I didn't think it smart to talk out loud.*

Martin sighed. Then, he saw Tara. His eyes caught hers and he quickly looked at his feet.

Oh, man. He thought.

What is it?

Just a girl. Nothing to worry about.

A loud sigh erupted in Martin's head.

Then why am I starting to worry?

Martin didn't respond. He looked up and saw Tara walking over to him.

"Hey, are you okay?" She asked.

Martin looked up at her. She was beautiful. Deep brown eyes and honey blonde hair. She wasn't a cheerleader, but you'd swear she was. She looked like the American high school dream, and right now, she was looking right at Martin.

"Yeah," he managed to say. "I guess I'm still kinda dealing with it, you know?"

She looked at him with a sad sweetness and put a hand on his shoulder.

"This is so fucked," she said.

"Pretty much," he replied shrugging.

She smiled.

"Let me know if you need anything, kay?"

"Kay."

"I should get back in line. I just wanted to say hi."

She smiled again and squeezed his shoulder. She turned and went back in line with her friends, who were all staring at Martin. He watched her go and actually began to relax a little.

Sweet, Stitch said in his head. *Does the ass match the voice?*

"Shut up," Martin said aloud.

The kid in front of him turned around and scowled at him.

"What'd you fuckin' say?"

Martin's head snapped toward the kid. It was Frank Losky, a senior football player. Not the brightest kid, but one of the meanest.

"Sorry, not you." Martin stammered.

"Right," Loskey replied, smirking. "Fucking right, *not* me."

Loskey turned back around and Martin took a deep breath.

Temper, temper Master.

That was your fault.

Please tell me you didn't resurrect me to help you date that girl.

Martin thought nothing but Stitch continued.

You did, didn't you, Stitch sounded angry.

No, Stitch, I didn't. Be quiet!

"You knew him, didn't you?" Loskey asked, turning back around.

"What?" Martin said surprised.

"Stu Fender. He was your friend, right?"

It took an actually effort for Martin to answer him. He really didn't consider Stu a friend. Not by any stretch of the imagination. James either for that matter. They were just…

"Well, I *knew* him."

"Bitch, yes or no."

Martin started to shake slightly.

"Er, yes."

Loskey glared at him.

"So, what happened to him?"

"I don't know," Martin stammered. "I just found out this morning."

"Bullshit," Loskey said simply.

Who is this asshole? Stitch asked.

Martin stared blankly at Loskey.

"You fucking know something, right?"

"No, I don't. Really."

Don't sound scared, Master.

"He was gonna out you or something, right?"

"Huh?"

"Out you because you're a sissy. He was gonna tell and you whacked him, right? I mean, we all know you're a sissy." Loskey started to laugh. "You don't think he still had copies of your famous picture?"

Martin's face flushed red. He was afraid and angry.

Master?

Martin gritted his teeth.

Not now, he thought. *Please not now.*

I'm sorry, was that for me or you? Stitch asked.

"Look a little embarrassed there, fag." Loskey said. "I mean, it makes no difference to me if you like a little dick, and we all know you *do*, but did you have to kill your pal like that?"

A few of Loskey's friends laughed.

Martin looked down, not knowing what to do.

"I'm still talking to you." Loskey said.

Tell him to fuck off.

Martin looked up, uncertain.

I can't say that, he thought. *He'll kill me.*

I don't know why I need to keep reminding you, but you are a master of demons, Stitch said. *He is decidedly not.*

Martin considered this for a split second and then thought,

What can you do?

"Did you hear me fag?" Loskey asked. "I said I'm still talking to you."

Martin looked up at Loskey. He fixed his eyes onto his and without smiling or even with a shaky voice spoke.

Martin said, "Fuck off."

Loskey looked surprised and then snickered. The small group of friends who were already laughing stopped.

"What did you say?"

"Turn around and fuck off." Martin said. "Last warning."

Loskey did a complete turn and leaned in close to Martin's face.

"You just wanted to see my ass, didn't you?" He smiled and said, "Ever been hit so hard, you shit your pants?"

Martin smiled back and said, "Did somebody say 'shit your pants?'"

Loskey's smiled faded as a loud flatulent sound erupted. He tried to giggle it off-it was just a fart after all, but it hurt somehow. His friends laughed. He stood up straight and the sound came again, this time louder. The sound was followed by a smell.

"Dude, fucking gross!" one kid said loudly. Loskey turned around as the kids in front of him followed suit. They were all equally disgusted, amused and chuckling.

"Man, he just shit himself," Loskey heard a girl yell. He reached around and felt the back of his pants. He felt wetness. He looked at his hand and saw...shit.

"Shit!" he exclaimed.

"Yeah, no kidding" he heard someone yell and there was more laughter. Martin stood staring at Loskey, who had all but ignored him. Another loud farting noise came and this time, Loskey doubled over, moaning.

A policeman in the front of the school came over.

"What's the problem?" he asked before seeing Loskey on his knees, now openly shitting himself and nearly screaming.

"It hurts, holy shit it *hurts*!" Loskey kept repeating. The policeman moved over to Loskey, but kept slight distance. Martin moved away as well, along with the other students.

How's that, Master? Stitch asked.

That's...awesome. Martin admitted.

Now, the question is, do we want him alive or dead?

Martin, impressed with this first flexing of this power, pondered this for a moment. He saw the agony on Loskey's face and although he hated the rotten bully, he couldn't help it.

Let him go for now, he thought.

Immediately, Loskey's pain subsided and he slumped over on the lawn. He closed his eyes for a moment and then looked around. The entire school had just watched him defecate all over himself. He fought back tears and stood up.

"You all right now?" The policeman asked him. The cop had a smirk on his face.

"I have to...get cleaned up," Loskey said and began to trot to the front of the school. The cop called over to the policeman watching the front door.

"Let him in, Billy. He's got some problems."

The entire line of students laughed, including Martin.

Kind of makes you wonder what that kid eats on a regular basis, doesn't it? Stitch asked and Martin laughed harder.

Quit making me laugh, Martin thought.

He snorted and then looked around him. Everyone else was still laughing, but not as hard as Martin. He didn't want to attract attention. He forced himself to stop laughing before anyone got any ideas.

But he held the smile just a little while longer.

CHAPTER 13

"You feel better, don't you?"

Stuart sat on the floor next to the remains of the young woman. The front of his shirt was covered in gore, and he was still chewing on a piece of breast.

"I do," Stuart said after he swallowed. "Boy, I really do."

In fact Stuart had never felt as good as he did right then even before he died. He felt like a new...thing. He felt powerful and strange, but in a good way. He was ready for whatever waited for him as long as he could feel this way.

"Perfect." Lord said. "Do you want to eat some more, or shall we get started?"

"Let's do it," Stuart replied, standing up. "What's the plan?"

"Simple. We find your friend and then we find Benial. *Then* we kill *your* friend and put Benial back into his place."

"Why can't we just kill him too?"

"He's eternal. But, there are fates worse than death, as you can attest."

Stuart considered this for a moment. Yes there were fates worse than death. But right now, he felt so good, he didn't really care.

"What's going to happen to me? I mean, I'm dead right?"

"Very much so, yes." Lord said.

"Well, what can I do?"

Lord didn't answer. Stuart looked around the room.

"Hello? You still there?"

"Still here."

"Okay. What can I do if I'm dead?"

Lord laughed.

"Don't worry; you won't be like that forever!"

Stuart felt relieved.

"Jesus, I thought I was gonna be dead for keeps, you know?" Stuart laughed.

Lord laughed again too.

"Let's worry about what you'll be later, okay? For now, we have some work to do. Where would your friend be right now?"

"School, probably." Stuart said. "So, I guess we can't go there now."

"No, but you know where he lives, right?"

"Well, yeah. But he won't be home right-"

"Obviously," Lord continued, "His parents would be home though, correct? At least one of them?"

Stuart smiled.

"Yeah, I guess they would be."

"Okay then," Lord said. "Let's find you a new shirt and maybe a basin for you to wash your face. You look a mess."

"What are we going to do?"

"We'll see," said Lord. "Who knows? Maybe you'll be hungry again."

CHAPTER 14

"First of all, Marty I want to say how sorry I am about your friends."

Martin sat in Principal Reece's office. He was seated right in front of Reece and two plain clothes detectives stood behind him. He surprised himself by not being nervous in the slightest bit. In fact, he was still pumped from what happened to Loskey. He tried to look maudlin and hoped he wasn't smirking.

"Thanks, Mr. Reece." He said, trying to sound sad. "It's just so...messed up."

"Yes, it is." Reece cleared his throat. "Since you knew Stuart and James, the police wanted to talk with you privately in my office. I don't want you to worry about anything, Marty. This is just to help us understand what happened. And considering what happened last year..."

Reece stopped because he ran out of any reason to finish his thought. He didn't know why he brought up last year and stopped abruptly. It took an actual effort for Martin to not glare, but he remained seated and nodded as if he understood.

What about last year? Stitch asked in his head. Martin remained silent.

Martin turned around and looked at the two detectives. They both looked serious as hell, except one of them had a denim jacket on. Martin turned around again to face Reece.

"I'll do what I can, sir." He said.

"Great. Let me get out of your way then. Marty, I'll be right outside."

Reece got up and one of the detectives moved into his place. Martin looked at him and again, tried to look sad. He hoped it was working because he was livid.

"Hi Marty," the cop with the denim jacket said. "My name is Lieutenant Weidlin. My partner back there is Detective Thoms. We're both working on this case and we hope you'll be able to help us out."

"Don't worry, kid." Thoms said behind him. "You're not on trial or anything."

Weidlin looked up at Thoms and glared.

"Forgive my partner, Marty. He's a little new at this."

Martin didn't have to look at Thoms to know his face was turning red. He fixed his gaze on Weidlin and tried to listen intently.

Here we go, Master. Careful.

Martin didn't respond.

"Now then Marty-or do you prefer Martin?"

The question took Martin completely by surprise. No one had ever asked that before; everyone just called him Marty. He really didn't know how to answer.

"Um...it doesn't matter really I guess," He stammered out.

Weidlin nodded.

"Okay, Marty. I just want to ask you a few questions. Routine, even. You don't need a lawyer or anything, but if you want one-"

"A lawyer?" Martin asked, nearly exclaiming.

"Nothing to be nervous about, really." Weidlin said coolly enough, but it rattled Martin.

Master, don't over-react. He's trying to shake your cage. Stitch sounded more pissed than concerned.

He knows something, Martin thought. *Should I get a lawyer?*

No, he's going to ask questions. If he knew anything about this, he wouldn't believe it anyway. Your parents are going to vouch for whatever you tell him. So, make it believable.

This calmed Martin down a little.

But not by much.

"Sorry," Martin said. "This day has just really...it's getting to me I think."

Nice one, Stitch thought.

"I understand," Weidlin said. "So, let's get started. Where were you last night, Marty?"

"I was home."

"You weren't with Stuart or James at all?"

"Well, we hung out for a little after school, but that was only for a little while."

"How long is a little while?"

"When it started getting dark. Around six thirty."

Weidlin looked down at his hands on the desk.

"Anyone vouch for your story?"

"Well, my folks."

"Were they home all night?"

Fuck, Martin thought. *They were out!*

Don't worry about that, Stitch replied back.

But-

Master, answer him already.

"Yeah, they were home all night."

"Did Stuart and James talk about what they were going to do last night?"

"Not really. They kinda made fun of me for going home early."

"Did they make fun of you a lot?" Thoms asked from behind him.

"Well," Martin started and stopped. If the detectives knew anything, they knew that Martin got made fun of a lot.

"Lots of people make fun of you, isn't that right?' Thoms asked.

"Um,"

"Thoms, why don't you go outside or something." Weidlin said suddenly.

Sighing, Thoms opened the principal's door and left.

"Sorry, Marty."

"Sure," Martin said. He had no idea what was going on.

"Thoms is...new." Weidlin said. "He's not really very good at this just yet."

"That's okay," Martin replied sheepishly. This time, it wasn't an act. He knew where the conversation was going.

"But, he's right. Your principal said you *do* get picked on a lot."

Martin's face grew red.

"So?"

"Well, it's just an observation. Principal Reece had mentioned to me the...*incident* last year."

Martin said nothing for a moment.

"That was last year."

"It's not that long ago though. Has it gotten any better?"

Martin swallowed hard. His throat started to feel tight.

"Kinda hard for it to get worse, isn't it?" asked Weidlin. Martin nodded.

What is he talking about? Stitch asked. Again, Martin didn't answer him. He spoke instead.

"It kinda sucks to talk about more than anything,"

Weidlin nodded and smiled slightly.

"You're right. Sorry about that, Marty." And then he added, "But it does need mentioning."

Although he felt like he was going to cry again, Martin smiled back and sighed. He took a deep breath.

"It's okay. Go ahead and ask me what you want."

Weidlin pulled a manila envelope out of a pile of paper's on Reece's desk. He opened it and produced an eight by ten picture. It was a picture of Martin, in a pair of white jockey shorts and a noticeable erection. It appeared to have been taken in the gym locker room. The look on Martin's face was one of horror. There was, emblazoned across the picture the words, "SOMEONE HAS A STIFFY!"

Martin's face turned scarlet. Weidlin put the picture away.

What did he show you? Stitch asked.

It's humiliating.

I'm sure, but what the fuck is it Master?

"It can't be easy to see again, Marty." Weidlin said.

Martin nodded, furious but in control.

"Any reason why you just showed it to me again then?" Martin asked.

Weidlin hadn't expected that kind of angry defiant response. He'd honestly expected the kid to cry.

Martin continued, "Because I just found out two of my friends are dead and you just randomly decided to show me the most embarrassing thing that has ever happened to me."

"I apologize, Marty. Truly." Weidlin said. "I'm simply trying to-"

"To what? They had *nothing* to do with that picture."

I gotta see this picture, Stitch thought into Martin's head.

Weidlin decided that he'd best change his direction of questioning. "What do your parents do for a living?"

"My dad is a trader."

"In New York?"

"No, from home. He got one of those TV things to trade online? He lost...*quit* his job last year."

"No kidding?" Weidlin seemed genuinely impressed. "I always thought that stuff was a scam. Good for him. You guys pretty well off then?"

"No, he's not that good yet. He does okay."

Be careful, he's trying to throw you off Master.

"What about your mom? What does she do?"

"She stays home too. She doesn't have a job."

"So both your folks are home right now?"

"Well, unless they went out, but yeah."

"Where were they last night?"

"Home," Martin said without hesitation.

"All night?"

"Yeah. I told you that."

"Right, right..."

Ask him what happened to your lackeys, Stitch suggested.

"So what actually happened to Stuart and James?" Martin asked.

Weidlin rested his chin on his hands and looked at Martin.

"They're both dead, Marty. That's all I really can tell you. It's nothing I can really talk too much about."

"But that's what we're talking about anyway, isn't it? Without actually saying it? Trying to see if anyone saw anything? I mean, that would explain showing me the picture, right?"

Weidlin smiled.

"You're right. You're a smart kid, Marty. But I really can't talk about the specifics of the case."

"Okay,"

Good one, Stitch said, sounding surprised. *That was really good. You threw him off.*

"When did Stuart and James stop picking on you?"

Martin swallowed hard. *Here it is again*, he thought.

"Well, they were always busting on me, but I did it back to them too. It's just how we are...were."

Martin put his head in his hands and sobbed a little.

Nice touch Master, Stitch thought.

Shut up, Martin thought back.

"Hey, I'm sorry. I have to ask these questions." Weidlin said softly. "Just a few more, okay?"

Martin sniffed.

Suddenly Weidlin's cell phone began to ring. Weidlin looked at it and answered it.

"Go," he said into the phone.

He listened intently to the speaker on the phone. Martin couldn't hear the conversation, but he thought Stitch might.

What's going on? Martin thought.

There was a pause, but at the same time Weidlin said "I'm on my way,"

Martin heard Stitch think rather loudly,

Son of a bitch!

"I think that'll do it for now," Weidlin said, standing up. "Listen, you take care of yourself, okay?"

Martin watched him get up and make a move to the door.

"What now?" he asked.

"Um," Weidlin started. He looked worried. "Your Principal will probably send you home later on. Sooner than later. Me and my partner are done here I think."

Weidlin ran out of the door. Martin heard him call for his partner.

"What happened?" Martin asked aloud.

We have to get out of here now Master. There is a huge problem.

"What?"

Your friend Stuart is apparently missing from the morgue and I think I know why.

"But...he's dead." Martin said, running to the door.

CHAPTER 15

Thoms was driving while Weidlin was yelling into his cell phone.

"So, someone walked into the morgue and *stole* the body? Is that what you're saying?"

Thoms was trying not to snicker and failing. He shook his head and smiled. Weidlin saw this and gave him the finger.

"We'll be there in a few minutes," Weidlin spat. "Try not to fuck anything else up." He closed the phone.

"That's some funny shit," Thoms said quietly.

"*How* is it funny?" Weidlin was getting furious.

"If that body hadn't walked, that kid Marty would be my prime suspect."

"I'm still waiting for the funny part."

"I guess they didn't have any news?"

Weidlin looked out of the window.

"None. Not even a time frame, although the security cameras stopped working apparently all at the same time."

"Well, that's something I guess."

Weidlin looked at Thoms.

"Just get us there," he said angrily.

Stuart stood behind Martin's house. Although he was dead, he felt exhausted. It was a longer walk from the crack house than he ever imagined. For one thing, Lord had kept taking over his body to duck behind buildings to avoid being seen. This was nearly impossible since it was still early in the morning. It was also starting to get annoying, since Lord would never tell him when he was going to 'take over and drive' as he called it. Whenever Stuart would protest, he would receive a jolt of terrible pain.

He was beginning to regret his arrangement, but because he was promised to be taken care of, he put up with it. He was still terrified and now, he was tired as well.

Lord couldn't seem to care less.

Still, he was getting tired. After all, he was being used to transport Lord around. Shouldn't he be treated a little bit better?

He sat down behind the front door and sighed.

"Hey Stu, are you okay?" Lord asked. It was that same stupid voice, Stuart thought.

"I'm fine," Stu said after a pause.

"Aw, come on, Stu." Lord said. "You can talk to me. If not me, who else?"

"You'll hurt me," Stu said.

The laughter that came forth was thunderous in Stu's head.

"Well, we'll see about that!" Lord said between chuckles. "Come on, fess up."

"You're just using me to haul you around. You don't have a body and you just want to get where you want to go. What am I getting out of the deal? I mean," Stuart stood up. "I mean, I'm grateful that you got me out of that morgue and stuff, but I feel so..."

"Used?" Lord finished.

"Yeah."

Lord said nothing for a long time. Stuart almost thought he had gone away.

"I appreciate how you feel Stuart, so I'm going to be a little sympathetic."

"Thanks." Stuart replied without thinking. Suddenly, he felt like his head was being ripped off of his body. He could look down and saw that the ground and Martin's house were getting smaller. Then he noticed, along with the pain, that he could see the entire neighborhood getting smaller.

"First of all, and let me be very clear on this; I *am* using you, but not for your body. We have a mutual enemy, my boy. I thought you could use some help. In other words, I was being nice."

The pain got worse, but at least the world stopped shrinking. He struggled, but couldn't break free.

"Secondly, you are being a little damned ungrateful for your position in this little joint endeavor of ours. I don't *need* you or your body for anything at all. I have one of my own, you see."

Stuart listened to this last piece of information and was processing it as he felt the pain in his head stop. He began to fall. He started to scream as he saw the world rising to meet him. Suddenly, he was suspended in midair, being held by something strong but invisible. He looked around but just saw the sky.

"What's this?" He asked.

"Look up and see."

He looked up and saw nothing for a moment. He looked at his leg to see if he could figure out what was holding him and saw that it was attached to something that looked like an...

Arm?

"Up a little more, Stu."

Stuart followed the arm saw that he was being held by something large, black and smiling at him.

"As you can see," Lord said. "I don't need you for transportation."

Stuart's jaw hung open as he began to make out what was attached to the arm. It was hard to actually see, but whatever it was had huge flapping leathery wings. The arm that held him was actually a leg that had a rather large and sharp set of talons. The rest of it was very large; black with yellowish colors and a head that looked like a smiling dragon. He wasn't sure really of what he was looking at, but it was enough to scare the hell out of him.

"Fuck," He said.

Lord opened his huge mouth and laughed loudly. Stu had never seen so many teeth.

"I don't think you want me to do *that*, Stu. You know what they say about us guys with big claws and teeth!"

He laughed louder. Stuart cowered and began to cry. Although no tears came, he cried.

"I see you're sorry, so I'll just let this one slide," Lord said finally. "Just remember one thing."

Stuart looked up at him. Lord pulled him up closer to his face. He was smiling, but not because he was happy.

"I really don't *need* you."

"Y...yes Lord," Stuart croaked. "I understand."

"Good. Now then, friends again?"

Stuart tried to say yes, but couldn't. He nodded enthusiastically instead.

"Well, let's get to work then, shall we? Your friend should be coming home and so should my friend. We should arrange a little welcome home party for them."

"Yes, Lord." Stuart managed. "Yes."

Stuart was gently lowered to the ground and Lord vanished, although his voice remained.

Lord said, "Always good to be clear about things, eh Stu?"

CHAPTER 16

Martin was running as fast as he could. Upon hearing that the undead Stuart was on his way to his house, he bolted out of the school without saying anything at all. Stitch, was regretting being in the backpack, but thought better of asking to be taken out.

"Can we get there any faster?" Martin yelled.

"I guess we're not being subtle about talking out loud then?" Stitch asked inside the pack.

"Stitch!' Martin yelled.

"Fine," Stitch said quietly. "You should be prepared though for what we find at the house."

"Like what?"

"First things first," Stitch said, as Martin suddenly began to levitate. Then, he began to soar, quickly. He felt his stomach swing and he fought back the urge to throw up. He did manage to open his mouth to say something, but several small bugs began to go down his throat. He looked ahead and then he looked down.

He could see the tops of houses and estimated that he was at least a hundred feet into the air.

"There's a good chance that your friend will be with Azaziel," Stitch said. "This will be a problem, but your parents may be able to hold them off for a while."

"Bugs!" Martin yelled. "Mouth!"

Stitch sighed.

"Turn your head, Master." He said.

Martin turned his head and opened his mouth. The bugs were still hitting his head, but no longer in his mouth.

"Who's Azaziel?"

"A very big problem. I can feel him nearby. He's made your friend his thrall."

"What does he want?"

"I don't know,"

"Well, what do we do when we get there?"

"Hope we beat them there." Stitch replied. "Or get there after they leave."

Stitch was worried. He wanted his old body, which was gone forever now in all likelihood. He wanted *any* body; something better than the pig skin. He'd be almost useless against Azaziel. He had some tricks, sure, but a showdown?

Not now. Maybe not ever.

Maybe.

"Master, was your friend an idiot?"

"Huh?"

"Was he stupid. You know what I mean."

Martin thought about it briefly and said,

"Yeah, he was dumb. Why?"

"We have an advantage then."

Martin looked ahead and got a bug in the eye for his trouble. They were close to the house.

"We're almost there," He said.

Stitch resisted the urge to sigh, and let Martin drop lower to land. Martin, of course had no idea what Stitch was doing, so he began to scream.

The drop was sudden and quick. Before he knew it, he was two houses away from his house and was dropped from ten feet from the earth into a pile of wet leaves.

"Ouch," Martin moaned. Stitch would have smiled and tried not to laugh.

He failed.

Martin rolled over and took off his back pack. He unzipped it and pulled Stitch out.

"What the fuck was that?"

"Sorry, Master. I can't really see in the bag." Stitch replied innocently.

Martin stood up and brushed himself off.

"Whatever. What's the plan?"

"We need to get closer to the house. We'll see how your parents did if your friend showed."

Martin started to carefully walk around a fence to get into the next yard.

"What did you mean by my parents holding them off?"

"They're looking for you. They would have tortured your parents to find out where you'd be. But, your parents aren't really easily swayed these days, Master."

"Explain."

"They are in my thrall remember? They're not going to tell them anything. In fact, they'll probably rip your friend to pieces."

Martin thought about this for a moment as he crossed the yard next to his.

"*My* parents? Really?"

"Really."

Martin reached the edge of the yard and looked at his house over a fence.

"Looks quiet," Martin said.

"That's not a good sign," Stitch said. "Can you see anything else?"

"No,"

Martin walked the small length of the fence to a spot where he could climb over.

"Go check it out." Martin said and drew his arm back with Stitch tightly gripped.

"What the fuck?" Stitch yelled and then he was airborne, sailing over the fence. He swore for four seconds until he hit the middle of Martin's back yard. Quickly, he got to his feet and looked around. He felt more vulnerable than he ever had before. Even when he was incorporeal, he still felt in control on some level. Safe.

Now he was six inches tall and made of swine. He couldn't see anything or anyone. He could still *smell* Azaziel, though. He'd been and gone already. Stitch relaxed slightly.

"Well?" Martin called from over the fence.

"Oh, it's all safe, Master. Thank *goodness* you sent me here first to protect you, seeing as I'm only six *fucking* inches tall."

"Shut up." Martin said, jumping the fence. "You still have to tell me about this Azaz...whatever his name is."

"Azaziel. Of course I will."

"Where are they?"

"Sniff the air. That's sulfur. They were here, but they're gone."

"Maybe my parents kicked their ass."

"Perhaps," Stitch said walking toward the house.

"Well," Started Martin. "Let's go in and see what happened."

Martin began to walk towards the back door.

"Sure you don't want to *throw me* inside first?" Stitch asked quietly.

Martin unlocked the back door and said, "Not this time, but thanks."

Stitch sighed and watched Martin walk inside. Instead of following him, Stitch walked around the yard, glad at least to be freed from the backpack.

This was bad, he thought. Really bad. He needed a body, but more than anything, he needed to keep Azaziel away from him until he had one. He was almost powerless against him in his current state. Not quite powerless, but enough to count when it all came down to it.

He sat down on a patch of grass and sighed. He tried to remember what it was like when he wasn't a chew toy.

INTERLUDE: HELL

Hundreds of thousands of them all knelt, praying and worshiping the same thing. It would have been beautiful and inspiring anywhere else…if it had been any *thing* else.

Demons.

Their huge leathery wings fluttered gently as they spoke in one voice against a backdrop of fire and smoke. In one voice, they spoke one word, over and over.

"*Cabal!*"

Atop a hill, stood a huge statue of Cabal, his wings extended and his arms outstretched as he received praise. In front of it, much smaller, but somehow more impressive was the real Cabal, in the same pose. His head was thrown back and his mouth open in ecstasy. Three demons stood behind him, arms crossed, watching the spectacle. Cabal's engorged member shot urine and ejaculate onto the worshipers. They cheered.

"I hate it when he does that," Benial whispered to Lilith, who winked, but kept her eyes forward.

"Silence!" Azaziel said. "Have you no reverence for Cabal?"

Benial smirked and again looked forward. He watched Cabal finish his 'blessing' and sighed. Cabal was his lord and master, no doubt. But he also knew Cabal made such displays for a reason. He had told him, after all, and Benial was no longer impressed.

Well, he was a just *little* impressed. He saw Cabal turn his head slightly to look at him.

Cabal winked and Benial hid a smile, as did Lilith. Azaziel frowned. Azaziel always frowned, Benial thought. He felt Lilith's scaly claws slide into his open palm and squeeze. Her claws dug into his flesh and he hissed in delight.

"Easy, lover." She cooed to him quietly. "Just a sample,"

Benial again, tried to hide a smile. Instead, he leaned over to Azaziel.

"You know *you* must clean the Master's blessing, Azaziel. Whenever he's finished that is,"

Azaziel growled, but nodded.

Cabal suddenly flapped his wings and flew off above the masses. Lilith released Benial's bleeding hand and followed. Benial looked at Azaziel and grinned.

"We shall see you soon, yes little brother?"

Benial launched off after Lilith and left Azaziel to his work, as the masses began to leave. When the three demons had flown out of sight, Azaziel screamed in anger and leapt off of the hill to begin cleaning up after the worshippers.

*

"My children," Cabal spoke from his throne. Lilith and Benial stood before him. "I have news from above."

"Good news, I pray." Benial said.

"The *greatest* news, Benial. Where is your brother?"

"He'll be along," Benial replied, smiling. "He's finishing a task for me."

Cabal laughed.

"You need not be so harsh on him. He will be a powerful demon one day."

"Pardon me for saying, Cabal, but I seriously doubt that."

"You'll see." Cabal said. "He's not anywhere near you or Lilith, but he will come into his own."

"He's a bit severe, don't you think?" Lilith asked.

Cabal considered this for a moment and said, "As were you and as was Benial. Azaziel is the future along with you two. He will come in handy with the news I have."

"What is the news?" Benial asked.

"Ah, we must wait for Azaziel!" Cabal said.

Benial sighed, which never failed to make Cabal laugh. There was a loud thud and Azaziel walked into the throne room. He looked exhausted and glared at Benial as he strode next to Lilith.

"Greetings, dear brother!" Benial said. He was smiling broadly.

Azaziel said nothing. Instead, he bowed in front of Cabal.

"Rise, Azaziel. Disregard your brother's teasing."

"Thank you, Master." Azaziel said.

Cabal stood up and walked towards the three demons.

"My children, today is a day to be remembered for all time. Today, we *rise*."

The three demons looked at each other, confused.

"How can that be?" Lilith asked. "We are *never* permitted to leave."

"We are now," Cabal replied. "I have spoken to He."

The three demons were shaken by this revelation. Cabal had not spoken to He in several millennia.

"He summoned me, and we spoke of our ascent. It will be limited, but again, we shall rise."

Benial frowned.

"What do you mean 'limited' Cabal?" he asked.

"There will be *rules* to our ascent. Still, enough room to spread our wings in a manner of speaking."

"Since when do *we* abide rules?" Benial asked. He was starting to become visibly angry.

Cabal looked him in the eyes, his stare severe.

"Since *now*, Benial. There is no negotiation. We have to follow rules."

"But,"

"Benial!' Cabal snarled. Benial drew back slightly. He'd never seen Cabal act this way towards him. Cabal softened slightly when he next spoke.

"We are offered *nothing* because of what we *are*," He started. "We are the bane of the universe simply for being what were created to be. Without this boon, we are nothing but a scapegoat for the favored in the human worlds." Cabal said 'human' with contempt. Benial understood, but didn't like it one bit.

"Unlike the last time, there will be rules," Cabal said, but then he smiled. "But like most rules, we will find a way to bend them. However, the rules must be in place."

Benial remembered the last time and what a time it had been. Just after the expulsion from heaven, Cabal and Benial waited for the next great failure from above-mankind. The first experiment with man ran into a snag when Lilith was summoned forth to be the first wife of Adam. When she refused, she was cast into the lovely abyss; a perfect fit for Benial. She was as betrayed as they all had been. As mankind flourished, so did the demons, frequently entering the human world to let loose chaos. Benial had become a legend of sorts himself, although the scholars of the time insisted on spelling his name wrong.

But, that was acceptable. Benial or Belial? It didn't matter. *He* was the "Angel of hostility" and 'The merciless one" and that was just fine for him.

When Azaziel had been created to find a similar fate with his name, the dynamic shifted. There was more wickedness in the human realm than had even been dreamed. It was a paradise for torment and evil.

And then, "He" flooded the world and cast all demons out. There were lovely souls to torment, true, but the ability to corrupt? Gone.

Until now.

Benial was distracted from his thoughts of the times previous by Azaziel bowing reverently.

"We shall heed the rules, Master." Azaziel said solemnly. Benial and Lilith rolled their eyes.

"What *are* the rules?" Lilith asked.

Cabal smiled and explained them in great detail.

Benial felt exhausted. He'd listened to the rules for hours, and although he was an eternal being, it felt like he'd never get that part of his existence back again. Lilith looked equally tired, but Azaziel was ever attentive.

As Cabal outlined and explained the conditions for demons entering the human world, a large stone grimoire imprinted the details in flame from behind him. It was all for dramatic show, of course; Benial understood this. The masses of lesser demons would all view the grimoire as a sort of sacred document. Because Benial, Lilith and Azaziel were all witness to the grimoire's creation, the three of them would be regarded as 'saints.'

Knowing this didn't change Benial's feelings towards the imposing of rules. It was all set up to protect the humans with almost no protection for him or his kind. There were annoying rules like the power of names.

"Cabal," Benial began. "If they speak our name, why should they be able to assume our power? What would the point of entering the human world?"

Cabal smiled.

"You aren't thinking clearly, Benial. Let me finish the rules. Then we shall discuss working *around* them."

Benial could have screamed, but held his tongue. He would wait. There was much he could still learn from Cabal, but he wondered exactly how much more he'd be *willing* to learn.

*

"Benial," Whispered Azaziel. "Must you call the master by his true name? Have you no respect?"

Benial, Lilith and Azaziel stood facing the burning landscape of what would later be known as hell in some religions. There were a thousand names for where they were and they were all wrong.

Benial sighed and looked at Azaziel.

"Are you trying to be funny?"

Azaziel looked as if he'd been slapped.

"I suppose not then," Benial said, answering for him. "Listen, little brother. You are a very powerful demon and you honor Cabal in your reverence. He has told me that he anticipates you being one of the most powerful demons someday."

Azaziel's expression changed to one of awe. Lilith had to turn away; she had begun to laugh.

"I had no idea," Azaziel said. He was nearly breathless.

"It is true, Azaziel." Benial said. He moved closer to his brother. "He told me so hours ago himself. You, little brother, are marked for greatness."

Lilith slapped Benial as Azaziel bowed his head.

"Benial, I..."

"No, no Azaziel. Don't speak. Just revel in your impending greatness." Benial said turning away from him so he could smile.

Azaziel looked up at Benial, who was turning to face him. His bottom lip quivered and blinked several times. He stood up full and opened his wings to their full length. Azaziel was nothing if not an impressive looking demon, Benial thought.

"Thank you, brother," Azaziel said. "I shall confer with you both later!" He leapt up and soared into the air.

Benial and Lilith waited until they could see him no more before they both exploded with laughter.

"How long," Lilith gasped "Do you think it will take him before he calls Cabal by his name?"

Benial laughed harder.

"I don't care, as long as it is done in front of us."

The two demons sat down and let their laughter die down. Benial allowed a dark frown cross his face. Lilith, who had been looking at him, spoke at last.

"What is it?"

"I dislike change, Lilith." He said. "I dislike change this sudden and I *especially* dislike it coming from above."

"What are we to do then? We have not been allowed to exist anywhere else but here for so long. It's a boon."

"It's a trap." Benial replied.

"Impossible," She snapped back. "*We* deceive, not them."

"Believe what you will. Mark my words, this will all go badly."

Benial stood up and continued.

"We are superfluous to the operation above. They are sent here for us to devour for eternity-for our pleasure. Why do we need to go up there at all?"

"But, we torment. Imagine tormenting them while they live! Don't you miss the corruption?" Lilith really enjoyed this thought and really had thought of little else.

Benial sighed.

"I do, but we can be pulled out of our paradise for the whim of those monkeys. We can go up and have our bodies destroyed by things that will *dare* speak our names aloud and then take our power. It sounds like torment for *us*, not them."

Benial extended his wings.

"I'm going to go flay someone. Are you coming?"

Lilith shook her head.

"Lover, listen." Benial said. "I just worry that this is the beginning of the end for us."

"They cannot exist without us," She said plainly.

Benial nodded and said,

"I wonder if that is really true, Lilith."

He flew off, leaving Lilith alone, facing the burning landscape that she adored as much as she did Benial. She would have wept if she had been capable. Instead, she dug her own claws into her leg until she hissed in glorious pain.

CHAPTER 17

Stuart was remembering something he had read about runners. It was probably something from one of his health classes in school. He had read that a runner uses his arms almost as much as his legs. The arms swing to help the runner keep balance and also to keep pace.

He thought about this while he ran, holding the stump where his right arm used to be.

People watching Stuart run down the street were shocked to see a young man missing an arm and dressed in zombie makeup. They moved out of his way with their mouths open, but oddly enough, forgot about him almost as soon as he ran past them.

Stuart was trying to get back to the crack house as quickly as possible. He couldn't believe what had happened and he really couldn't believe that Lord had abandoned him in the house.

"Hey Stu, how are you holding up?" Lord said out of nowhere. Stuart didn't try to look for him this time. He knew he wouldn't find him. He was just a voice again, not the huge dragon like thing that had nearly taken his head off. He continued to run.

"Come on, Stuart. It's just a set back."

"My arm," Stuart said. He saw the crack house at the end of the block and ran faster.

"Yeah, I know." Lord said. "But you haven't even seen your face yet. You look terrible." Lord laughed at his own joke.

Stuart stumbled up the steps of the crack house and crashed through the front door. He fell hard on the floor in front of the stairs leading up to the upper floors. He took a moment to kick the front door closed and sat up on the floor. It was difficult using only one arm. He was in agony.

"You should get upstairs," Lord suggested.

"Fuck you!' Stuart yelled.

Lord laughed out loud.

"Oh Stu, you're funny. Especially after our little talk."

"No, fuck you." Stuart said. "You totally fucked me over in the house. Where *were* you?"

"I watched the whole thing." Lord said. "It was just awful."

"Why didn't you help me?"

"There was no way I could have helped you, Stuart. Don't you think I would have?"

Stuart sniffed and tried to stand.

"You almost tore my head off, and you couldn't fucking *help* me?"

"Listen," Lord said. "You are my in my thrall. They aren't. I'm not allowed to touch anything I'm not in control of. It's part of the rules."

"Rules?" Stuart spat as he started to climb the stairs. "You're like, the Devil and you're following rules?"

"There are rules for everything." Lord replied. "Besides, it was *your* job to take care of your friend's parents."

Stuart said nothing. He slowly climbed the stairs with his head down. He held onto the wall since he couldn't hold the railing. He was exhausted.

He just wanted to die.

When he got to the sixth floor, he went to the room with the dead girl. He wasn't surprised to see that she was still very much dead. He sat down hard next to her corpse. Even though she had been dead for only a few hours, she still looked freshly killed. He looked at her sadly.

"Lucky," he said quietly.

Lord appeared in the room, crouching. Stuart looked up at him. He should have been afraid, he realized, but he wasn't.

"Hi son." Lord said cheerily. "Why so glum?"

"Just leave me alone,' Stuart replied.

"Afraid I can't do that and I'm also afraid you can't either." Lord said flatly. "You kind of belong to me."

"Then why don't you just kill me already?"

Lord smiled widely.

"Because you're already dead, Stuart." He leaned down closely to Stuart. "Listen to me carefully. *I* did not kill you. *I* did not leave your soul inside of your dead corpse. I *saved* you from being tortured and buried. I gave you a chance to avenge yourself and you want me to put you back where you were a few hours ago?"

Stuart looked up at him.

"She ripped my arm off," Stuart moaned. "She fucked up my face and you didn't do anything to help me."

"I couldn't help you. Benial put your friend's parents in his thrall. I couldn't touch them. When we find Benial, I'll be able to help you more. That's why I need *you* to help *me*." Lord smiled a very large smile and said, "When you help me, you're really helping yourself."

To Stuart, it made sense and he resented it. He was angry and in pain, but he didn't have any options. He was, after all, a one armed zombie with a fucked up face. He looked down at the dead girl next to him.

"She really is lucky, isn't she?" He said finally. "She's just dead. I'm going to just keep falling apart and shit, right? I can't die, can I?"

He glared at Lord.

"Can I?"

Lord sniffed.

"You'll only be able to die once I take care of Benial. He is the one who did this to you. Him and your friend. We find them, and then we can take care of you. Once and for all."

Stuart said nothing for a long time, until he finally lowered his head.

"Just as long as I can die."

Lord nodded and smiled. He clapped his clawed hands together loudly.

"Great!" He said. "I'll be back later. You sit tight!" And Lord disappeared. Stuart sobbed tearlessly. He went back to looking at the dead girl. He put his hand on her cold leg and squeezed.

"I'm sorry," he whispered. He pulled the leg closer to him as he leaned over and began to bite into her thigh.

*

Stitch opened the back door to Martin's house. For some reason, he was feeling stronger. He'd gotten to use some of his power and it felt good. He almost thought he might be able to face Azaziel if he had to.

The feeling faded as he looked around the kitchen.

Martin's father sat on the floor, eating an arm. He was sitting in an inordinate amount of blood, apparently not his own. What was left of Martin's mother was sprawled out next to the refrigerator. *Guess it's her blood*, Stitch thought. Both of her arms were attached however. He looked back at Martin's father, who looked up long enough to acknowledge him.

"Hi Master," he said cheerily enough.

Stitch sighed.

Three feet in front of him was Martin, unconscious and lying on the floor.

"What happened?" Stitch asked.

Martin's father dropped the arm and stood up.

"It was Marty's friend, just like you thought might happen. Of course, he wasn't expecting *us*." He looked at his dead wife, or what was left of her. "He managed to kill Polly I'm afraid."

"I see that," Stitch said. "Is that his arm then?"

"Yes. I thought you wouldn't mind."

"Not at all." Stitch said. He gestured to Martin. "Can you pick him up? He probably shouldn't be in here when he wakes up."

"Sure," Martin's father said. "But what if his friend comes back?" He dropped the arm and stood up. There was blood all over his legs.

"Pity you couldn't have kept him here. Was there anyone else?"

Martin's father bent down and picked up his son.

"The one you spoke of, Azaziel. He watched, but didn't do anything."

"He couldn't, but that's good." Stitch said, satisfied. "Um...What is your name?"

"Bill,"

"Bill. Of course it is." Stitch said. "Bill, after you put the Master in the living room, I'll need you to take care of your wife."

"Can I eat her?"

"Do whatever you want, just get rid of her quickly." Stitch snapped. "We don't have a lot of time. Put her in the basement or something, but do it. Go."

Bill smiled and carried Martin out of the kitchen. Stitch waddled over to Martin's mother. Her lower half looked as if it had been shredded. Nothing was recognizable at all. He took a small hand, dipped it into the pool of blood, and drew something on the floor.

"Me venire cito. Mihi vobiscum." He said, and then added, "And be fucking quick about it."

He stood back and waited.

Nothing happened. He glared at what he drew on the floor.

"Come on!" He spat.

*

Martin was dreaming again. This time, he was not engulfed in flames. He was sitting on a hill by himself, looking down at the small town where he lived. There were people moving silently up the hill towards him. Not in a threatening way, but there were enough people to make him a little nervous. In the front of the group was James. He was smiling and waving. And Losky was there too, looking happy to see Martin for some reason. His school and all the teachers could be seen.

Tara was there, smiling.

They all were coming to see Martin. And they were all happy. He saw Stitch riding on Barky. He couldn't tell, but maybe Stitch was smiling too. Everyone was happy. Even Martin. He looked up at the sky. Everything was good.

Suddenly, the bright summer sky darkened. The whole town however seemed to silently explode in a bright orange blossom. All at once a voice buzzed in his head.

"You're gonna reap just what you sow," the voice said. It was the voice of his mother, who...

"...didn't make it through the attack. Are you listening to me?"

Martin snapped awake to find Stitch standing on his chest.

"There you are. We have problems, Master."

"What the hell happened?" Martin croaked.

"You saw your mother on the floor and your dad was eating your friend Stuart's arm. You passed out. Not too surprised at that, actually. Now then, we-"

"*What?*" Martin shouted and sat up, throwing Stitch onto the floor. He saw that he was on the couch in the living room. He kicked his legs over the side and stood up.

"My mother is *dead?*" He shouted.

Stitch sighed.

"Master," he said, picking himself off of the floor. "Your mother has *been* dead. We don't have time-"

"I want to see her now." Martin said, sniffing.

"We have to go, Master. We have to find your friend before he finds us."

Martin looked at Stitch. This wasn't going anywhere near where he had wanted it to go. Not in the least bit. He looked around the living room and saw pictures of his family. The picture of him and his father playing a really bad game of basketball when Martin was ten. Neither of them knew how to play. His mother had laughed relentlessly at both of them. The picture of him and his mom at grade school graduation from two years previous. She had been so proud of him that day. He was the top student in the class and she had told him that high school would be a great adventure.

"You'll make friends," she had said to him. "And even if you only make one, well, that'll be enough."

He looked down at Stitch.

"You're not my friend," he said in a hollow voice.

Stitch said nothing.

"Where are we going to go?" Martin asked. His eyes were wet with tears, but he was forcing himself to not cry.

"We're going to meet up with *my* friend," Stitch said.

Martin straightened up.

"I have to get some stuff from my room. I'll be back." Martin said and walked quickly to the staircase. He grabbed a picture of him and both of his parents taken last year from their vacation at Wildwood. He didn't look at it.

When he reached his bedroom door and opened it, he saw Barky, cowering in a corner. When Barky saw him, he leapt up and ran over to him. Martin dropped to his knees and let the big dog lick him. He hugged the dog hard.

"Hey boy!" He said, genuinely happy to see him. "Good dog, good dog."

Barky let a few small barks out and let Martin stand up. He ran in small circles, like he wanted to play.

"No, we're going." Martin said, grabbing some clothes and shoving them into a large duffel bag. "You too."

Barky gave a quick yip as if he understood.

Martin looked on the floor and saw his copy of "Raising Demons: Millennium Edition" and put it in the bag. He gave his room a quick look and saw his yearbook from the year previous. He grabbed that as well and looked at Barky.

"Let's go," he said, and walked out of the room. Barky followed.

Stitch stood in front of the small pentacle he drew on the kitchen floor. Nothing had happened and he was furious.

"Where are you?" He asked, glaring at the pentacle.

The pentacle seemed to glare back at him, silently.

"Who are you yelling at?" Martin asked, appearing in the doorway. Stitch looked up at him. He noticed Martin's eyes were red from crying again, but he seemed to have pulled himself together somewhat. He also noticed the dog.

They just couldn't kill the fucking dog, Stitch thought.

"No one in particular, Master." Stitch said finally, and then added. "Are you okay?"

Martin ignored the question.

"Where are we going?"

"Are we bringing the mongrel?"

"Of course. Where?"

"Somewhere safe. An old place I don't think Azaziel knows about."

Martin nodded. He heard something in the basement and had an idea of what it was.

"What happens to my father now?" Martin asked.

Stitch shrugged.

"What would you like to happen to him?"

"Just end it, okay?"

Stitch sighed.

"It might be better if-"

"End it. Now." Martin said firmly.

"Done." Stitch said and a thud came from the basement. No other noise followed it. Martin bit his lip, but did not make a sound. He nodded, and picked up Stitch.

"Tell me where we're going," He said, shoving Stitch into his backpack. "And start talking to me about Azaziel."

CHAPTER 18

Barky stood at attention in front of a large cave. His eyes searched the woods eagerly, as if he were waiting for someone. He let out a small whine and tucked his tail slightly in. He was scared, no doubt about it. But, he was more scared for his Master than anyone else. Before they had left with the nasty little chew toy (*whom Barky could sadly no longer chew on for some reason*) he had heard horrible things going on in the house. Since his master had locked him in the room for most of the day, he had tried to sleep. There was screaming and yelling. He could tell it was his master's masters doing the yelling, but it didn't seem like them at the same time. Very odd.

Barky looked at the trees again and saw a rabbit. He readied himself to chase it and then fought the urge. He had to protect the master at all costs. He turned around and barked into the cave. He could hear master talking to the ugly chew thing. Master was angry at the chew toy. He didn't know what they were saying, but he could tell that Master was really angry. Master had gotten really angry at him once when he peed on the floor three years ago, but he was even angrier now. He wondered if the ugly chew thing had peed somewhere he wasn't supposed to...

"I don't see why you're so pissed at me," sniffed Stitch. "You brought me to life for your bidding, not the other way around." Then after a thought he added, "No offense."

"You killed my parents!" Martin screamed. "*Twice!*"

Stitch said nothing. He'd heard this line of anger from the boy for the better part of two hours. He had spent most of the two hours hoping that the boy would become distraught and kill himself. He had the first part, but the suicide wasn't going to happen. He felt very unlucky.

"Are you listening to me?" Martin screamed again. "My parents are dead!"

"I know, Master. Dead twice. I know all of this. We're being counterproductive."

They were both standing in the dark, wide and damp cave that Stitch had led them to. It was where, 200 years previous, Stitch had hidden himself when he was first brought to the human world. The bones of all of the children had long since gone, but the smell had remained.

Martin stood leaning against a flat side of the cave, just out of reach of the light coming from his upended flashlight. He had stopped crying, but his eyes burned. He had never been angrier. But he was really unsure of just who he was truly more angry with-Stitch or himself.

"I never told you to kill them, Stitch."

"You did the last time."

"Well...I mean before that."

"And honestly, I only killed your mother once. Your friend did the second one."

"Whatever!" Martin's hands went to his face. "God damn!"

Stitch sighed.

"I'm pretty sure he has, Master."

"Fuck you!" Martin snapped. "This is all your-"

He stopped himself. He knew whose fault it was and there wasn't anything he could do about it. No arguing about it, it was his fault. All the way around. Every single bit of it. He took a deep breath and let it out slowly.

"Better?" Stitch asked.

"What do you care?" Martin asked back.

"You're responsible for everything that has happened today, very true indeed." Stitch began. "But there's so *much* more to do. So much more you're capable of doing. Things you can make happen. For example, the reason you conjured me in the first place."

Martin took another deep breath.

"You never have told me what that was, Master. Perhaps we can address that and maybe it may aid us in what we need to do about Azaziel. Tell me. What happened last year?"

"You need to tell me about *him*," Martin said quietly. "Why is he after me?"

"He's after me, not you." Stitch replied. "He's...my brother."

Martin stared at him.

"Your *brother*?"

"Yes, my little brother. He's the one who put me into the book where you found me."

"Why is he after you then, if he's your brother?"

"I'm still trying to figure out why he put me into the book in the first place," Stitch said, then added "But I think I have a pretty good idea."

Martin sat down on the damp earth.

"Let's hear it then."

"I'm not sure it's relevant to our-"

"*Now!*" Martin spat loudly. There was no mistaking the tone in his voice, Stitch observed. He was getting used to being a demon master, even if he had no idea what he was doing.

"Your brother is after you, so he's after me too. *We* need to stop him. How do we do that?"

"I don't know," Stitch said.

"So, why is he after you?"

"Because you let me out of the book."

"I got that. Why did he put you *into* the book?"

"Because he's too sensitive."

Martin picked up what he thought was a rock and hurled it at Stitch. It hit him hard and knocked him over. There was a cloud of white as the object bounced off of Stitch and hit the cave wall. Martin looked down and gasped. He was sitting next to a small pile of bones.

"Nice throw, Master." Stitch said, face down. He let out a small cough.

Martin ignored the comment.

"Talk."

Stitch righted himself and did as he was told.

*

It began to rain softly and Barky put his head down from inside the mouth of the cave. There was the faint sound of distant thunder. He let a small whine escape as his eyes continued to look around the forest. It was cool and the slight breeze was almost comforting. Another rabbit scampered in the distance and this time, Barky had no desire to chase it.

He could hear the chew toy talking from inside of the cave. He hated the chew toy so much. He couldn't understand why the Master wanted to keep it around. Everything was going wrong. He whined again.

Barky decided to get up and go to the bathroom when everything suddenly went dark. He couldn't move. It felt like someone was standing on his head. He was going to growl. There was a sharp, quick pain and then nothing.

It began to rain harder and the thunder came closer than ever.

*

"So, this Cabal is your ...*Dad?*"

Stitch sighed.

"No. Cabal is my god. He was in charge of everything. He's what you monkeys call Satan. The main guy."

"So, who's your Dad?"

"What difference does that make?"

"Well, you said this Azaziel was your brother. Is Lilith your sister?"

"I told you this was a waste of time, Master." Stitch said, disgusted.

"It's my time to waste," Martin replied coldly. "Answer my question."

"No, she is *not* my sister. Yes he is my brother. No, Cabal is not my father."

"All right," Martin said, slightly satisfied, but still confused. "Explain to me how you and your 'god' got put into the book. And tell me why your brother is after you."

"Azaziel resents me. I was higher up in the pecking order and he always hated me. He's still a jealous little bastard, but now..." Stitch stopped and then said, "We might consider getting Cabal out of the book, Master."

Martin looked at Stitch even more indignantly than ever.

"You've got to fucking be kidding me," Martin said.

"But Cabal might have a better chance against Azaziel. I'm practically useless like this."

Martin nodded.

"True. What about Lilith?"

"That's who I was trying to contact before we left the house. Besides, she wouldn't fare much better."

"Can she help us at all?"

Stitch sighed.

"Not if she doesn't answer her calls, she can't," Stitch replied. "Maybe we can find Cabal in the book. Did you bring it Master?"

Martin reached out and grabbed his backpack. He unzipped it and pulled out the book.

"How do you spell 'Cabal'?" He asked.

CHAPTER 19

Adam Maldetto washed his face in the sink of his small bathroom. No soap, just cold water and he hissed at its coolness. He looked at himself in the mirror and sighed.

He hadn't shaved in days and his eyes had been bloodshot for just as long. He felt horrible. Grabbing a towel, he wiped his face dry and walked into his dining room, where his laptop waited for him.

He sat down and looked at the screen.

Blank.

He sighed and put his face in his hands. It had been three days since he'd been able to write anything, including an email. He was blank again and it was maddening.

He leaned back in his chair and glared at the ceiling. It was a useless feeling that washed over him and he closed his eyes. The muse would arrive he knew. He was unsure if that would be a good thing or not; his muse was demanding. Upon arrival, the writing would be constant until whatever was in his head was exhausted.

He considered going back to bed, but it was two o'clock in the afternoon. I could drink, he thought, and opened his eyes.

Blinking on his screen was a sentence. He hadn't typed it-he was sure of it. After reading it the third time, he knew where it had come from. It read,

You must leave the apartment and not return until I tell you.

Adam looked around, knowing he'd see no one.

"Why?" He asked out loud.

The sentence deleted itself and a new one appeared on the screen.

Because, I said so.

Adam gave a small chuckle. He got up from his chair and walked into the kitchen. He grabbed a cup on the sink and filled it with tap water. He drank two cups full and went back into the dining room.

The screen was blank. Adam chuckled again. He hated the muse and loved the muse at the same time, but sometimes, she was a bitch.

He went into his bedroom to lie down. Maybe I'll take a nap and go see a movie later, he thought.

*

"We'll need to get to a computer," Martin said, repacking the backpack. "We can look up the name and address and go from there."

"Fair enough," Stitch said, in the most non-committal way he could muster. "But we still need to be careful."

"Right," Martin said, grabbing Stitch and shoving him in the backpack. Stitch let out a quick curse. Martin started his way to the opening of the cave.

"It sounds like it's raining," Martin said.

"Master," Stitch said slowly. "Take me out of the pack."

"Why? We're almost-"

"I smell blood."

Martin stopped and took the pack off of his shoulder. He opened it and Stitch hopped out and scurried to the opening of the cave, which was still a hundred yards away.

"Stay there, Master." Stitch called to him. Martin was confused, but stood there.

"Maybe Barky caught a rabbit," he yelled after Stitch, but Stitch was surprisingly fast and did not answer.

When Stitch got the mouth of the cave he looked and saw that it was raining hard. The smell of blood, which was still strong, was fading. He looked, but didn't see the dog. He moved forward, trying not to get wet and looked for anything. It didn't take long, and it wasn't hard to miss.

Barky had been torn into shreds. What was left was unrecognizable and messy; a patch of wet fur here and there, but he had been reduced to a mushy pulp.

Worse, he had been turned into a message. It was from Azaziel. It could be from no one else.

"Stitch, what's going on?" Martin yelled, moving quickly toward the cave opening.

"Master, you may not want to see-"

"What the *fuck*?"

Martin looked at what was left of Barky. He didn't cry and Stitch was surprised. His fists clenched and he shook, but he did not cry.

"Your brother?" Martin asked.

"Looks that way. He's gone, but he wants us to know he can find us whenever he wants."

Martin nodded and glared at the message left for him and Stitch, which simply read,

HI THERE!

"Let's find a computer," Martin said through his teeth.

INTERLUDE: HELL

Benial stood quietly over Lilith, her sexual energy spent. She lay bleeding and sleeping quietly. Benial smiled and wiped the blood off of his own chin. He turned and walked out of the room and into the main cavern.

He extended his wings, stretching them and they stung; glorious pain. Lilith was good, no doubt about that. He wanted to go back and give her some more, but there was work to do.

He sighed.

There was always something to do.

Benial walked to the edge of the abyss and looked out at the beautiful sulfur sky. He couldn't help himself and smiled again. He was a lucky demon. Second only to Cabal himself; the favored son. He had the sadistic affections of Lilith, who had been made some kind of god apparently during her brief tenure with the monkeys. "Goddess of Death," she'd told him, grinning ferociously. He had nodded and was happy for her, but Benial had made it clear he wanted nothing to do with that place.

A demon's place was here, now. Among the damned and among his own kind. No need for the human race-he'd see them eventually when they came below. There was no rush for an eternal being.

He sat down and kicked his feet over the cliff's edge. He heard a flapping of wings and knew who it was at once.

He sighed.

"Greetings, brother." Azaziel said, landing behind him.

"Greetings," Benial said in a monotone.

"May I share your moment of introspection?"

"It's hardly introspection if you share it," Benial replied, but did not protest when Azaziel sat down.

There was a long silence until Azaziel finally spoke.

"You hate me."

"I wouldn't say hate,"

"But you don't like me."

"We are creatures of hate, born of hate. Am I *supposed* to like you?"

Azaziel paused for a moment.

"I've always looked up to you."

"That's because I'm much taller than you."

"You know what I mean."

Benial sighed.

"I hate it when you sigh like that,"

"What do you want me to say, brother? Has the time you spent with the monkeys done something to you?"

"What do you mean?"

Benial turned and faced his brother.

"I mean you were simply intolerable before, but since you've returned you are now *also* contemptible. You've become more arrogant. Normally, that would be a sign of improvement, but for you..."

Azaziel frowned and then glared.

"*You* are the most arrogant demon here," he said quietly. "Who are you to judge arrogance?"

Benial stared at his brother and then casually pushed him off of the edge of the cliff. He got halfway down before he extended his wings and flew back up to hover in front of Benial.

Azaziel screamed.

"Go back to the monkeys, little brother." Benial said laughing. "They remain the only creatures that fear you. Perhaps they can provide you with the affection you so desperately seek from me."

"This is *not* over." Azaziel growled. "You have shunned me for the last time."

"Then your lesson is learned, dear Azaziel! Your constant absence will ensure I can never shun you again!" And Benial laughed as loudly as he could while Azaziel flew away, fuming.

Benial was still laughing when Lilith slithered up behind him.

"You're laughing without me," she cooed.

Benial kept laughing.

CHAPTER 20

Stitch felt like crying, although he'd never actually done it before. He had laughed until tears fell openly from his eyes (*when he had eyes*) but never out of frustration or anger.

Or fear.

They were acting on Martin's hunch; finding the author of the book to see if they could bring back Cabal. It was futile. Azaziel, as stupid as he is, was also too arrogant to leave an untied loose end like Cabal. There was no way possible.

And yet, here he was, reduced in size and dignity, standing in an apartment building in New York waiting to knock on some bastard's door. He tried to visualize the confrontation. In each scenario, it ends badly, mostly for Stitch. He was becoming resigned to the fact that he was not only stuck in his useless body, but that he'd also be stuck with Martin.

Until Azaziel found them both and killed Martin. He could only imagine what he'd do with him in his current state.

One thing was for sure. Martin was angrier that Azaziel had killed the mongrel. Stitch couldn't understand. Both of his parents were dead. Not severely wounded, dead. Murdered. *Twice*. This fact alone made Martin much more prone to mistakes out of anger and hurt. Anger was a good tool if you knew how to use it, but Martin didn't understand this fact. Anger is the path to the power he wanted, or the power he thought he wanted. Stitch had tried to tell this to Martin to no avail. He was just shoved deeper into the backpack.

Stitch was glad the dog was dead.

They had gone to the library to look up the author of "Raising Demons for Dummies" online. Martin had wasted a good twenty minutes looking up Adam Maldetto before Stitch decided to do something against his own nature.

He told Martin where he could be found.

Martin looked at him dumbfounded.

"Why didn't you just tell me?" he demanded.

"Because really, I'm not supposed to Master." Stitch hissed. "I just wanted to hurry this along. It's no longer just your neck on the line."

That earned him a punch through the backpack. It was worth it and worth it even more when Stitch suggested he 'fly' them to Maldetto's apartment. The screams for the first ten minutes had been worth every punch.

Now, they were at their destination.

"Well, I guess I'll knock." Martin said after looking at the door for almost two full minutes. Stitch simply sighed from inside of the backpack. Martin took a moment to punch the bag, and then knocked on the door.

There was the sound of movement and then the lock disengaging. The door opened and a medium sized man with ratty hair stood there, smiling.

"Can I help you?"

Martin cleared his throat.

"Um, yes," he started. "I'm looking for Adam Maldetto."

If possible, the man in the door smiled even larger.

"That's me, all right. Come on in." Maldetto moved out of the way and let Martin walk into the house.

Martin took the room in at once. It was a shithole, but it felt like a powerful space for some reason he couldn't identify. He thought this and directed it at Stitch who said nothing.

"Something to drink?" Maldetto asked. "I'm afraid all I got is orange soda."

"Um, sure." Martin said. "Listen, I have some questions for you if you don't mind."

"Not at all," Maldetto said, walking into the small kitchen. "Say, is it really windy out or something?"

Martin frowned. He looked around the little apartment until he caught his reflection on a mirror hung crooked on a wall. His hair was in a million directions. He tried to smooth it, but failed.

"Yeah, kinda." Martin said, abandoning his hair. "I have some questions about your book."

Maldetto beamed.

"Which one? Man, this is cool! You know, you're the first."

"The first what?"

"The first fan to ever find me. Man, this is awesome!" Maldetto did a little dance and ran into his kitchen. Martin heard a little scream come from the kitchen.

"He can't be serious," Stitch said from in the bag and waited for a punch that didn't come.

"So, what's your name?" Maldetto called from the kitchen.

"It's Marty...I mean, Martin,"

He noticed the laptop on the table in the dining room. He walked over to it and looked at the screen.

It read in large font that blinked,

GET OUT NOW!

Martin blinked as he looked at the screen. The font disappeared. He frowned and looked into the kitchen. He saw Maldetto pouring the orange soda into two cups. He asked Stitch a question in his head.

Did you see what was on the computer screen?

What, through the book bag? No Master, I missed it.

Martin fought the urge to punch the bag again.

It was blinking a warning for this guy until I looked at it. Then it went away.

What did it say?

Get out now. Do you think its Azaziel?

No, he'd be here. But, it's someone. Can you smell anything?

Just this weird guy's apartment. Why?

Take me out of the bag Master.

Okay, but behave.

Stitch said nothing. Martin reached inside and put the demon next to the laptop.

"Hey, that's pretty cool!" Maldetto said, coming out of the kitchen. "Is that for me?"

"Um, not really." Martin replied, taking the soda. "But it's kinda why I'm here."

Maldetto frowned.

"Hmmm. Please, sit down."

Martin did and sighed heavily. He looked up at Maldetto, who was still grinning.

"You wrote "Raising Demons: Millennium Edition, right?"

Maldetto's grin vanished instantly. He looked like someone had just slapped him with a hand full of shit. He tried poorly to recover.

"Well, I've written scores of other things...like "Timeless-"

"You did write it though?" Martin said, cutting him off and pulling his copy out of his back pack.

Maldetto frowned and sat down.

"Who sent you?" He said almost sadly. "It's a joke, right?"

"What?"

"Come on kid, who put you up to this, huh?"

Martin realized that Maldetto was embarrassed. Humiliated even.

"No one." Martin said. "I got the book a year ago and used it."

Maldetto laughed.

"Right, sure kid. And let me guess, you want your money back." Maldetto stood up. "Get out. This isn't funny."

Martin fought the urge to stand up, but decided to remain seated. He looked up at Maldetto.

"Sit down." He said firmly. "I don't have a lot of time."

Maldetto laughed even harder.

"Oh, this is still part of the joke, right? A kid just happens to roll into my pad with the single most embarrassing p-"

"I said sit." Martin said. "*Now.*" The tone and inflection of his voice made Martin shudder a bit, but he was losing his patience. With the anger in him rising he felt something new.

Powerful.

Maldetto glared at him, although the voice coming out of the kid was a little unsettling.

"I didn't come here to make fun of you," Martin said, lightening his tone. "And I didn't come to get an autograph. I'm looking for a particular demon in this book. Can you help me or not?"

Maldetto sat.

"The book," He started, "Doesn't work. That thing you brought in. It's a totem, right?"

Martin nodded.

"Right there is your first problem. It's too small. Any demon you try to conjure is just going to be pissed if you conjure it into that little thing."

"No shit," Stitch said.

Maldetto looked at Stitch and Stitch looked at him. He pushed himself up on the table and stood, seeming to glare at Maldetto.

"But, the book works." Stitch said.

Maldetto looked at Stitch and then at Martin.

There was a small silence before Maldetto fainted and fell out of his chair and onto the floor.

Martin and Stitch sighed at the same time.

CHAPTER 21

Stuart had stopped crying, but was still upset. The rest of the girl he had been eating was shoved into a corner. He'd need someone new and he didn't dread the thought as much as he thought he would. In fact, he was getting hungry again. Lord had suggested waiting a while to whet his appetite and possibly eat Marty when he found him.

That wasn't likely to happen any time soon he feared.

"Marty," he said aloud for no reason. This was all his fault, wasn't it? He wouldn't have done any of this shit if it weren't for Marty. Fucking Marty.

He looked at the dead girl and wondered what her name had been. He couldn't remember if she was a pretty girl or not. It was strange that if she was pretty, he had chosen to kill her rather than try to have sex with her. He'd tried to have sex with just about every girl he'd ever met since he was twelve. He tried to imagine having sex now. He looked at the girl and touched himself. He'd never actually had sex other than with himself (*which was almost in normal circumstances, constantly*) and knew he'd never actually have it now that he was a corpse.

He looked at the girl and continued to touch himself.

He surprised himself by discovering that he wasn't completely dead after all.

Stuart began to stroke himself through his jeans until he realized he could have sex with the girl. This thought was replaced with two other thoughts; the argument that she was dead. This was followed by another stronger thought that he said aloud.

"But, I'm dead too,"

He stood up slowly and walked to the dead girl in the corner. He grabbed a leg and pulled her out into the room. He kicked her legs apart and looked at her. He smiled thinly as he realized that for as much of her he had eaten, there was a surprising amount of her left available. Stuart fumbled with his jeans with his remaining hand and got ready to dispose of his virginity.

*

Maldetto was in the exact spot where he had fainted. He looked up at the ceiling and heard part of a conversation.

"We don't *need* to kill him," the boy said. "Maybe he's a wizard or something. He could help us."

"He's not a wizard," the other voice said. "He's a fucking *tool*. We find out what he knows, and get rid of the tool. Simple plan, yes?"

Maldetto couldn't believe his ears.

"There's been a lot of death today, Stitch."

"There's going to be a lot more. I'd like us not to be included in the final tally."

There was a pause until the boy said,

"Yeah, I guess you're right. Can you wake him up?"

Maldetto tried not to scream. He stayed as still as he could.

"He's up and listening," Stitch said. Maldetto heard little feet padding over to him. It nearly sounded cute until a sharp pain exploded from the side of his head. He screamed. His hand went to the left side of his head. It felt like someone had torn his ear off. He stood up quickly and looked down. Stitch was holding his left ear in his little hands. He was also holding it up to his crudely sewn mouth.

"Can you hear me now?"

Stitch threw the ear casually to the side and looked up at Maldetto.

"We need Cabal."

"You ripped off my ear!"

"Yes I did," Stitch said. "And now that he's off from school, I have the rest of the afternoon free to see what *else* I can rip off."

"Cabal." Martin said. "You need to tell us how to resurrect Cabal."

"This is insane," Maldetto cried. He held the place where his ear used to be and he felt blood pouring out over his fingers. "Totally insane. You *can't* resurrect demons. The book was a *joke*."

"It is a joke," Stitch admitted. "But not in the way you think. Cabal was sent there too. We need to conjure him."

Maldetto sat down.

"The book wasn't supposed to work," he said, starting to cry. "When she was telling me what to write she said it wasn't supposed to work."

"Who's she?" Martin asked.

"M..my muse," Maldetto said. "She came to me and said if I wrote the book, my other books would finally make me successful. She was right...kind of."

Stitch sighed.

"What does your muse look like?"

"Never met her. Just through the computer. She leaves me messages. Can I go get some ice? Can I have my *ear*?"

"No and no." Stitch said. "What does this muse call herself?"

"She said I'm not supposed to tell anyone."

"Did she now?"

Stitch walked closer to him.

"Did she threaten you?" Martin asked.

"She said my suffering would be unimaginable."

"Can I tell you something Mr. Maldetto?" Martin moved over the chair where he was sitting. Maldetto seemed less frightened at the boy, so he nodded.

Martin bent down to his remaining ear and whispered.

"I resurrected this demon last night. Since then, the two closest things to friends I had are dead. My dog was torn to pieces a few hours ago. Both of my parents are dead and the demon that put *my* demon in your book is after us." He backed away from Maldetto and stood back up. Maldetto looked at him.

"Your book made me a sixteen year old master of demons." he said. "My demon and I are *not* in a very good mood."

Maldetto looked at Martin and at Stitch, who was climbing up his pants leg. Stitch jumped at Maldetto's head. He covered his face and waited for an impact that never came. He moved his hands away from his head and then reached for his missing ear. It was back and the pain was gone.

"I can take things off and put them back whenever I feel like it." Stitch said, standing on Maldetto's legs. He then added, "Or not. Name of muse. Now."

Maldetto swallowed.

"Lilith," said Lilith from behind them.

Martin turned and looked. He was horrified at the sight, but he didn't flinch. Her wings were curled in to give more room and she was smiling. Or, Martin thought, that's just what her teeth look like. Stitch didn't bother turning around.

"I knew it," he said.

"Hello, lover. Making new friends I see."

Stitch turned around. Martin looked at him and frowned.

"What..." Martin started.

"Introduce me to your Master, Tiny." Lilith said. "Oh, I'm sorry. *Stitch*, I mean."

"Master? Lilith. Lilith? Master."

"Charmed," she said and extended a claw. Martin backed away slowly.

"I believe you know this one," Stitch said. He nudged his head to Maldetto.

Lilith hissed and Maldetto covered up.

"I didn't tell! I didn't tell!" he cried.

"You betrayed me. You betrayed Cabal, but you betrayed *me*." Stitch said. He couldn't believe it.

"It wasn't betrayal." Lilith said. "If anything, it was torment. We are demons. It's what we do."

Stitch jumped onto Maldetto's shoulder and looked at him. He ripped the ear off again. He screamed. Stitch turned slowly.

"Any time I want," he said to Maldetto and started to move towards Lilith. He casually tossed the ear to the side.

Lilith turned and looked directly at Martin, who was still staring at her. She laughed.

"You've never seen a real demon before have you? Just this little used-to-be." She spread her wings out to half extension, knocking over a table. She growled and bared her teeth and glared at Martin. Martin to his surprise, and to Stitch's, stood his ground.

"Now that you're up close to one, what do you think?"

Martin's heart was racing, but his mind was clear in a way it hadn't been in days.

"You're kinda leathery," he said, not blinking.

Stitch didn't sigh.

He laughed.

Lilith snarled inches from Martin's face.

"So, you helped put Stitch in the book, huh?" he simply asked. "And Cabal too. Isn't he like, your god or something?"

"Who do you think you're talking to?" She said through her considerable mouth of teeth.

"Teneri sermons meos et metuant." Martin said clearly and loudly right in Lilith's face. Her eyes rolled back into her head as her wings folded up. Her long powerful arms went inward, tight to her body and stood rigid. Her face, already a rictus of horror now revealed something else.

Fear.

"What are you doing?" she squealed.

"Containing you for a moment," Martin said. "Be quiet, would you?"

Martin turned and looked down at Stitch. Stitch looked back up at him.

"I absolutely hate myself for saying this," Stitch began, "But well *done*, Master."

Stitch also hated the lack of contempt he heard from his own voice.

"How are you able to do this?" Lilith hissed in pain and frustration.

Martin ignored it.

"Tell us how to free Cabal."

"Tell me why I should? I am *eternal*"

Martin blinked. He didn't have a verbal response. But, he smiled and said two words.

"Deus nocet."

Lilith threw her head back and roared in agony.

After a moment, she stopped. She was heaving. Martin stood right where he had been and spoke.

"Eternity is a very long time, wouldn't you agree? I'm sixteen and can keep doing that for at least another 70 years I think. You know, with pee breaks and stuff, but Stitch here? He's got all the time in the world. He can do that when I die. Sure, he wouldn't have to if I was dead, but I get the feeling he wouldn't mind at all. Would you Stitch?"

"Everyone needs a hobby," Stitch said.

Lilith looked, not in horror, but in awe at this child and her former lover.

"You wouldn't."

Stitch walked closer to Lilith.

"We're demons," Stitch said. "We torment. It's what we *do*."

Lilith whimpered. Maldetto, watching from the floor had every question he wanted answered in that simple sentence.

"Let me find it!" Maldetto barked from the floor. "I can find it if you let me look for it, but please don't kill me!"

Lilith, Martin and Stitch turned to look at him.

Maldetto grabbed Martin's copy of the book and began to flip through it, not knowing what he was looking for, but trying to find it anyway. His ear (what was left of it) throbbed, but he worked past it. He saw every word he had written and recognized none of it. It was a million years ago.

"You don't even know what we're looking for. Just thought I'd mention that, stupid." Stitch said.

"No, you said you were looking for Cable. I can find it!"

"*Cabal*, not Cable." Martin corrected.

"Whatever! Just don't kill me!" He looked over page after page and began to cry. None of it was recognizable.

"I …just…don't know this…" he said through streaming tears and a small croaking voice. Stitch regarded him for a moment and then looked at Lilith.

"You shut him out of it. Didn't you?" Stitch asked. "You used him to write it, but wiped his memory clean."

Lilith turned her head away and said nothing.

"Master, what was that you said before? The one where Lil got all screamie sounding? Boy, I think I could listen to that sound all day."

"Hmmm…" Martin said, mimicking forgetfulness. "Not sure what you mean. Was it in Latin maybe?" Martin got close to Lilith-something that few humans dared to ever do. "Maybe I do know, but maybe you could keep me from saying it."

Lilith was whimpering, but snapped her head violently at Martin and roared. Martin didn't move an inch. In fact he smiled.

"I will torture you for *eons* boy!" She snarled.

"Deus nocet," he said casually and she convulsed and screamed for nearly ten minutes this time.

When she stopped, Stitch walked over to Lilith.

"He's good, isn't he?" He asked, cheer in his voice. "You know, just a few hours ago, I'd all but given up on him, but look at him now! Top notch. I think he's enjoying this. Hell, I think even *I'm* enjoying this."

Lilith was too exhausted to respond but she glared at him, heaving.

"Do me a big favor Lil," Stitch said in a sweet voice. "Keep resisting. I'd forgotten how much agony agrees with you."

Martin looked around the room and took a moment, just one small moment to take in what had brought him here. He had conjured a demon and trapped it in a small homemade doll. He'd watched people he knew die. He allowed his parents to be slaughtered by this evil little doll. His dog, his only real friend...

And for *what?*

Martin remembered why he had done all of this and he couldn't justify it. His cheeks became red and hot. He didn't feel like he was going to cry, but he felt…

"Sorry," he said. It was in a very small, barely audible voice.

"Huh?" Maldetto said, still going through the book.

"I'm sorry," Martin repeated.

Stitch slowly turned from Lilith.

"Who are you talking to Master?" Stitch asked.

"I don't know," Martin replied. "I'm just…sorry."

"Master?"

Martin looked around and saw a chair. He grabbed it and sat down. He put his face in his hands for a moment. Then, he looked back up.

"What am I *doing*?" He asked no one in particular. "Really, I don't know."

Lilith began to growl and tried to stand.

"Moveare sordes," Martin said absently and Lilith slumped to the floor. She did not move. Stitch looked at her and then at Martin again

"Master?"

"I…I'm so sorry but I don't know what I'm doing."

"You're a Master of demons now," Stitch said. "You can do anything you want."

"But what if I don't *want* anything? Not anymore. What if what I want is…*pointless*?"

"Master, these things are new to you." Stitch said. He felt revulsion at what he was about to say. "You'll grow into it in time."

"Can Cabal help me?" Martin asked.

Stitch sighed.

"Help you *what*?"

"I want to see Cabal."

"I thought that's why we were here."

"I know, but he won't show up."

"What?" Stitch was getting angry.

"He's not in the book." Martin said, shifting in the chair. "I have to call him."

Stitch glared at Martin. Then he walked over to Maldetto, who was transfixed on Martin. Stitch reattached his ear, but Maldetto didn't seem to notice until it was ripped off again. He screamed and fell to the floor. He began to crawl toward the kitchen.

"Master, maybe I should have been specific. You are the Master of a demon. Not all of them. Pretty much just me."

"I stopped Lilith."

"True,"

"I can bring him here."

"No Master, you can't."

Martin closed his eyes; he looked like he was finally going to cry. When he opened his eyes, he said, "He's here."

"Right," Stitch said. He turned to follow Maldetto into the kitchen.

"You need to have a bit more faith, Benial," said Cabal. The voice came from nowhere and everywhere it seemed. It wasn't booming, but casual.

Martin looked around. Maldetto screamed. Stitch froze.

"Did you hear me?"

"I heard you, but I don't believe it." Stitch said.

"Is that him?" Martin asked.

"I'm the one you've been looking for," Cabal said.

"Bullshit." Stitch said. "Show yourself."

The voice of Cabal chuckled.

"You will never *ever* change even when it serves your interests. It's a trait I have always admired about you," He said, adding. "Although it seems that your brother has embraced quite a bit of change, yes?"

"Azaziel remains an idiot. And I still don't believe it's you. You were trapped in the book."

"Ah the book. Pretty interesting, isn't it? Convenient how your brother trapped me in there, along with you and so many others. How do you think he's done so far in my absence?"

"He sucks," Stitch replied.

Cabal laughed again.

"Wait, this is Cabal talking to us? Really Cabal?" Martin asked Stitch.

Stitch walked over to Martin.

"Master, its' probably Azaziel just playing with us. We should go."

"If it were Azaziel, he'd be bragging over your corpses. Well, over the ones who can die. It's *me*."

Stitch sighed. Cabal laughed.

"He does that constantly, Martin. I'm sure you've noticed."

"Excuse me," Maldetto said, from the other room. "But this is really a lot to take in. Can you go now so I can kill myself or something?"

"Get in here so I can rip that other ear off,"

"Stop it," Cabal ordered. "I can use him."

Stitch ignored the request.

"You're *not* Cabal,"

There was a sharp change in the air; it felt electric and the lights dimmed. A putrid stench filled the room. Maldetto started and stopped screaming. He began to choke. He began to thrash. All of this went on out of sight to those in the living room. Martin stared bewildered at what was happening to Maldetto.

"I think we should go." Stitch said.

"Not yet. I think I know what's happening."

"So do I Master, that's why we should *fucking go*."

Maldetto's body suddenly burst into the living room from the kitchen with his eyes closed. He stood for a moment and then, his eyes opened.

Except they weren't Maldetto's eyes. They weren't anyone's eyes. His eyes were gone; what remained were the sockets, but there was a faint light in the holes.

He looked at Martin and Stitch and smiled.

"Would you mind giving me his ear now?" asked Cabal.

Without meaning to, Stitch dropped the ear. Cabal laughed.

"Ah, how I have *missed* you!" Cabal said. "We are demons to be sure, but I have very much missed you."

"How did you escape the book?" Martin asked. He had a feeling that what he had just spent the last 20 minutes involved with would be important somewhere else today, but couldn't figure out where or why.

"Book?" came the reply. "Where did you get that idea?"

"The big thing on the floor behind you," Martin shot back. "She said Azaziel trapped you in the book. We were trying to get you out."

"Well, that's almost sweet." Cabal said. "Except I wasn't in the book."

Stitch broke his silence.

"Where were you then?"

"Everywhere, my son, absolutely *everywhere*." Cabal said.

"Glad you had a great vacation, but where the fuck *were you*? We thought Azaziel destroyed you. At least that's what I thought. You just vanished."

"You sound like a lost child. Like your young master there." Cabal said. "I left because I *chose* to go. I wanted to see which one of you would pick up the ball. I hoped it would have been you. How sad I was to have been wrong."

Stitch was now furious. He padded over to Maldetto's standing, smirking, talking corpse and stood in front of it. He raised an arm to Cabal's amusement as if to strike when Martin reached down and grabbed him.

"Stitch, there's no time for this." Martin said to Stitch and put him on the fireplace mantle, swearing. Cabal laughed.

"Ah, the young master and his little charge, making things right!"

"I have a lot of questions, Cabal. I'm hoping you can answer them." Martin said to Cabal.

Cabal seemed amused, but dropped the smile.

"Ask away, young master."

Martin took a deep breath.

"Everything I've done today...can it be reversed?"

"No."

"Can you bring my parents back?"

"That falls under the reverse question, so no."

Martin closed his eyes on that one.

"There's no going back at all?"

"No there isn't."

"How do I kill Azaziel?"

"You *don't*."

"Then how do I get rid of him?"

"Ah! Now you're thinking like a master! I can tell you how to do that, but your charge Stitch will need to do much of the work."

Stitch glared at Cabal.

"Master, I-"

Martin ignored him.

"Just one more question, really, and we can get to work." Martin said. "Am I evil?"

"Child, that is a question only you can answer." Cabal said. "What you are is up to you. If you choose to be evil, then yes, I suppose you are. But if you need to ask, then who am I to tell you? *You* conjured a demon after all."

Martin nodded.

"I just don't know any more I guess," Martin said. "But I have to finish this or it wasn't for anything at all, right?"

Cabal grabbed a chair and sat. He invited Martin to sit as well. When he sat, Cabal looked at him with almost sympathy.

"Why would a sixteen year old boy need his own demon?" he asked.

Stitch jumped from the mantle and ran past Martin straight to Cabal.

"What is this?" he asked. "What are you doing?"

"I'm talking to your master," Cabal said. "And one would think that a conversation between two masters would be enough to warrant a bit of respect."

Stitch was briefly quiet, and then he said,

"You have got to be kidding me. You vanish for nearly 300 years, leave me to rot and just show up and-"

Cabal picked Stitch up and casually threw him next to where Lilith still lay. He waved a hand and Stitch was quiet. Cabal turned back to Martin.

"Sorry. Family issues," he said and smiled. "Now then, back to my question."

"Why did I want my own demon?"

Cabal waited.

"It's hard to explain," Martin said. His throat was tightening again. Cabal reached out and put his hand on Martin's shoulder. Martin felt an electric surge and then felt better. Free, was how he felt.

"I know what happened," Cabal said. "You can tell me if you want, but I know."

Martin looked at Cabal, eyes moist, but not crying.

"You *know*?"

"I know everything," Cabal said. "But you may feel better if you tell me."

CHAPTER 22

Stitch, next to Lilith, couldn't move, but he could still think and see. What he was looking at was Lilith's face. If he could have spit, he would have; he was furious.

You bitch, he thought.

How could you do this to me? Lilith thought back to him. The thought slammed into Stitch's head.

How could I do what to you? He replied back telepathically. *You betrayed me. Me, of all demons. And don't give me the "I'm a demon it's what we do" shit. This is me we're talking about.*

Benny, Cabal was gone and you did nothing about it, she replied. *I was left alone. What was I supposed to do?*

You let Azaziel fuck me over.

I didn't know it was him that put you in the book.

No, Stitch thought. *It was you who put me in the book. And you've become a terrible liar.*

Lilith said nothing.

As I thought.

I didn't put you in the book. I was just the custodian of the book. And besides, you got out. How do you think that happened? Lilith thought.

When I get a body of some kind, I'm going to tear Azaziel apart. Then I'm going to come for you.

Good luck with that, Benny. Lilith laughed in Stitch's head. *You're practically a child's toy. You'll do nothing but be torn to shreds and be put back into the earth like the non-corporeal ungrateful hunk of shit you are.*

No sweet talk, Lil. You're going to pay for this.

I'd like to see that, came Lilith's reply.

Stitch was then picked up roughly. He couldn't tell who had picked him up, and he still couldn't move. He called out mentally.

Master?

You're useless aren't you? Lilith answered. *Call your master like a dog.*

Stitch sighed. It was true after all. He was a child's toy. No nameless one anymore-not in the way he had liked so much. Just a random useless pile of old pigskin. The kid would get a new dog, and he'd be a chew toy. An eternal one at that.

Stitch was taken out of the pocket. It was Martin who had picked him up. He was placed on the fireplace mantle again.

"I know you've been talking," Cabal had said, still sitting. "What have you heard?"

Stitch was able to move and speak again.

"Are you done being a guidance counselor, Cabal?"

"Why, actually I am. If you had been listening, you'd know that. How's Lilith doing over there?"

Lilith was still unmoving, but Stitch still heard random curses being hurled at him.

"Apart from the fact that she's not in tiny little chunks, she's fine," Stitch replied. "Do I get to ask you questions now?"

"That's up to your master," Cabal said, looking and smiling at Martin. Martin looked less harried and calm. He looked at Stitch.

"We don't really have time, Stitch." Martin said. "We have to take care of Stu and Azaziel and fast. They know we're here. We have a few things to do before we take care of them."

"Yes, master," Stitch said. He was furious, but the feeling of being resigned was creeping in instead.

"Martin, I would like to take a minute to talk to your small charge for a moment if that's alright with you. Won't take a moment." Cabal said.

"That's fine. I'll wait outside." Martin grabbed his book bag and his book and walked out of Maldetto's apartment.

Cabal looked at Stitch and smiled.

"You have no idea how silly you look, Benial. I'm very disappointed."

"You're disappointed? I've been trying to get you out of that book, thinking that my true master was wasting away to a mere after-thought and you were just out running around?"

"Benial, were you worried about me?" Cabal mocked.

"I was worried about *me*!" Stitch shot back. "Look what you let happen. First, you made that awful deal with He, and then you just disappeared, leaving me to watch Azaziel."

"Looks like he was watching you, wasn't he?"

"Yes, it looks that way, doesn't it." Stitch said. "I thought He had revoked your little deal for us to rise up. Still can't believe you allowed that to happen."

Cabal stood up.

"Would you like to know a secret, Benial? A secret I have told no other demon?"

"That would be something new," Stitch said. "Please, oh *absent* Master, tell me something I do not know."

Cabal smiled.

"There is *no* He."

"Of course there is," Stitch said.

"No actually, there isn't."

Stitch was silent.

"There is only *me*. I made no deal."

"I don't believe you. Why-"

"Why would I deceive you? That's an easy one. It's what I do. You could say, Benial, that my ways are mysterious."

Stitch let the import of this sink in and he did not like them one bit.

"I was testing you, your brother and Lilith." Cabal continued. "You failed yourself and me. Azaziel stepped up. Now, however, he has gone ahead and screwed it up. I need *you* to fix it. This is your chance."

"Wait a minute," Stitch said, nearly stuttering. "Did you just admit you are *God*? Is that what you just said?"

Cabal smiled.

"You believe what you want to believe. But I need you to take care of Azaziel. If you want your chance that is."

"Chance of what?"

"Taking my place. There needs to be balance. Plus the tension is enjoyable, isn't it?"

Stitch sighed.

"I need my old body back."

"No."

"I need to be rid of being in that boy's thrall."

"No. You need him."

"*What?*"

"You heard me. We can discuss you getting another body if and when you have finished your task at hand."

"And what the fuck is my task at hand?"

"Ask your master. But don't screw this up, Benial."

"Or what? Since you're He, doesn't that mean you can just make everything the way you want it?"

"No, but it means I can make any demand of you that I want and you'll do it."

Stitch looked at Cabal and knew he was right.

"What do I need to do?"

Cabal walked to the front door and opened it.

"Again, *ask your master.* He's up to speed and knows what he has to do. Guide him as best you can, but he is in charge. Understand?"

"I suppose," Stitch began as he jumped off of the mantle onto the floor. "It doesn't matter if I understand or not. But I'll do what you ask."

"I'm not asking," Cabal said smiling.

Stitch walked over to Lilith.

"What about her?" he asked.

"You can leave her here. It's up to your Master what'll happen to her."

Stitch heard Lilith scream in his head. If he had been able to smile, he would have.

"At least there's that," Stitch said and padded over to Martin. Martin picked up Stitch and put him in his book bag. He looked up at Cabal.

"Thanks Cabal," Martin said, smiling a little.

"You'll be okay, child. Just remember what I told you."

"I will," said Martin and ran down the hall.

Cabal closed the door and looked around the apartment. After a moment, Maldetto's body collapsed to the floor and Cabal was gone. The apartment was still and quiet save for the intermittent breathing of Lilith's large demon body.

CHAPTER 23

Stuart leaned back against the wall and looked at the girl. He was smiling. Four times. He had sex four times, each time a little longer and a little better than the last. He was a little tired, but he felt better. His missing arm didn't bother him as much anymore. He was hungry, but didn't want to keep eating the girl.

He'd have to get someone new.

The thought of this nearly made him aroused again, but he stayed against the wall.

"Why you dirty little *birdy*!" Lord said. Of course, it was just his voice, but he saw it all, Stuart knew. He didn't care. He chuckled.

"Hi Lord."

"You've been a busy little undead boy haven't you?" Lord said. "How do you feel?"

"I feel pretty good, Lord." Stuart said. "Hungry, but I don't want to eat her anymore."

Lord laughed.

"Well, we can't have you starving, can we? You can take care of that later though. Our two little problems are on the move. This time, I'd like to actually intercept them. What do you say?"

Stuart had plenty to say, but simply smiled, saying only, "Can't wait."

"You *rock*, Stu! You are really stepping up, my man."

"Thanks."

"So, get yourself dressed and we'll get going, kay?"

Stuart started to stand. It was hard because of the missing arm, but he managed. Lord sighed.

"Gonna need to get you a new arm. Can't have my number one guy running around without two arms."

"How does that happen?" Stuart asked, struggling with a t-shirt.

"Get dressed and go into the hallway," Lord said.

Stuart got his clothes on as quickly as he could. The hardest thing, he found, was getting his shoes back on, but he managed to do it. He was grateful he wore Velcro sneakers. He lumbered in the hallway and saw a very large black man lying unconscious on the floor. His head was literally split wide open. Stuart would have salivated if he could have and Lord chuckled.

"Chow time later, arm time now, my boy!" he said, and the corpse moved. It slid across the floor and up the wall opposite Stuart. Stuart was about two feet shorter than the corpse at its full height and the arms were frighteningly muscular.

"This guy is fucking huge!" Stuart said. "Look at those guns, man."

"I know," Lord said. "Thought you might do better with a bigger replacement. Stand back a bit."

Stuart did so and the corpse's right arm rose up and began to twist at the shoulder. He heard the bones crack and the flesh make a noise like a towel being wrung. It nearly made two full turns before the arm was ripped from the corpse. It hung in the air, dripping.

"How do I get it on?" Stuart asked.

"Okay Stu, lift up your shirt. This is really gonna hurt."

Stuart struggled, and wondered why he had bothered to put his shirt on in the first place. No sooner did he have the shirt off, then what was left of his stump began to split and fray. Stuart didn't scream, but Lord was right. It really hurt. It hurt more when the black guy's arm slammed into the stump. And it hurt further still, when the bones began to fuse and the flesh began to mesh itself together. After a minute, the arm was on. Stuart's eyes were closed and he slumped against the wall.

"Open up those black eyes, Stuart and see what Lord done *brung ya!*" Lord said, sounding satisfied.

Stuart did and looked at his new arm. He tried to use it and it responded. It felt powerful. *He* felt powerful. He flexed, and although it was tender, he already felt…new.

"Kick ass," Stuart said, smiling. He punched the wall in front of him and his fist went nearly all the way through the wall. He pulled it out and looked at the hand.

The word "LOVE" was tattooed on the knuckles.

"I always wanted a tattoo," he said.

He looked at the corpse, still suspended against the wall, blood dripping from the stump. He pulled off a loose piece of skin and put it in his mouth. He chewed loudly.

"Okay kid, snack time is over," Lord said. "Time to go to work. There's a jacket on the staircase you might want to put on when you leave. You *do* look a little funky right now."

"Kay," Stuart said still chewing. "Where am I going?"

"Pine Barrens," Lord said. "We're going to have us some fun."

CHAPTER 24

Weidlin looked out of the passenger window at the sky. It was raining lightly against the window. He was nearly slumped in his seat. After spending his entire day on this case, he wanted to drink an entire bottle of gin and pass out for a year.

Thoms drove quietly, occasionally tapping his fingers on the steering wheel. He's a decent enough partner Weidlin thought. A little thick headed, but all right. Zero cop instinct. This last thought made him smirk a little.

"I was thinking," Thoms said. Weidlin sat up slightly surprised.

"Yeah?"

"There's no way that kid did that, back at the house. Not a chance."

"No shit," Weidlin said.

"But," Thoms continued. "I think he's involved somehow."

Weidlin sighed.

"Of *course* he's involved. His parents are dead. And his two friends were found dead at the fucking grave yard."

"I think he had a hand in it." Thoms said.

"For all we know, that hand he has in it is the one we found in the house. You remember, on the detached arm?" Weidlin asked. He was disgusted.

Thoms remained steady.

"It's not the kid's arm. Guarantee it."

Weidlin looked at his partner.

"Guess we'll see."

"Guess we will." Thoms said smugly.

Weidlin slid back down in his seat and looked out the window again. He was dreading a lot of things, and that included writing the findings from both the school and the new crime scene at that Marty kid's house.

It was fucked to the sky, as his father had been fond of saying. His gut told him that if he had kept rattling Marty's cage, the kid would have slipped up. It was all over his face. Why they chose to call him over to that kid's house to head the crime scene he would never know.

He'd been up since three am and had already worked the goddamn graveyard scene and then this bullshit. It was making his head hurt just thinking about it. But the sheer coincidences involved were impossible.

Which is why he didn't believe in them.

"What did you say?" Thoms asked.

"Shut up and drive," Weidlin said. "Let's go to the graveyard again."

CHAPTER 25

"Why are we back here?" Stitch asked. He'd asked it at least three times and Martin had not spoken a word to him since leaving Maldetto's apartment, other than "Get us back to the cave."

Martin sat cross-legged on the floor, next to the bones and stared into the fire he'd made. Stitch had been pacing for nearly forty minutes, swearing and kicking little rocks on the cave floor.

"We are *targets*, Master. We need to go somewhere *else*. I was thinking that your friend might just rot apart and we would only need to deal with Azaziel, which is bad enough. But if they have to look for us, it would buy us some time."

Still, Martin said nothing. He just stared, not blinking into the fire.

Stitch sighed.

"Are you *meditating*?"

Martin closed his eyes and then opened them.

"No, I'm not meditating." He said.

"Oh, welcome back, Master. Remember me? I'm the demon you conjured. We have some issues, like not getting destroyed. Glad you're awake now."

"Shut up. We're not going anywhere."

"Why not?"

Martin stood up and looked at Stitch.

"Because we're ending it here," he said.

Stitch looked up at him.

"*Sure.*" Stitch said.

"Cabal is right," Martin said. "You don't have any respect."

"Are you surprised?"

Martin closed his eyes again and then opened them.

"We are ending it all here. Tonight."

"So, are you going to kill yourself? Or are you going to let your friend do it for you? My brother will try to kill me. Probably will, or at least tear what is left of me apart."

"I'm not killing myself. You're going to destroy Azaziel. I am going to take care of Stuart."

Stitch laughed.

"And I'm sure you have a solid plan. That's what the staring into the flames thing was all about, right?"

"Something like that."

"What did Cabal say to you?"

"I'm not allowed to tell you all of it." Martin replied.

"What?"

"Cabal said 'Don't tell Stitch anything we talked about,' and I'm not going to. We're going to be okay, but I do need your help." Martin walked over to Stitch and picked him up. "When we're done with this, I'll release you. But it has to be done my way. The worst-case scenario is you go back to having no body and floating around aimlessly. You'll still exist and I'll be dead, probably."

"Great plan,"

"Stuart will come first. I'll take care of him. Azaziel is able to attack me, but he won't. He wants you."

"Master, he can't attack you." Stitch said. "Those are the rules."

"The rules have changed," Martin said. "The one thing I can tell you what Cabal said is *that*. Didn't you hear him? He *never* arranged anything like rules because he *made them up*. There aren't any rules."

Stitch looked at Martin.

"So, I'm *not* in your thrall?"

"Okay, *mostly* no rules. You still answer to me."

Stitch pondered this for a moment.

"What's the plan?"

"Actually Stitch, I think you'll like it a whole lot."

"How so?"

Martin explained the plan to Stitch. He spoke quickly and quietly. He was very direct. When he was done he looked at the little doll.

"Well?" Martin asked.

"You can't see it," Stitch said. "But I'm smiling on the inside."

"I thought you might like it."

"Does Cabal know what you're planning?"

"Probably. He said he knows everything."

"Fair enough. I should get started then."

Martin, instead of dropping Stitch, lowered him to the cave floor. Nothing really needed to be said, but Martin called after the little demon as he walked slowly to the mouth of the cave.

"Stitch, good luck."

Stitch resisted the urge to sigh.

"I'll be back as quickly as I can." He began to walk again and stopped. "Master?"

"Yeah?"

"The Latin you used to hurt Lilith won't work on your friend. I'll write one that will on the floor. I can't say it."

He grabbed a stick and scrawled something on the floor.

"Don't hold back using it," Stitch said. "It'll be…*hilarious*."

And he left.

Martin looked at the path to the mouth of the cave for a long time after Stitch left. Then he started to cry. He wanted to go to sleep. He wanted it all to be over. He wanted everything to be the way it was before he raised a demon. He wanted to be dead.

He sat down hard on the cave floor and looked into the fire through tears. He knew what he had to do, but he just wanted it to be over. He wanted to see his parents and above all he wanted to vanish from his life.

"I'm sorry," he sobbed to no one at all. "I'm so sorry."

CHAPTER 26

"That's enough," Weidlin said. He and Thoms walked back to the car slowly. The graveyard was a bust, he knew. There would be no more clues and nothing else, as far as Weidlin was concerned, could be done until they found either Marty, or the allegedly dead kid from the morgue.

"Told ya," Thoms said, but his tone didn't match his words. He sounded defeated. As much as he liked to argue with Weidlin, he was just tired now and wanted to go home.

They got into the car and Weidlin slumped down into the passenger seat again.

"Home?" Thoms asked. "It's starting to get slightly late."

Weidlin gave a non-committal shrug. Thoms started the car and slowly crept away from the graveyard. After a minute, Thoms said, "You know, they wouldn't have pulled that shit in a cemetery."

Weidlin grunted. He didn't care.

"A cemetery," Thoms continued. "Is looked after and shit. Not a lot of vandalism, you know? Kids these days ain't got no respect."

"There were two dead kids in that graveyard," Weidlin said quietly. "I don't think respect plays a part in a whole hell of a lot these days."

Thoms took his turn to grunt.

"So what do you think happened?"

Weidlin sat up a little and looked out of the window.

"I really don't have any idea," he said. "I mean, I know I don't trust Marty. He's my suspect number one, but I'm fucked to know why. There isn't a single thing that makes any kind of damn sense."

Thoms chuckled.

"Well, it is the Pine Barrens. All kinds a goofy shit goes down here."

Weidlin allowed himself to laugh a little as well.

"Yeah, that's no lie." Weidlin said. "And we're right near the woods now too. Watch out for goofy shit."

The two cops shared a laugh which died quickly when they saw what looked like a big teenaged kid walking briskly ahead of them. He was wearing a jacket, but it looked like there was something wrong with his right arm.

"What in the good name of Christ is up with that kid's arm?" Thoms asked.

"Let's slow up and see what's up," Weidlin said. "Because I don't like the look of this one bit."

Thoms grunted and slowed down slightly.

CHAPTER 27

Stuart walked with a confidence he had never had before; a sort of swagger that only came with age and experience. He had neither of course, but he felt like he had. The only thing he knew was that he couldn't die and he had gotten laid. He knew that if something fell off (*or was torn off*) it could be easily replaced. He looked at his new arm. God *damn*, he thought. I am so gonna fuck Marty up. Then I'm gonna eat him while he watches.

He smiled.

As he walked briskly toward the tree line, a slow moving car pulled next to him and gunned its engine. Stuart kept walking, but turned his head to see who was screwing with him.

"Hey kid, can I ask you a question?" the passenger said through the open window. Stuart smiled and stopped. The car followed suit and Thoms put the car into park.

"Go right ahead," Stuart replied. "It's your life."

Weidlin stared in disbelief at the kid he saw before him. His skin was a dark bruised purplish color, and through the kid's jacket, his right arm was grotesquely larger compared to the other. The kid's clothes were tattered and bloody. And the kid was smiling.

"What's your name?" Weidlin asked.

"Stuart. What's yours?"

"Stuart what?"

Stuart's smile expanded wider. His mouth seemed to be splitting on one side, exposing more teeth along the side of his head. Weidlin swallowed something greasy and foul that was in his mouth. Thoms got out of the car and drew his gun. He pointed it at Stuart from across the roof.

"Put your hands on the hood kid," Thoms barked, "And don't make me tell you twice."

Stuart walked slowly to the front of the car. Weidlin found it took an actual effort to open his car door, but he did and hurried out, reaching for his gun.

Stuart stood in front of the car. Thoms stood to the side, gun drawn and still pointing it directly at Stuart.

"I said put your hands on the hood." Thoms said through his teeth.

Stuart raised both of his hands. Both Thoms and Weidlin did a double take as they notice that the right hand was huge.

And it appeared to be darker in color. Stuart rotated that hand in particular and made a fist. He then drove it into the hood of the car. The hood buckled and the car shook. Thoms and Weidlin looked dumbfounded. Stuart then began to shake the car, and began to lift it off of the ground. He got the car up three feet and dropped it, smiling. There was a chunk of skin missing from Stuart's large hand, but no blood. The engine suddenly landed on the road with a thud.

Thoms cocked his gun.

"Don't you move or you're dead."

"And what are you gonna do if I *am* dead?" Stuart asked, moving toward Thoms.

"Fuck *this*," Thoms said before shooting three quick rounds into Stuart's chest. Stuart kept moving and Thoms lowered his gun.

"Cut it out, you're gonna make me laugh!" Stuart said. He then lunged forward, reaching for and grabbing both of Thoms' arms. The gun fell from Thoms' hands and he began to struggle. Weidlin snapped out of what he was seeing and pulled his gun. "Let him go now!" Weidlin yelled. Stuart yanked both of Thoms' arms, hard and Weidlin heard a large wet snap. Stuart yanked again, and more snaps were heard. Thoms screamed as he dropped to his knees.

"I said stop!" Weidlin yelled and shot Stuart in the back. Stuart didn't budge. Instead, he put his left foot on Thoms' chest. He turned his head to Weidlin and said, "Make a wish!" and pushed with his leg while pulling the arms. Thoms tried not to scream but failed. Weidlin shot Stuart in the side of his face.

Thoms' right arm came off with a surprisingly loud snap. Stuart and Thoms both collapsed. Weidlin was hyperventilating and shaking, but he did not move. He looked at Thoms, who wasn't moving and at Stuart who was getting back up. He looked directly at Weidlin and smiled.

He took Thoms' arm and used it to wave at Weidlin. He casually threw the arm to one side. The left side of Stuart's face was now missing most of the skin from the gunshots. It looked like he was laughing.

Weidlin took a step back.

"I don't have any more time for you," Stuart said. "Run away or shoot yourself, but I have more killing to do. Oh, and you pissed your pants."

Stuart turned and walked into the woods.

Weidlin stood there, staring at the space where the worst thing he had ever seen had been just a moment ago. He couldn't move. Wouldn't move, until something rational popped into his head. His gun still extended, he just stood there, like some poorly made statue.

CHAPTER 28

Martin had stopped crying. It was almost time. He stood up and began to walk to the edge of the cave to read the word Stitch had left for him. He stopped when he saw Stuart standing there. He looked awful and dangerous. A chill ran through him.

"'Sup Marty," Stuart said.

"It's *Martin*." He replied.

"No, I think its Marty, *Marty*. I'm really going to enjoy hurting you."

Martin stood there and put his hands behind his back. He swallowed hard.

"How is it being dead, Stu?"

Stuart hadn't expected how calm Marty would be and he paused.

"It sucks. I'll have Lord bring you back so you can see how bad it is."

"But you're smiling."

"Some fucking cop shot half my face off."

"That sucks."

"Told you."

"Who's Lord?"

"My Master."

"Where is he now?"

"Don't you worry about where he is," Stuart said. "You need to worry about where *I* am right now."

"I just wondered where your Master was. No need to get all crazy." Martin had an idea. "What's it like to have a Master?"

Stuart was silent.

"I mean, *I'm* a Master. I just wanted to know what the other end of it feels like."

"You're no Master," Stuart said.

"Oh, but I am. I *am* a Master. You have no idea what I can do these days Stu."

"Shut up, Marty."

"Maybe you could call me Master if you can't say my name right." Martin said. "You have to call your Master Lord and not by *his* name. Do you even know his name?"

"It doesn't matter what his name is,"

"Names are power, Stu. I know your Master's name."

"And I know *your* demon's name. What's the difference?"

"The difference is," Martin said, walking closer to Stuart. "If you knew your Master's name, you might be able to finally die and move on. If I knew my demon's real name, I'd *still* be a Master and you'd still be a fucking bag of meat."

Stuart growled.

"This bag of meat is gonna kill you like I killed your mother."

Martin paused and then said.

"Was that before or after she ripped your arm off?"

Stuart leapt at Martin. Martin dodged him easily and tried to run down the cave to the opening. Stuart hooked a foot and tripped him. Martin landed face first into the hard dirt.

Martin tried to crawl away, but felt a strong hand grab his ankle. He was being dragged backwards until he actually left the floor of the cave. He was thrown hard all the way to the back wall of the cave and landed hard on a pile of bones. His back was in agony. He pulled himself up to a sitting position to see Stuart about ten feet away from him, still snarling.

Martin's eyes were wet with tears but he backed himself to the wall of the cave and tried to push himself up.

"Oh, just stay down, Marty," Stuart said, "But, I'd really like it if you would just beg me not to kill you."

"Did you beg Azaziel to kill you?" Martin asked. Stuart stopped.

"Who?"

"Your Master. Did you beg *him*?"

Stuart was stunned.

"His name?"

"It's a gift, Stuart. I feel bad for what happened to you and to James."

Martin's back and legs felt like they were on fire, but he was surprisingly calm. He knew he was dead, and almost welcomed it.

"I'm not going to beg you not to kill me," he said. "I *want* you to kill me. But I want you to have some peace. You don't want to be a bag of meat anymore, do you?"

"I...what was his name?" Stuart was still in shock where three loud gunshots rang through the cave. All three hit Stuart in the back and he whirled around.

Weidlin stood there still aiming.

"Don't you move!" He yelled. Martin recognized him at once. It was the cop from school. His mind raced.

"What's the word written on the floor?" Martin yelled to him.

Weidlin didn't acknowledge the question.

"I don't care if you're dead, do not move."

"You can shoot me all day, fuck-tard," Stuart said moving toward Weidlin. "I don't die."

Martin managed to get to his feet and yelled again.

"Read the word on the *floor*!"

This time Weidlin looked down. A few feet in front of him, something was scrawled on the floor of the cave, but there was a footprint in the middle of it. He carefully moved forward, switching his eyes from the floor to Stuart.

Stuart began to run to meet Weidlin. Weidlin shot once, directly into Stuart's forehead, but it didn't slow him down. Stuart stepped over the written word and grabbed Weidlin by the throat. Weidlin made a gurgling sound as he was lifted off of the ground. His feet kicked in the air and Weidlin dropped his gun. Smiling, Stuart slammed Weidlin into the wall of the cave, three times. He felt Weidlin's neck snap. Satisfied, he threw Weidlin down towards the entrance of the cave. He landed dead, with a thud. Stuart stood over him for a moment and turned around to face Martin.

"You *really* think some word is gonna stop me?" Stuart asked. He moved forward and looked down at the word. He read it a few times and looked at Martin. He started to laugh.

"You gotta be kidding me!" Stuart said, laughing harder by the second. "Holy shit, that's funny!"

Martin looked at Stuart.

"What?" Martin asked.

Stuart couldn't stop laughing. He began to laugh harder and harder. He sat down on the cave floor and started to punch the ground. His laughter was starting to boom and echo.

"Stu?" Martin called, but Stuart was shaking with laughter. Stuart's entire body was vibrating as he laughed. The look on Stuart's face however was changing.

His face had begun to decompose at a rapid pace.

Stuart put an arm out to pull himself up. He tried to stand, but couldn't; his newly attached arm fell off. Stuart began to flail violently and still he laughed. With his good arm, he began to claw at his throat. His fingers scratched through his neck and Martin watched as Stuart pulled his voice box out. Stuart began to wholly rot and decompose before Martin's eyes. The body still shook with laughter, although now it was just a series of high-pitched intakes of air and gurgling. Stuart slumped face first on the cave floor as he turned quickly into a black pool of wetness and tattered clothes. What was left of his arm-his good arm clawed at the dirt until it too, became black goo.

There was silence for a long time. Martin stood, mouth opened at what was left of Stuart. He limped carefully over to where Stuart had mercifully and finally died and looked on the floor at the word Stuart had read to himself.

From what was left of the word, he could tell that it said simply, "BOO."

Martin, in spite of the pain, sighed and began to chuckle.

CHAPTER 29

Martin managed to get his backpack on and limp out of the cave. It was pitch black, but his eyes adjusted quickly to the night. He didn't want to risk using the flashlight, so he found a walking stick for support and attempted to get out.

He made it twelve feet when he heard the voice.

"Hey there Marty!" Azaziel said.

Martin stopped and looked around.

"Azaziel." Martin said.

"Yep, that's me." He replied. "You've caused me an awful lot of problems."

"I could really say the same about you,"

Azaziel laughed.

"Well, I hate to point fingers Marty, but you started it."

"Fair enough," Martin said. "And my name is Martin."

"Oh, that's *right*. A demon Master should be called by his true name, right?" Azaziel laughed again.

"You can't touch me." Martin said.

"Well, I wouldn't say that." Azaziel said. "But I just wanted to talk. Where's your little bitty demon buddy?"

"He went looking for you."

"I know, but I got so wrapped up in watching you and Stu go toe to toe, I lost track of him. Where is he?"

Martin looked around.

"Where are you?"

"I'm everywhere."

"No, you aren't." Martin said and then added, "Show yourself."

"Now *that's* funny."

"I said show yourself."

"Getting cocky aren't we?"

Martin said nothing.

"Boy, you are a demon Master. *One* demon. But certainly not me."

"Deus nocet," Martin said sharply.

Martin had never heard laughter as dark as the kind he heard now.

"Oh, Marty you are a little *gem*!" Azaziel said. "I'm going to really like hearing you squeal."

"You can't touch me, Azaziel." Martin said again, this time sounding like he was trying to convince himself.

"But I know someone who can!" Azaziel said, cheerfully.

From out of nowhere, a huge black thing landed with a thud in front of Martin. As the wings opened and closed, Martin knew in an instant who it was.

Lilith's mouth opened in a rictus smile. In her teeth, were the remains of Stitch's sewn body, still intact, but not moving. Lilith spat the little doll onto the ground and growled in Martin's face.

"Hey babe," Azaziel said casually. "I'm sure you have some business with him, huh?"

Lilith flapped her wings, never taking her eyes off of Martin.

Azaziel laughed as Martin tried to run, but instead, limped about four feet and fell onto the ground, hard. Lilith grabbed Martin up with one clawed hand and brought him right to her mouth.

"Oh, this is gonna be great!" Azaziel said. "You have to tell me how Benial went first. I'm sure Marty here wants to know that too!"

Lilith snarled directly into Martin's face. Martin screamed in terror.

"Wait, I need a body!" Azaziel said. A moment later, the corpse of Detective Weidlin walked gingerly out of the cave, the head hung limp to one side.

"The head is a little fucked up, but it'll work!" Azaziel said through the mangled mouth of Weidlin. "Throw that kid down for a sec and tell me how Benial died."

Lilith ignored this and opened her mouth, exposing her teeth. She roared, lifting Martin above her head. The Azaziel/Weidlin thing laughed and cheered. He clapped his hands.

Lilith dropped Martin onto the ground. Azaziel walked over to Martin, who was scrambling to get away from Lilith. Azaziel put his foot on the back of his neck. Martin screamed.

"I can touch you *now* boy!" The Azaziel/Weidlin thing said. "And we are gonna have us a *good* time. Maybe we won't kill you straight away. Maybe I'll just have you around to be my bitch. Maybe, I'll bring back Benial and stick him in *your* body. Boy I'd love to fuck with him."

Azaziel looked up at Lilith.

"So how did you get Benial? I can't wait to hear this!"

Lilith sighed.

She grabbed the Azaziel/Weidlin thing by his torso. Lilith pulled him up right to her face. Martin rolled over and looked up at Lilith, squeezing the Azaziel/Weidlin thing.

"She didn't, brother." Stitch said through Lilith's mouth. "But I'll tell you that it is very satisfying to see the look on your stupid face right now. *Suspendisse!*"

Lilith/Stitch let the Azaziel/Weidlin thing go, and it stayed suspended in the air. Weidlin's body shook and wiggled as Azaziel's voice cried in frustration.

"Master," Stitch said, nodding with Lilith's head. Martin sat up watching and looked at Lilith.

"It's about time," Martin said.

"That's just a little bit ungrateful, Master." Stitch said. "How'd that word work for you?"

"Fine, but 'Boo?'" Martin asked, trying to stand.

Stitch/Lilith chuckled.

"It's not the word, Master, but the symbol under where I wrote it. I could have written anything there. The word was just the trigger."

"Hey!" the Azaziel/Weidlin thing screamed.

"Sorry, Azaziel. Almost forgot about you."

Stitch/Lilith grabbed one of the kicking legs of the thing and yanked it off. Azaziel/Weidlin thing screamed.

"Hurts, don't it?" Stitch asked. "I have a little surprise for you, brother."

"I'm going to destroy you, Benial!"

"Maybe," Stitch/Lilith said. "Not today. But *that's* not the surprise."

The small, tattered totem that once housed Stitch began to move. It stood up and mended itself. It hobbled over to the other two demons. Martin looked in disbelief.

"Hello, Azaziel." Cabal said, though the totem.

A look of disbelief and then pure hatred spread over Azaziel's borrowed face.

"No," Azaziel/Weidlin thing said. "You're gone. You're in the book! It's not *you*!"

"This body really doesn't suit me." Cabal said.

"Tell me about it," Stitch said.

"No need," Cabal said. "I need to correct something first."

Azaziel snarled at Stitch/Lilith.

"This is your surprise?" it asked.

"Actually, no it isn't."

There was a flash of light so bright, Martin had to put his arms over his eyes. It sounded like an electrical discharge he had heard once when a power transformer exploded during a storm. When the sound died away, everything was the same.

Except, it wasn't.

"This is much, much better." Cabal said. Except, the voice came from Lilith's body. Martin's eyes darted to the totem. The totem, looked at itself once, then again.

It sighed.

"Damn you," The totem said.

"Master!" Azaziel/Weidlin screamed. "*Father*, please!"

"And you *did* please me, Azaziel. You certainly did." Cabal said. "But I've decided that the time has come for me to return. I can't have you and your siblings running amok up here. I demand balance."

"Yeah, dear brother," Stitch yelled from the ground. "Apparently Cabal is God. *That's* the surprise."

"*What?*" Azaziel/Weidlin thing asked. "That's impossible. Master, what do you-"

"Silence!" Cabal bellowed. "You're going back home, Azaziel. Say goodbye to your brother."

"Benial," Azaziel/Weidlin thing began. "I-"

"Buh bye." Stitch said, and the corpse of Detective Weidlin dropped to the ground. Dead again, and devoid of Azaziel.

Martin sat and watched it all. His head was pounding. Lilith turned and faced them both.

"Now. As for you two."

Martin swallowed.

"Martin, tell Benial."

Martin swallowed.

"His name is Benial?" Martin asked. "Shouldn't it be Belial?"

Stitch stamped a little foot.

"You find out my real name and you *criticize it?*" Stitch yelled. "Just destroy me already."

"Stitch. I mean, *Benial*. I release you from my thrall. You're free."

Stitch felt a weight lift from him and fully expected to be released from the small, pigskin body.

It didn't happen. He looked up at Cabal.

"Why am I still in this body?"

Cabal ignored him.

"Go on Martin."

Martin took a deep breath.

"I conjured you so I could kill everyone in my school." He said. The words hung in the air. For a moment, all was silent. And then Stitch exploded with anger.

"Are you *kidding?*" Stitch asked. "That's it? That's why you trapped me in his little doll? You wanted to *kill your school?*"

Stitch began to pace in a little circle.

"All of this? Because you wanted to kill your stupid *fucking friends?*"

"They aren't my friends," Martin said.

"Why didn't you just do what every other stupid, lonely, asshole does and get a gun and blow your fucking head off?"

"I didn't want to die!" Martin screamed. "But I hated them! I hated them all. I don't *have* friends. No one at all! Not even my dog anymore."

"Well," Stitch said. "That's kind of your fault isn't it?"

Martin began to sob.

"My parents are dead, my dog is dead. I may as well be too. I'm sorry. I just want-"

Stitch sighed.

"And stop fucking *sighing* all the time!"

"You're *not* my master anymore!" Stitch said. "Which means, I can-"

"Enough." Cabal said firmly, cutting off Stitch. "Martin, I'm going to give you a choice. I shouldn't but I'm going to."

"I just want to die," Martin said sobbing.

"I can help," Stitch said eagerly.

"No, that's too easy." Cabal said. "I can reset this. *All* of this. Make it like it was before. But you'll always remember. You'll carry that with you forever, and you will answer for it one day. But, today you're getting a second chance."

"*What?*" Stitch couldn't believe it. "Cabal, be serious. Be-"

"Be silent!" Cabal said. "Not another word."

Stitch remained silent.

"Why do I have to remember?" Martin asked.

"Because you're being punished. I'm bringing you back to where this started. If you go through with conjuring Benial, I will let the course run. You may succeed in getting your school killed, and you may not. But it will run its way through. Your parents will die, your dog and so will any chance you have at redemption. Understand?"

Martin looked at Stitch and at Cabal.

"Will they ever be punished?" Martin asked. "The ones who hurt me? The ones who took that picture? Everybody who laughed? What about *them*?"

"What *about* them?" Cabal asked. "They didn't kill anyone. *You* seem to have the only actual body count. Why should they be punished so harshly?"

"But not at *all*? It wasn't right!" Martin was screaming.

"Martin. It's not your call to deal out justice. Lousy things happen to good people. It will always be this way, but there is a balance. There always is a balance. Maybe not right away, but there is one. You have to trust that, child."

Martin said nothing for nearly a minute.

"What do I need to do?" Martin asked.

"The right thing," Cabal said, and in a flash, Martin disappeared.

Stitch looked up at Cabal.

"That's it then?" He asked. "That kid gets to learn from his mistake? Do it all over again?"

"It is my will, Benial." Cabal said.

"I don't think I like you being God." Stitch said.

Cabal laughed.

"We are what we are, Benial. Even you."

"So, what. We go back home now? Big family reunion?"

"Not quite," Cabal said. Lilith's body fell to the ground. Cabal had vacated the body.

"Um," Stitch said, looking around. "Still here?"

"I'm always here, Benial. I'm everywhere."

"What happens to me?" Stitch asked.

There was a moment of silence, until Cabal finally said,

"I think you will make a great successor to me in Hell as my attentions will be more directed to the...other side."

Stitch couldn't believe it.

"You mean-"

"In charge, yes."

"Thank you Cabal!" Stitch bowed.

"Is that reverence?" Cabal asked. He sounded genuinely surprised. "How unlike you."

Stitch righted himself.

"It is what I have always wanted," Stitch said. "Come, let's go!"

There was another moment of silence.

"I don't think I like what you're not telling me, Cabal."

"Benial," Cabal said. "Favored over all the others, you will be my chosen successor. But for now, I want you here. I want you to learn."

"Learn what?"

Cabal laughed.

"Humility,"

And with that Cabal was gone.

Stitch looked around. He was alone. The corpse of Detective Weidlin vanished. Stitch imagined that was just the beginning of the changes. Since Martin never resurrected him, or made the pigskin, all of the work that had been done would be undone. He waited patiently for his small body to vanish as well. He was a little relieved to go back to being a non-corporeal being. He hated the body.

He waited.

And waited.

Stitch looked around him. There was nothing but forest and darkness. The fire in the cave vanished.

Stitch was alone and still in doll.

He knew.

He was trapped in this body until Cabal came for him, whenever that was going to be.

Instead of becoming angry, he made one quick resolve.

He was leaving New Jersey. If he had to be a small ugly chew toy, he damn sure was going to do it somewhere else and not in the Pine Barrens.

The first rays of dawn would be coming soon. A small breeze had begun to pick up. He thought he'd better start moving. He walked to a clearing and shot up in the air. He looked down at the place where it all had finished. Stitch sighed, and flew in the direction of the wind.

CHAPTER 30

Martin walked home, his mouth bleeding, but otherwise, he was okay. He knew tomorrow was going to be a hard day at school. He knew that it may be worse for him at school than ever before, but he was alive. James and Stuart took turns hitting him after he refused to try and raise the demon. Every punch he took meant that James and Stuart would still be alive in the morning. He didn't know if that was a good thing, but he felt better knowing they weren't dead because of him.

He wept a little, but not too much. The pain was a reminder. He unlocked the back door to his house and let himself inside. He wanted to clean himself up and go to bed.

He looked and saw the note on the table, telling him that his parents would be home late. He reached in his backpack and took out the book. He looked at it.

Raising Demons For Dummies: Millennium Edition.

He tossed it in the trash can by the door loudly and then he heard a bark. This was followed by heavy paws bounding for the kitchen.

Barky.

Marty, not Martin smiled.

CHAPTER 31

Pittsburgh

Kat didn't speak or have any reaction to the tale whatsoever. She had sat attentively and listened. After Stitch was done, she figured she was up to speed. Stitch paused for a moment and Kat spoke.

"So, what you've just told me is that the Devil is actually God," she said.

"I'm still trying to get that into my head too," Stitch said.

"Okay, just so it isn't just me. Go on."

"Go on *what?* That's all. I got here, you took me home, and here we are. Satisfied?"

Kat just looked at him and slowly shook her head.

"And you need my help to learn humility?"

Stitch sighed.

"I need *your* help to get a new body. Fuck humility."

"No no no no no," Kat said. "Cabal told you that you needed to learn humility. Don't you think that's what you should be doing?"

Stitch stood up.

"No I do *not.* Demons are *not* humble. We humiliate, we are not to be humiliated. It's…unnatural."

"I think supernatural would be more like it." Kat said.

"It doesn't matter what it is, I'm not doing it." Stitch said. He was nearly yelling.

Kat said nothing. She just looked at the little doll.

"What?" Stitch asked after nearly a full minute.

"You're like a little kid," she said. "Throwing a tantrum because you can't get what you want."

154

"I want a new body. I want to go home!" And this time, Stitch did yell.

"So much like a little kid," she said.

"If you're not going to help me, tell me now and I'll find someone else."

"Oh that's smart. Little Pooky in the snow in Pittsburgh jumping out of a snow drift. 'Hey! Can I have a new body? Please, so I can go home?'" Kat laughed then she softened. "What you need to do is *listen* to Cabal. Humility. I can help you with that, and then maybe? The other thing."

Stitch walked the length of the couch back and forth twice and then hopped on the floor. He walked to the front of Kat's chair.

"You can't be serious," he said.

"As serious as I can be with a talking doll,"

"You're going to teach me humility?"

"How can you *not* learn humility?" she said. "You're surrounded by it."

"That *smell* is humility?"

"No, that's stale smoke. Speaking of which," Kat said, getting up. She grabbed her cigarettes from the coffee table and walked into the kitchen. She lit up.

She had listened to Stitch's story for a long time-it seemed like hours and she had gotten up repeatedly to get cigarettes from the kitchen. Stitch had asked why she didn't just bring them into the living room, but for some reason, she refused to answer.

"Cabal, your God or your daddy or whatever he is, wants you to take over the evil side of the job from what you told me," Kat said. "You just need to *learn* something before he gives it to you. I imagine that would get you the body you want." Kat snickered a little.

Stitch considered this for a moment.

"*That's* what you got from that?" He asked.

"How the hell could you *not* get that from that?" Kat asked back. "I mean, come on. You didn't think he'd just *give* it all to you, did you?"

"He gave it to my brother,' Stitch replied, sounding a little pouty.

"No, Pooky. Your brother *took* it. Big difference."

"Stop calling me Pooky," Stitch said

"Your little brother did what you were just dying to do, didn't he? For all your bullshit, you did actually respect Cabal and you're pissed…" She stopped suddenly and started to smile. "You have *Daddy* issues. Holy cow you do."

"He is not my Daddy,"

"Dude, he turned back time and fixed everything *except* you and you're pissed. The older son rejected in the eyes for the younger one. He is *so* much your fucking Daddy."

Stitch said nothing, but Kat could see he was getting angry. She kept on talking.

"Not even to mention your girl Lil."

"Lil*ith*," Stitch said.

"Whatever. I mean, how else does she go from you to him? Because he went ahead and just *took* her. You had everything taken, Pooky. Your chick, your job, your entire *life*. Or whatever it is you have. You got owned."

Stitch stood up and looked like he was going to say something but didn't. He started to shake and then sat down again.

"You know I'm right," Kat said, but not without a little sympathy. "And you know it's not any new information either. You got comfy being Cabal's right hand. Didn't think anyone could touch you, right?"

"How do you know all of this?" Stitch asked, his voice not quite as booming.

Kat took another drag from her cigarette. She looked at Stitch and smiled. She was relaxing, because she was talking about something she knew about and that made her happy.

Well, happier.

"When you take your eyes off of the prize, someone comes over and yanks it from you. Sometimes it's someone you never even heard of, and sometimes it's your sister. Sometimes, someone you didn't expect is living your life. I know exactly what happened to you. And so do you. How does it feel?"

Stitch was still for a moment. Then he stood up and hopped off of the couch. He padded over to Kat and said.

"It sucks." He said.

Kat, surprising herself, bent down and picked Stitch up. She held him to her face and smiled again.

"That, Pooky, is humility."

"Stop calling me Pooky." Stitch said without any real fire behind it.

"You can cry if you want to," Kat said.

"Fuck you."

"Really. I won't listen."

"Thanks and again, fuck you."

Kat dropped Stitch onto the floor and walked back into the kitchen.

"That's no way to talk to me if you want me to help you find a new body." Kat said. Stitch pushed himself up off of the floor.

"Why not just toss me into a wood chipper or something? I can't die. Get rid of this body and I can go back to floating around aimlessly."

"Then how do you get your happy ending?"

Stitch heard this and didn't hear it at the same time.

"*What?*"

"Your happy ending. Everyone should have one, you know."

"I'm sorry," Stitch began. "Maybe somewhere along the way of your dime store analysis you forgot that I'm a demon."

"Kinda hard to forget actually," she said. She was eating a toaster pancake. She held it up. "I'd offer you one, but you're a demon with a doll body and no mouth. Didn't wanna be rude."

"I meant demons don't have happy endings."

"How would you know?"

"For one thing, we don't have ends. Second, we're pure evil."

"You were happy when you were with Lilith," Kat said though a mouthful of pancake. "At least it sounded like you were."

"She betrayed me,"

"You betrayed her first."

This time, Stitch was mad. He flew up from the floor and onto the kitchen counter in front of Kat. She nearly choked on some pancake out of surprise.

"I betrayed *no one!*" Stitch said. "As soon as I was out of the way, she went right to Azaziel. Didn't even try to help me, so don't say I wasn't betrayed."

"You didn't take your shot at the prize and you wound up leaving her behind. You betrayed her by ignoring your destiny. Or at least what you thought should have been your destiny."

"That's bullshit!"

"That's the truth. And she did try to help you from what I can see."

"And how is that?" Stitch asked. The two of them were face to face and yelling at each other in the kitchen. Had Kat stopped to think about it, she would have laughed at how absurd this was getting. "After hearing an hour or two of something that you came to the conclusion that she tried to *help me?*"

"The book, you jagoff." Kat said. "You said that the guy who wrote the book told you the stuff wasn't supposed to work. And yet, the spell to bring *you* back did? How does that happen when the demon who helped write it was...oh wait, *your* fucking girlfriend!"

Stitch held a little arm up to protest and he held it there for a few moments but then put it down.

Because he knew she was right.

"And," Kat said, still nearly yelling. "You go and hijack her body and use it like a shake and bake bag. So you tell me, *genius*. Where is she now, and how do you think *she* feels?"

Stitch physically shook his head and looked at this woman in front of him.

"Where the *fuck* did you come from?" he said. "Shouldn't you be cowering in fear or something? You were crying a little while ago. Now you're..." He couldn't think of the words.

"Humility is a bitch, isn't it?" Kat said, smiling. "The old you is fighting this new feeling you have. It'll take some getting used to." She took a deep breath. "Listen, I don't like yelling. I'll argue till the cows come home, but don't make me yell, okay?"

Stitch stared at her blankly.

"Whatever," he said finally.

"Good." Kat said, "Now, we just need to wait for the blizzard to be over and we can start."

"Start what?"

"Looking for your new body and getting you back to where you belong."

"And just where is that?"

"In hell with your old lady I guess," Kat said, walking back into the living room. She put what was left of her pancake in her mouth and then grabbed another cigarette. She jumped on the couch and patted the cushion next to her.

"Come on Pooky. Let's watch a movie."

"I'm not a cat and stop calling me Pooky."

Kat smirked.

"You're starting to like it just a little," she said.

Stitch sighed. Then, he jumped down from the counter and walked over to the couch. Kat looked down at him and picked him up.

"That's a good little demon,' she said.

CHAPTER 32

Stitch looked out of the window and glared at the snow, as if he could make it stop that way. He had been in existence for eons. He heard Kat snoring lightly behind him on the couch. He turned and looked at her.

Something told him she could help him and he acted on it, for the first time. Every part of him resisted the urge to hide in that stupid comic shop, but it seemed like the right idea and it had brought him here.

Squalor.

He sighed and looked back out the window. He watched cars stop in the middle of the street. A volley of horns would go off and the driver would get out and run to move a chair in front of the sidewalk. Then the driver would hurry back into the car and park. It was amazing. These people were insane, Stitch thought.

He stopped looking and hopped off of the windowsill. He looked at Kat again. There was something about her he couldn't quite place. And he also couldn't decide if it was something he should be worried about, and that bothered him.

The movie they had been watching still played while Kat slept. She had fallen asleep twenty minutes into it and Stitch decided to let her sleep. Mainly, so he could look through her things without any protests from her. He managed to decide that he wouldn't kill her for now and that at least felt good. He wasn't in anyone's thrall either, so he had control of his actions. Making a simple decision was a small measure of control.

There was a perpetual cloud of blue looking smoke that ran through the house since there was almost no ventilation and this woman seemed to smoke constantly while she was awake. Stitch didn't care, but it was more annoying than anything. He looked at the things in her living room through the thin smoke.

Mostly, it was books, movies and empty packs of cigarettes. Every square inch had DVD's, old labeled VHS tapes and books of every kind, just stacked or shoved onto shelves. There weren't any family pictures on the tables except for one. A younger version of Kat and an older girl who looked almost like her. The furniture- what furniture there was anyway- was simply a couch and a worn recliner. Aside from the coffee table, that was it. There were other chairs either folded up or covered with paper. The only real pictures on the walls were horror movie posters.

He left the living room and went into the kitchen to look for her purse. It was easy to find. It was a small pink thing that looked like a bowling ball bag. He jumped up onto the wraparound bar that divided the living room and the small eat in kitchen. He padded over to the purse and opened it up.

It was a small purse, but still slightly taller than he was, so he kicked it over. Not much spilled out; car keys, a can of pepper spray and a cell phone.

He looked in the purse after moving the big items out of the way and noted that there was no money in there at all. Not that it meant anything, but it did explain why her house sucked.

He came back to the phone. It was a touch screen phone that sprung to life when he touched it. It lit up and displayed all of the options he had including a password to look unlock the phone.

He nearly kicked it, but he didn't want to wake Kat up just yet. He needed a password. Judging from what he knew about her so far, he used words describing what he saw in the house.

He typed in the word 'mess.'

Nothing.

He tried 'fucking mess.'

Nothing.

He growled a little and looked around him. He looked at the movie posters and the movies. He tried nearly a hundred things and none of them worked. He was eternal, but Kat's nap was not.

He looked at the screen.

It said, "Please enter password."

He was about to kick it and then, without thinking, typed 'password.'

The phone granted him access. It took everything he had to not launch the phone across the room, into a wall and into a million pieces.

He instead, looked at his options. He could go on the internet, or take a picture or look at pictures or,

Pictures. He figured he'd take a look.

He quickly pushed the icon for that function and started to look through the pictures.

It was mostly crap.

No people, just things. A dead rat on the sidewalk. A car crash. The dashboard of a car from the driver's side. A spider web.

No good, Stitch thought and went to look at the phonebook. Instead, he found the text function. It pulled up a screen that had an inbox, and outbox and a draft box. He went to the inbox and saw 13 messages.

He started at the top. There was a message from someone listed as "Dickbag." It read, 'dnt txt me agn.' He went to the next message. And the next. And the next. After ten minutes, Stitch figured out the story behind the texts from Kat and the appropriately named Dickbag and began to laugh.

He was about to try something new. He would text Dickbag, which would of course show up under Kat's name. He was about to try when suddenly there was a clang and he was flying. It took an actual effort to figure out what was happening, but by that time, he flew into a wall and bounced, landing on the floor in the living room.

"You little mother*fucker*!" Kat yelled, holding an iron skillet. "How dare you go through my stuff?"

Stitch pushed himself up from the floor. He looked at Kat in the kitchen. She was furious, of course. He wouldn't have expected otherwise.

"How was your nap?" Stitch asked.

Kat was glaring at Stitch then at her phone. Her pale complexion went red as she saw what Stitch had been looking at specifically.

"Who is Dickbag?" He asked.

"Right now it's you!" She said. "How could you do that?"

"Do I really have to go into the whole 'I'm a demon' thing again?" Stitch asked. "Because that's getting tiresome."

Kat stuffed the things that had been spilled out back into her purse. She then took the purse and put it on top of her fridge.

Stitch was going to tell her that he could still get to it if he wanted to, but decided against it. She turned around and glared at him.

"I should throw you the fuck outside," she said, not quite yelling. "But you're right. You're a demon. That's what you do."

She walked across the room and picked up Stitch. She held him up to her face.

"And this is what I do," she said and threw him across the room and into the opposite wall. As soon as he hit the floor, Kat followed and picked him up again. He started to squirm but she threw him again against the opposite wall.

When he hit the floor, he got up and darted under the couch.

"What the fuck is wrong with you?" He asked from underneath in a muffled voice.

"You're a demon. You're just being you. Well, Kat is just being Kat. So, don't make me come under there and get you, Pooky." She began to tap her foot impatiently and from under the couch she heard a sigh. A moment later, Stitch pulled himself from under the couch.

"What do you want me to say?" He asked.

"You *know* what I want you to say." Kat replied.

Stitch thought about it for a moment and just as he was about to actually apologize, an idea struck him very hard.

"Dickbag." Stitch said.

Kat's jaw tightened.

"That is decidedly *not* what I wanted you to say," she said coldly.

"No, no." Stitch began. "You don't like this guy Dickbag, right?"

"Wrong, I *did* like that guy. That's the problem, or didn't you get that far in snooping my phone to know that?"

"I think that's when you started hitting and throwing," Stitch said. "But, we can use him."

"For what?" She asked, but as soon as the words left her lips, she knew. Her tight jaw dropped.

"You know for what," he said. "It's perfect."

"No. Absolutely not. I'll stitch you a new body myself if I have to, but not him."

"But it really is perfect. You know him, so he'd come see you and then I could-"

"First of all, genius, he *won't* come and see me," Kat said. "He doesn't *like* me. He doesn't *want* me, so he's now a *dickbag*, thus the nickname. Second, the answer is still no."

Stitch walked slowly towards Kat.

"I thought you wanted to help me."

"No, fucker. I said I *would* help you, but I'm starting to re-think that idea now." Kat said and walked out of the room. She trotted upstairs, leaving Stitch in the living room alone. He looked at the purse on top of the fridge and then looked away. He was screwed and worse, he was beginning to see how much it was his own fault.

He walked slowly to the window again and looked outside. His face was pressed against the glass. He began to replay the last thing Cabal had said to him.

I want you to learn.

Learn what?

"Humility," Stitch said quietly and watched the cars slosh past as the snow began to fall harder.

CHAPTER 33

Bruce had decided not to watch it snow all morning while doing his inventory. As much as he hated inventory, it was a good way to see movies he hadn't seen in ages. Which, of course interrupted his inventory and as he pulled it from the shelf to watch in the store, he laughed the laugh of the lazy.

He was nearly all the way through the movie when he looked out of the store window. He blinked several times as he saw quite possibly, the most attractive woman he'd ever seen walk in front of the store. She had deep red curly hair that was flowing over everything it seemed. She wasn't bundled up in Pittsburgh winter wear either. It looked like leather. His heart skipped and then sank.

There was no way she was coming into the store.

As was typical for Bruce, he talked to the girl as she walked past the window.

"That's it, just keep walking. Nothing but heartache in here for you, baby." Bruce chuckled as he watched the girl walk past the door.

He shook his head and looked back at the movie. Thoughts of the girl vanished as the movie took its hold on him again. He thought that as big as this guy's sword was, he should have maybe just a little more trouble swinging it around like that.

The bell to his door jingled. He didn't bother to look up.

"You have until the end of this movie to look around and then I'm closing up shop. Ten minutes or so, okay?"

"Then maybe you should tell me where all the heartache is,"

Bruce swallowed hard. His head darted to the direction of the voice, and there she was, standing right in front of the counter. All that red hair and leather. Her eyes were so green as to nearly be cliché, but it still worked. To Bruce, she was flawless.

And she was tall!

"Well," Bruce said, trying to think of something clever. "What can I interest you in, Red?" He leaned casually on the counter.

"Oh don't worry," she said. "I'm already interested. If I see something I *want* I'll let you know."

Bruce melted. He thought for a fleeting moment that he was asleep, but he wasn't. This was turning into a very good day. He looked out of the window to see the snow still coming down in huge chunks. Maybe, he thought, I can get snowed in here with her for a few days. He smiled. He looked back and the girl was still in front of the counter, looking at him.

And smiling.

Bruce's heart was pounding hard in his chest. He'd only read about these things happening. Hell, every movie he loved had stuff like this happen and it looked like-

"Bruce, you don't have to daydream about me. I'm right here in front of you," the girl said, slowly inching closer.

"Well," Bruce said absently, almost in a daze. "So you are."

At the point of where their lips would actually touch, the girl abruptly stopped.

"Where is it?" she said, losing some of the seduction.

"Huh?"

"The doll. It was here. Where is it?"

Bruce hadn't even realized he had closed his eyes, but he had. The girl had backed up and was now looking though the discount bin of stuffed oddities. He shook his head. Did he miss the kiss?

"I'm..." Bruce started to say but stopped. The vision of womanhood in his store-the future Mrs. Bruce Ballard-was throwing merchandise on his floor.

"You're what?" She asked, not even looking up at him.

"I'm wondering why you're fucking up my display actually," Bruce said finishing his thought and ruining his buzz. Where was the sexy fun from seconds ago?

She whirled around, smile almost gone on her lips. In fact she looked kind of annoyed.

"Where is it? Little ugly thing. Pretty hard to miss."

Bruce had no idea what she was-

"Wait!" he said, light bulb clicking on in his head. "Really ugly fucking thing, brown with button eyes?"

The girl beamed and dropped the cute puppy with chainsaw stuffed toy. She sauntered back over to the counter again.

"Interested again," she cooed. "Give it to me now,"

Bruce, glad just to have a happy reaction, smiled.

"Well, baby, I can't just *give* it to you. I gave it away this morning. But, I think I can-"

He was cut off abruptly as her arm shot out and grabbed his neck, which Bruce thought odd for a brief moment because she was roughly six feet away from him.

"I said, give it to me. How hard is that?" She asked. She pushed Bruce against the wall behind the counter. She was still walking toward him and Bruce's eyes were wide with surprise.

He tried to speak, but gurgled instead. The girl rolled her eyes and loosened her grip. Bruce took a gasping breath.

"What the fuck! What the fuck! What the-" Bruce was cut off again as the girl tightened her grip again.

"I let you breathe and that's what you choose to say? Oh dear, you're so much dumber than I thought." The girl said, disappointed. "Now, I'm going to let you go again and this time, you tell me where the doll is, okay? There's no need to tell me you're scared, because I already know."

She sounded less like a sexy thing and more like a mom. Somebody *else's* total bitch mom. Bruce wasn't as scared as he was confused until she said that she knew he was scared. He started to shake, but promised himself he would not freak out.

167

She loosened her grip again. He took a deep breath.

"Ok," He said, trying to not sound scared and really trying not to freak out. "It isn't here. I gave it to someone this morning."

The girl smiled.

"Much better," she said. "Did it say anything?"

Bruce opened his mouth to speak and paused. He thought carefully about what he was going to say.

"Did you just ask if the doll...*said* anything?"

The girl smiled, but it wasn't because she was happy.

"I spoke very clearly. Yes that's what I said."

Bruce shook his head and still wondered if he had heard her correctly.

"Very well," she said and let go of his neck. "Where can I find this person?"

Bruce slumped and grabbed his neck. Jesus, she was strong. He thought about her question and thought about who had the doll.

"What do you want with it?" he asked her.

"Does it *matter* why I want it?" She asked, almost snarling.

Bruce swallowed.

"I guess not, but it's a fair question."

"You wouldn't believe me and now I'm starting to get a little pissed."

"Sorry," Bruce said. "But you're asking me to tell you where a customer lives and that's not cool, especially since you just nearly took my head off. No offense." He was slowly but surely trying to move away from behind the counter.

"I *could* take your head off," she said. "And I could eat it and learn everything I need to know and have a snack in the process."

She looked at him and he stopped moving.

"Or, you can make this a whole lot easier. What do you think?"

"You'd eat my head? You'd need a pretty big mouth, sister." Bruce said, and then his hand shot up and covered his mouth.

She walked over to the door and flipped the "Open for Bid'ness" sign to read "Closed An' At" to anyone coming to the door. She pulled the shade down over the door and waved a hand toward the big store window. It covered with frost and was impossible to see in or out.

Bruce swallowed again.

"Oh fuck," he muttered though his hand.

"Oh fuck is *right*. And, your head is pretty big," she said and smiled. "But I think I can manage."

She started to change her appearance in front of him. Her tight leather dress, complete with little spikes, seemed to spread over her skin and then seemed to fuse with her hair. She also seemed to start to grow. Bruce stared in horror as the dress seemed to go under her face and dissolve the beauty of it, and then expand it, giving the girl a rictus smile of sharpened teeth. Teeth that gnashed together and made a spark. The girl/thing was now spreading huge wings that looked like the tight dress with the little spikes all over it. Her whole body looked like a vicious brutal beast that in all of his life, Bruce had never thought actually existed.

The entire change took fifteen seconds but to Bruce, it was forever. When it was done, he suddenly knew what it was that he saw.

And it was looking right back at him.

Bruce cleared his throat.

"Well, I guess you *could* eat my head if you wanted to," he said quietly.

"Clearly," she said through her teeth.

CHAPTER 34

Kat had spent the better part of an hour doing what she always did when she was upset. She was cleaning her room. She was very upset, and the cleaning of her room usually meant that one large pile of things was simply moved to a different part of the room while another pile of things took its place. Not very effective, but she often found loose change this way.

Today however, she was actually cleaning. When she found actual trash, she threw it into a large construction trash bag. The one she was currently using was nearly full. The pile of dirty laundry had made its way into the hallway to allow her to move around the room. She had even done the unthinkable and opened the blinds to let light into her room for the first time in months not by accident.

She looked out of the window for a minute to watch the snow and sat on her bed. She let out a very big sigh.

"Usually, that's what I would say." Stitch said from the hallway. Kat didn't bother to turn around.

"What do you want?" she asked.

"I wanted to see what you were doing." He said.

"What does it look like?"

"Looks like you're not doing anything."

"Wrong. Go away."

Stitch turned to leave and then stopped.

"Are you going to come back down?"

"What the fuck do you care?"

"Good point," Stitch said angrily. "Thanks for reminding me." He stormed off as best he could for his size.

Kat shook her head and kept looking out the window and then blinked.

"Wait. What?" She looked in the hallway and saw Stitch jumping down the stairs. She walked to the doorway of her room and didn't notice that she could do it without tripping over her clothes. She did have to kick a path in the hallway, but she did and rushed down the stairs.

"Hey," she called out. "Where are you?"

She heard something fall and looked in the living room. Stitch was on the windowsill again. He had knocked over a small and quite dead plant to do it.

"Why did you come upstairs? Come out here." She said.

Stitch said nothing.

"I said come out here."

"I heard you."

"So?"

"I'm busy now."

"Doing what?"

"What do you care?"

Kat chuckled.

"Are you fucking kidding me? Get your little spooky ass out of my curtains."

Stitch sighed and hopped down from the window.

"What." He said.

"Why did you come upstairs?"

Stitch said nothing.

"You are pretty transparent for a demon, you know that?"

"And how many demons do you know?" he asked.

"Just you, but I think you've spent too much time around us. You're picking up all of our nasty little habits."

Kat was feeling better because she wasn't thinking about the situation. She was reacting to it now, which kept her calm.

"What are you talking about?"

"You came up to apologize to me."

This time Stitch chuckled.

"Now that is funny."

"Is it really?" Kat asked. "Because the demon learning about humility just randomly wanted to come upstairs to see the human who was mad at him?"

Stitch said nothing.

"Yeah, as I thought." Kat said. "Humility feels weird, doesn't it?"

There was a moment of silence, broken by Stitch who said only, "Yes,"

Kat nodded.

"And there we have it." She said. "You're learning, Pooky. How does that feel?"

"I told you not to call me that,"

"Yeah, you did but I don't listen so good sometimes. And you don't have to apologize to me."

"Was that what I was going to do?" Stitch asked, but he wasn't being sarcastic. "I don't know what's happening to me," Stitch looked up at Kat.

"You're a demon. Not used to this kind of stuff."

"I don't think this is supposed to happen to demons. Something is wrong."

He was going to say something else when he turned toward the window.

"Something is here," he said and he leapt back up to the window.

"What is it?" Kat asked. She was back to feeling nervous again.

"That guy from the store. How well do you know him?"

"Bruce? Known him a few years. Good guy, why?"

"Well," Stitch said, jumping down from the window. "Two reasons. One is that he's walking up your walkway and two, I think he's dead."

Kat heard this and didn't hear it at the same time.

"Come again?"

"Look out of your Judas Hole"

"My what?"

Stitch stomped his foot.

"For fuck's sake, the little hole in your door to see outside? It's called a Judas hole. *Look*!"

Kat hurried to the door and looked through the hole. She saw Bruce and Bruce looked awful. More to the point, by the way his head was lolled to one side, he really looked dead.

"Oh my God," she said softly. She started to unlock the door.

"No!" Stitch yelled. "Keep it locked. He's looking for me."

Kat looked at Stitch briefly and then looked back through the door. Bruce was almost to the door.

"But..." she started to argue, but Stitch motioned for her to move away from the door.

When the first slow, hard knock came, Kat thought she'd scream. She covered her mouth and whispered, "What do we do?"

"For one thing," Bruce's voice came booming from the other side of the door. "You don't have whisper. I already know you're home."

Kat started to tear up a little.

"What happened to you Bruce?" She asked.

"Let me in and I'll tell you."

"No," Stitch said to Kat. Kat looked helplessly at the doll.

"Ah!" Bruce exclaimed. "The creepy ass doll *does* talk. No shit. Kat, you have to let me see that thing."

He knocked again, three times, slowly and hard. This time, Kat let out a small squeal with each hammering hit.

"Who sent you?" Stitch asked.

"Guess."

Stitch sighed.

"No, really. You have to narrow it down. Was it Azaziel? Cabal? Who was it?"

"Lilith," Kat said quietly. "Is it Lilith?"

They heard what sounded like clapping on the other side of the door.

"Ah, my sweet Katrina. You do have sight beyond sight."

"Don't you quote 'Thundercats' to me," she said and nearly opened the door.

"Where is she?" Stitch asked, ignoring the exchange.

"She's everywhere." Bruce said, knocking on the door again, this time nearly taking the door off of the hinges. "She's everywhere and nowhere. All around you, Benial. All the time."

Stitch looked at Kat.

"Benial is my name," he said.

"Yeah, I kinda figured that out. Thanks, Captain Obvious."

Kat had backed away from the door and started to look for something to use as a weapon in case -when- Bruce came inside. There wasn't anything more dangerous than a large disposable lighter in the shape of a candy dispenser with a cartoon dog head on top.

She grabbed it anyway, and decided that now was a great time to smoke.

"You're *smoking*?" Stitch asked.

"If these things were made for anything, it's for shit like this," she said through a cloud.

"That'll kill you, honey." Bruce said and knocked again.

"Why isn't Lilith here? Why doesn't she show herself?" Stitch asked.

"Because," Bruce replied. "She wants you to think about it."

Knock.

Kat screamed.

"I won't hurt you, Kat." Bruce said. "Just him. Has he hurt you?"

"What?"

"The fucked up doll. Has he hurt you?"

"No, he hasn't. Look Bru..." She was going to suggest he go to a hospital, but stopped herself. She honestly didn't know what to say.

"I know," he said. "I...just *know*. It's too late for me." Kat let out a small cry.

There was a moment of silence broken by Stitch.

"When is she coming for me?" He demanded.

Bruce pounded on the door.

"Way to fuck up that moment!" Bruce yelled. "Damn it man, I wait for five years for a tender moment with the woman of my dreams and you totally kill it."

"Shut up," Stitch snapped back. "What does she want?"

Knock.

"You wanna play it like that, I'll tell her you're good and ready to get fucked up. Happy?"

Stitch didn't know what to say.

"Bru?" Kat called out. "Why don't you tell Lilith to come here so she can talk to him?"

"What?" Both Stitch and Bruce asked at exactly the same time.

"Seriously," Kat said, taking a drag. "I know what this is about."

"You are insane!" Stitch yelled. "Why would you invite her here?"

"I gotta go with him on this, babe." Bruce added. "She really hates this little prick."

"Maybe *I* want to talk to her," she said calmly. "Maybe she can fix you Bruce. Maybe we can work it out so nothing else bad has to happen."

"You really *are* insane," Stitch said.

"Unlikely," Bruce added.

"Tell her," Kat said firmly.

There was another moment of silence.

"I told her I'd do this as long as nothing bad happened to you," Bruce said.

Kat shook her head.

"It's okay Bruce. I'll be okay."

"You know I've always loved you right?"

"I know."

Stitch pretended to clear his throat.

"You know," was all he managed to get out when Kat walked over, picked him up and threw him across the room into the wall. He hit the ground with a small thud.

"Go get her, Bru."

"Ok," and with that, Kat heard Bruce shuffle through the snow. Kat inched to the door to look out of the Judas hole to see Bruce one last time. Although she never loved Bruce, she felt like her heart was breaking. She looked and saw nothing but black. She unlocked the door to open it and look outside.

"No!" Stitch yelled from across the room as Kat opened the door.

She looked out to see Bruce, slumping away and rounding a corner. She felt tears again but held them back. She looked around. The neighborhood was otherwise empty. No cars, no people. Just a shitload of snow that was still coming down. She caught a chill and closed the door, re-bolting it as well.

She turned and saw Stitch standing right in front of her. They stood there for a moment, staring at each other. Kat cocked her head to one side.

"I know this is gonna sound stupid, but since you're made out of a football with emotionless button eyes, I have to ask. Are you *glaring* at me?"

"Yes."

"Okay."

"That's it? Okay?"

Kat looked away and walked into her kitchen. Stitch stood where he was still glaring and then followed.

"I don't know why you're glaring at me," Kat said. "But she's going to show up here sooner than later I imagine and you need to think of what to say to her."

"That's actually why I'm glaring." Stitch said. "I'm furious."

"You're not used to being emotional." Kat said, grabbing a box of mini cupcakes from the cupboard. "I'd offer you a cupcake, but I don't think you can eat them. They usually help me." She shook one out of the box, opened the little cellophane package and popped it into her mouth. She chewed it slowly and meticulously. Her eyes were closed. She swallowed finally and opened her eyes. Looking at Stitch, who still glared at her, she said, "Man, I'm getting a little emotional myself. Those things are fucking good."

"You invited her here." Stitch said.

"You're welcome." Kat said, debating a second cupcake.

"No, you *invited* her here. What the hell is wrong with you?"

She smiled.

"Plenty is wrong with me, but we're working on you, Pooky." She decided to put the cupcakes back. "You have an opportunity to talk things out with Lilith. Why wouldn't you take it?"

And there it was. The question hung in the air as if it had a physical presence. Stitch stared at Kat and couldn't find an answer he liked. He couldn't say anything at all he found. So, he stood there.

"Well?" Kat asked.

"I'm leaving," Stitch said suddenly and turned around.

"Why? She'll be here soon."

"Exactly. I need to be long gone from here."

Kat stayed where she was and watched Stitch. He wasn't leaving. He was pacing.

"You're nervous. That's almost cute, but you would have left already if you wanted to-"

"Why do you keep analyzing me?" Stitch asked, nearly yelling. "*Your* life is a train wreck. A total fucking joke and you're going to figure *me* out? What makes you think you have any idea of what you're talking about?"

Kat was stunned by the brutality of what Stitch was saying.

"I have been trapped in this house with you for hours now and all you do is tell me about me. And here I am fucking *listening* to it. Then you invite a demon who wants to ..." Stitch stopped.

"What? Wants to what? Kill you? You can't die, remember?" Kat was nearly in tears but she held it back. "You little jagoff. I'm trying to *help* you. You aren't trapped. Get the fuck out if you want, but no one's making you stay here. You're the one who wanted to learn humility. Well guess what? Lots of other shit goes with being humble. Like being scared. And you are scared like it or not."

"I hate this." Stitch blurted out. "Humility. I'm an eternal being. What good is humility to me? What am I supposed to do with it? It does nothing but-"And he stopped. He couldn't think of the word he was looking for, but Kat found it.

"Hurt." she suggested. Stitch sat down on the floor in front of the couch.

"I hate this," he repeated to no one in particular.

"I'm sure you do," Kat said, not without a little sympathy. "The question *still* is what are you going to do about it? If she comes here and you give her something she doesn't like, or say something she doesn't want to hear, you're screwed."

"Thanks for the recap," Stitch said. "I need to leave."

"You're not going anywhere," Kat said.

"What are you going to do about it?"

"Nothing. You've been 'leaving' all day. Still here. I should go take a nap or finish cleaning my room. Let me know when she shows up."

Kat started to go up the stairs.

"No, don't." Stitch nearly whispered.

"I'm sorry?" She asked.

"Don't."

Kat smiled and then frowned slightly.

"You've never really had these feelings, have you?"

"Once. An experiment. Humility is new, but some of the other ones..." He paused.

Kat was confused.

"You experimented with feelings? What, like in Devil College?"

Stitch sighed.

"To help us torment better, we were given different emotions to try out. Demons can't feel some things by design. Pity, remorse, regret. Things like that. A few of us volunteered for it. It was terrible."

"Why terrible?"

"Take a real good fucking look at me," Stitch replied. "Now, think about what's coming after me."

"Lilith was there too?"

"And my brother. Actually..." Stitch stopped for a moment. He stomped his little foot. "Fuck!"

Kat remained confused and bent down. Her neck was starting to hurt looking down all of the time.

"What?" She asked.

"I'm an idiot!" Stitch yelled and started kicking things in Kat's living room. He picked up a leg of Kat's coffee table and tried to flip it over, but Kat stopped him.

"Stop trying to wreck my place, you little prick." She said, kicking Stitch away from the furniture. "What is it?"

Stitch pushed himself up from the floor. He looked at Kat and he was vibrating.

"We were set up," He said finally and there was something in his voice that sounded foreign to him and odd to Kat. "Me, Lilith and my shithead brother. We got set up for *all* of this...son of a bitch."

"I'm trying to follow what you're saying, but I don't get it."

Stitch was furious. He started to pace again and once again, he was dealing with things he never thought in all of his millennia of existence he'd ever have to.

"Pooky?" Kat asked, but Stitch just stormed around the room. Kat decided to sit on the couch and have a cigarette. She couldn't understand what he had been rambling about. She grabbed her pack and shook out a smoke. As she put it in her mouth and reached for her lighter, Stitch growled.

"Hey," Kat said. "No growling. Yell, scream whatever, but do not growl."

Stitch stopped pacing and looked at Kat again.

"The three of us were part of that stupid experiment of Cabal's. Everything started getting shitty right after it. It was one of the last things I did before I got conjured in New Jersey by the witch. It was all a set up."

"I thought your brother screwed you. You already knew it was a set up."

"It was," Stitch said. "But it wasn't my brother. The arrogant prick got set up too. It was Cabal the whole time."

"But, Cabal's God I thought." Kat said. It sounded very odd to say that and now she knew what was different about Stitch's voice.

He sounded betrayed.

"He's no god," Stitch said. "At least not the one he says he is, but I think he wants to be. This was all part of his little project. He used me."

Kat took a drag from her cigarette and exhaled slowly. She coughed and said, "I'd offer you a drag of this if you had a mouth."

And then the front door exploded.

CHAPTER 35

Kat was on the floor of her kitchen, trying to think of something witty to say. Something, anything to make her want to open her eyes. She ran down a few in her head like "You could have used the doorbell," or even, "What, you can't knock?" But, none came to her and she was usually good about these things. *This is too much*, she thought. *This is over load. This is overkill and I am not opening my eyes.*

"Open your eyes," a voice said.

She refused.

"Please, open your eyes."

The voice was calm, even pleasant and seemed to come from inside her head. Still she kept her eyes shut tightly.

"Fine then," the voice said. "I know you're scared but you don't have to be."

"Right," she murmured and tried to squeeze her eyes closed even harder. The voice laughed.

"Suit yourself, Katrina. But you're going to open your eyes sooner or later. I'd sure like to help you."

"Please, get out of my head. If I'm still alive, you shouldn't be in my head." Kat said quickly.

"Well," the voice said softly "This is a private conversation. We wouldn't want anybody else to hear."

Kat was feeling slightly more disoriented than after the front door explosion. She didn't want to open her eyes, but she really didn't want this voice in her head either.

"There is nothing but pain coming your way, Katrina." The voice continued. "Terrible pain, but I can help you. I truly can. Do you want to know how?"

It may have been the way the voice had said the last part-the 'Want to know how?' part that started to piss her off. It certainly had a little to do with her front door blowing up, but her anger was starting to reground her.

"I want you to get out of my fucking head," she said loudly. Not yelling, but not whimpering either.

"Ooh, we got a live one!" the voice said, still in her head. "And people will think you're talking to yourself."

Kat squeezed her eyes tighter and gnashed her teeth.

"Fuck *off!*" she yelled.

The voice laughed, this time outside of her head.

"I really like you, Katrina. You're funny!"

Kat heard a thud as something large seemed to set foot on the floor. The heat from the explosion was giving way to the cold coming in from outside and she actually could hear the wind. And whatever just stepped into the house.

"And pretty dishy looking too," the voice said.

Kat realized that she couldn't stay on the floor anymore and keep her eyes closed. She opened her eyes.

She had been thrown with her head away from the front door and other than how roughly she had landed, she didn't seem to be really hurt. Her house on the other hand looked worse than usual. Everything that had been anywhere near her front door was now on or around her couch. This included the coat rack, the window from the door, shoes and part of the rug.

She moved and sat up. Behind the large dragon looking thing, she could see snow through the gaping hole in the door.

Kat blinked twice.

Kat assumed it was what a demon actually looked like. This one had a large head full of teeth and looked almost like a terrier with scales and crappy ears. It had a long neck with fading yellow scales on black looking flesh. Its body was gargoyle like, and had huge leathery looking wings coming from its back. It was jittery and very much alive and looking right at Kat. She couldn't tell if it had so many teeth it just couldn't close its mouth, or if it was just smiling.

"Hi there!" the thing said. "Boy howdy, are you a cute one!"

Kat fought hard to resist the urge to scream but failed. She screamed good and long and loud. She tried to look away but couldn't and she began to try to crawl backwards but was blocked by the fridge.

"Why, don't be scared of little old me," the demon said. "Let me introduce myself. I'm-"

"Brother," Kat stammered. "His brother."

"Very *good*, Katrina. I wasn't sure he'd talk about me." Azaziel said, this time not as happily. "And where is my *big* brother hiding? How odd that his first line of defense was you."

Kat swallowed hard and tried to think. It was easier to speak when she couldn't see this thing in front of her. She looked around the room and just saw rubble. Two feet away from her, she saw her still smoldering cigarette. Her eyes went wide and she picked it up. She took a long drag and relaxed as she exhaled.

She closed her eyes for a moment to collect her thoughts. She exhaled and took another drag. She shot a quick look at the thing again and blew out her smoke. She casually shook her head and took another quick drag from her cigarette. The demon's smile dropped.

"Excuse me," Azaziel said. "But have you lost your mind?"

She opened her eyes.

"Oddly enough, no." Kat replied. "Sorry about that, but I guess I never realized just how addicted to smoking I really am. I mean, look at this," She held out a hand. "Rock steady. I'm terrified, but I'm okay, you know?"

Azaziel stood there, not really knowing what to say. He actually looked behind him to see if she was maybe talking to someone else as Kat continued.

"Here's the thing. Nicotine is a stimulant. I don't know if you know what that is, but it makes your heart rate go faster right? Well it *relaxes* me, because in my head, I've convinced myself that it calms me down.

I guess that's part of the addiction and why I don't think I'm ever gonna-"

"Quiet!" Azaziel said sharply. "You were screaming a minute ago."

"Hey, you're still all scary and stuff. I'm just...getting used to it I guess."

Azaziel stepped closer and emitted a low growl.

"Where is Benial?"

Kat was confused for a moment, and then she chuckled.

"No wonder he wouldn't tell me his name." She said, more to herself than anything else. "It sucks."

Azaziel blinked.

"Where is my brother?"

She looked in the general direction of where Stitch had been standing.

"He is probably buried under all the stuff from when you blew up my door. And he's probably pissed."

Azaziel looked at the pile of rubble and laughed.

"That's kind of funny," Azaziel moved toward the pile and Kat saw that in addition to the wings, there was a short stubby tail.

"What happened to your tail?" She asked. Azaziel turned to look at his tail and looked at Kat.

"There's *nothing* wrong with my tail. It's always looked like that. And what do you know about demon tails anyway?"

"Does Lilith have a stumpy tail like that?"

From deep under the rubble, Kat and Azaziel heard something that sounded like a quick sharp laugh. Azaziel growled and began to dig through the mess. He extended a long claw nail and stabbed it into the pile and pulled out Stitch, who was now impaled on the claw.

Stitch was still laughing.

"What's so funny?" Azaziel snarled.

"Your tail *is* stumpy," Stitch said, nearly snorting as he laughed.

Kat was horrified at seeing Stitch on the claw. It looked like there were chunks of splinters in him as well.

Azaziel ignored this.

"So, you got to keep your little puny body. *Lovely!*" Azaziel said.

"And you got your stumpy tail body back. Gotta admit, I thought for sure you would change bodies when you got back."

Azaziel snarled.

"I wouldn't be so judgmental if I were you,"

"Why? If you destroy this body, I go back and apparently get my old body. Win win situation, asshole."

Azaziel laughed.

"And what if I destroyed your body while you've been gone?"

"Well then," Stitch began. "I supposed I could scoop your bullshit out and try on a stumpy tail suit."

Azaziel hurled Stitch against a wall and then instantly regretted it as Stitch hit the ground running.

"Dumbass," Kat heard Stitch say as he ran. Azaziel roared and began to tear the living room apart. Kat took one last drag from the cigarette and stood up. She looked for her coat and boots in the rubble behind Azaziel as he tore through her things.

Azaziel worked his way to the far side of the living room as Kat found her boots. Stitch was in one of them. He held a small hand up and said "Shhhh," Kat nodded and looked for a coat. And then, Kat had an idea.

"You know, we thought you were Lilith," Kat said to Azaziel, who didn't bother to turn around.

"What?" He asked. "What about Lilith?"

"She's here, looking for your brother."

Azaziel stopped and turned around.

"Lilith is *here?*"

"Well," Kat continued. "On her way here I suppose. Not here yet, but she's pretty pissed at Pooky as well."

Stitch couldn't believe his ears and repeated himself.

"Shhhh!"

Kat dropped the boot with Stitch still inside.

"Pooky?" Azaziel said. "*Pooky?* Are you kidding me?"

"It's just a nickname. Anyway, yeah, she's looking for him. He's going to apologize to her."

Stitch tried to crawl out of the boot, but Kat put her foot over the opening and put all of her weight on it.

Azaziel stared at her.

"Impossible. He's a demon. We don't apologize. Not even him. Especially him."

"Sure he does," Kat continued. "He's a different kind of demon these days. You know, after that thing Cabal did to you three, he's really a different guy."

Azaziel actually shook his head and growled.

"Katrina, he is a demon. Like me. Like Lilith. *Unlike* a human."

"Yeah, he's still a demon." Kat said. "But he's not like you."

Azaziel dropped part of the doorjamb and turned around completely to face Kat.

"What do you mean he's not like me? I'm evil, he's evil. We are brothers."

"He's been chosen by Cabal to take over. He's a little different than you I would think."

Azaziel laughed.

"The little thing he is now will *never* take over. I've been in charge since Cabal left."

"And now that he's come back? Who's in charge?"

Azaziel said nothing for a moment.

"I will be soon again, I can tell you that." Azaziel said finally. "I just need to take care of Benial first. And if Lilith is looking for him too, it'll be easier than I thought."

Kat laughed.

"You don't get it. He's going to apologize to her. He loves her,"

The movement inside of the boot was getting more and more furious. Kat stomped the boot and she could hear a muffled sigh come from below.

What are you doing?' Stitch's voice exploded in Kat's head.

'*Trust me*,' she replied in her head. '*And don't sigh. That's really annoying.*'

"Love? Oh, sweetie pie, you've been *had*!" The game show host voice had come back, except it was scarier watching the demon's mouth move while he talked. "Demons have enough emotions to just get by. The fun ones. Jealousy, hate, spite. I'm afraid love got left behind with loyalty and being nice."

"He told me about the experiment with emotions and how you all changed afterward. Lilith and your brother fell in love." She paused and looked at Azaziel. "And so did you."

Azaziel looked Kat squarely in the eyes and did nothing for nearly a minute. Then he roared with laughter. Kat held her arms up to her face as the laughter also carried with it gale force wind and it seems, spit. It was appalling, and the breath was actually worse than she could have imagined, but she knew she hit a chord.

When he had stopped laughing, she jumped right back on it.

"It all makes sense now. Your beef with him isn't about Cabal at all. He made you look bad in front of Lilith."

"That's enough now," Azaziel said, still chuckling.

"I mean, hell, you had her attention for hundreds of years and she still wanted him. You were in charge and it was still all about *him*."

"It was *never* about her, Katrina. Now, where is he so I can take him and we can be on our way?"

Kat wouldn't drop it.

"How horrible for you being one of only three demons able to feel different things like love and you get the short end of the stick like that. It's kind of sad. Aren't there any other demon girls where you're from?"

"Shut the *fuck up* already and bring me Benial!" Azaziel exploded. His wings opened and gave a quick flap, knocking everything down that hadn't already been knocked down. Kat recoiled, taking her foot off of the boot. Stitch flew out of the boot and hovered in the air between Kat and his brother. He spun around and said to Kat quickly, "I'll take itn from here," He spun back around.

"Hello brother," Stitch said. "Got a thing for Lilith? Does she know?"

Azaziel bared his teeth and snarled.

"Oh, how I've missed you doing that," Stitch said cheerily. "I truly enjoy making you furious. I'm nearly giddy to do it again."

"I'm going to keep you in that body for as long as it holds together." Azaziel said. "and if I have to, I'll make another one, and nail you to a tree for the next ten thousand years as an example for humiliating me."

"Oh, you do such a great job of doing *that* on your own. You don't need help from me."

"Well, you're hip deep in humiliation in your little doll body," Azaziel shot back.

"That's just it. You can't humiliate me anymore than I already have been. Seriously. What could you do that would be worse? You're going to be the one looking like an asshole - like always - for tormenting me, when in all honesty, I won't care. Lilith may not want me for anything other than revenge, and she is due that, but she doesn't want you for *anything* whatsoever."

"So it is true," Azaziel said, almost whispering. "You're going to apologize to her? Really? That's...*offensive*."

"Tell me about it," Stitch said. "I don't know what's happening to me, but I hate it. I also can't stop it. But I can still love to make you furious."

Stitch waved a hand and a large chunk of the door flew directly into Azaziel's right eye. Azaziel roared again and fell backwards.

Stitch spun and faced Kat. "Get out of here *now*."

"But what about you?"

"I got this. *Go*."

Kat grabbed her boots and slid them on. She grabbed a coat near the front door and jumped into the snow. It had slowed to a flurry, but there was a lot of snow on the ground. She got about ten steps before she realized she had nowhere to run to that was nearby. She turned and looked at the gaping hole in her house. She blinked. She blinked again.

The hole was gone. It was her front door. Nothing wrong with it in fact.

Good as new in fact.

"What the fuck?" she said out loud.

She looked up and down her street. Nothing. Except...

The foot prints from Bruce were still there, although covered up from the falling snow. She could still make them out thought, and franticly started to follow them. She got thirty feet when they abruptly stopped.

Bruce had fallen into the snow. For a moment she assumed he finally died and was about to mourn him when he moved and made a muffled noise. She reached down and brushed snow off of him. His face was nearly frozen along with the rest of him, but he was struggling to get up.

"Fuck," he said. He didn't sound like a man who was cold. He sounded like a man who had been paralyzed and was trying to work through it. "Hep. Hep. Fuck."

"What?" Kat asked franticly. She was slapping his face.

"Hep!" He repeated. "Don't hit, *hep*. Hep me up."

"Oh, shit," Kat said, getting it now. She grabbed an arm and started to pull him up. Eventually, he was standing upright.

"Your house," he said and they shuffled towards it.

"Where did they go?" Kat asked.

"No idea, but Lilith is on her way." Bruce managed to say. "Need to get warm. By the way, being dead sucks," he said.

They got to her front door and she opened it carefully.

It looked as if nothing had happened. It wasn't clean-it *never* was clean, but it didn't look like the front door had been blown off either.

When they were both in, Kat closed the door and locked it. Bruce made his way to the couch and collapsed on it.

"What can I get you?" She asked.

"Warm," he replied. She took the two blankets from her couch and covered him.

"I'll make you coffee or something, okay?"

Bruce groaned his answer.

Kat took off her coat and threw it on a chair on the way into the kitchen. She saw her cigarettes and grabbed them.

She lit one and took a deep drag. She looked around the house. There was no evidence of anything unusual happening. Well, except for the Bruce-thing on the couch. Other than that, it was normal.

She thought about Stitch and what might be happening. Where the hell did they go? She suddenly had a thought.

If Lilith was on her way, what was she going to do when she got here?

And would she fuck up her doorway again?

She took another drag and opened her freezer door for the coffee. She was still throbbing from the explosion that happened before, and wondered why the pain couldn't have been fixed along with the house.

She closed the freezer, turned and walked right into Lilith.

Kat had been so startled she fell backwards onto the floor, spilling coffee grounds everywhere. She looked up at the woman, standing in the kitchen. She thought she looked like a really pretty Viking and Kat nearly laughed.

"Where's my thrall?" she demanded.

Kat had lost count of how many times she had tried to keep her cool. She was trying again, but it was getting more and more difficult.

"Lilith?" Kat asked.

The woman just glared at her.

"You don't look like a demon is all. That's why I'm asking."

"Where is-"

"If you mean Bruce, he's on the couch thawing out." Kat pushed herself up and stood in front of the human form of Lilith. "I don't appreciate you killing my friend."

"I didn't kill him. He is in my thrall, that's all. If he's dead," she started and looked at Bruce, on the couch, "he has nothing left to lose. Therefore, useless."

Kat couldn't stop staring at her.

"Gotcha. Smoke?" She looked at the cigarette in her own hand. It had gone out from her trip to the floor. She tossed it in the sink and grabbed the pack from the counter.

"You got here a little late," Kat said lighting up. "Azaziel was here."

Lilith frowned.

"Azaziel?" Lilith seemed to get angrier. "Why is *he* here?"

"Well, he's not. He *was* here. He burst in and starting fighting your boyfriend and then they-"

Lilith's hand shot out and grabbed Kat by the throat. Kat dropped her cigarette and Lilith picked her up off of the floor.

"*What* did you say?" She asked.

Kat tried to respond but couldn't. She grabbed Lilith's arm and pulled. Lilith suddenly dropped her and squatted over her body. Kat gasped for air.

"What did you say?" She repeated.

Kat coughed, and managed to say, "Boyfriend,"

"Benial is a lot of things," Lilith said. "A boy isn't one of them and a boyfriend is not even on that list."

Kat looked into Lilith's coal black eyes.

"He loves you," she said. Her throat was killing her.

Lilith smiled.

"I'm sure you believed that when he said it, but we're demons, stupid."

"He didn't say it," Kat said. She was catching breaths in bigger gasps, but it was still hard.

Lilith looked puzzled.

"If he didn't say it, then-"

"Look, you need to help me up or something because you really fucked up my neck here." Kat was now franticly trying to stand and was clutching at her neck.

Lilith grabbed Kat's arm and pulled her up. She put a hand on her neck and massaged it slightly. Kat screamed as best she could, but it sounded almost like a squeal. As the squeal went on, Lilith massaged

Kat's neck until the squeal turned into a scream of pure agony. She let go of Kat's neck and arm. Kat fell back to the floor.

The pain had been terrible, but she could breathe easily and her throat no longer felt like she had tried to swallow a baseball. She looked up at Lilith.

"Well?" the demon asked.

"Well what? You want a thank you or something?"

"Tell me why you think Benial is in love with me,"

Kat got up off of the floor and looked for her cigarettes on the counter top.

"I know he is," Kat said, not looking at Lilith. Looking at her too long made her angry for some reason she couldn't define. "I could tell when he talked about you. He tried to deny it but not very well."

"Do you know what he did to me?" Lilith asked.

"Yep." Kat responded and grabbed her smokes again. She shook out a cigarette and then thought about it for the first time. She put the pack and the smoke on the counter. She grabbed her coffee pot and walked to the sink.

"And?" Lilith asked.

"And *what?*" Kat said, back to the demon. "Don't tell me you feel like a victim because in a fight he couldn't win, he took your body to try. And you're hurt now? I thought you said you were a demon." She poured the water into the coffee machine and stuck the pot underneath. She grabbed a filter and reached into a cupboard to get some coffee when Lilith reached over and spun her around.

"Look at me!" Lilith said nearly screaming. "You know *nothing* about being a demon and you think you can speak to me with such authority about it? You know nothing."

Kat again looked Lilith in her eyes.

"And neither one of you know *anything* about love, so I guess we're even. So, are you going to help get him back?"

Lilith's eyes went wide.

"Help? *Help?* After what he did? Are you-"

"Insane? Nearly. I've made friends with a demon trapped in my apartment for the better part of a snow day. He possibly saved my life and at the very least, *he* didn't do *that* to my friend," She said the last part, pointing at Bruce, still on the couch under the blanket. Lilith looked at him and Bruce, still looking blue, waved at her.

"So don't talk to me about insane. I'm up to my tits in insane today. If you're not gonna help, then fix my friend and be on your way."

Lilith growled. Kat growled back, taking the demon by surprise.

"Don't think that after everything that's happened to me today that a little growling is going to get you what you want, toots."

"You have no leverage to intimidate me," Lilith said.

"Sure I do. Benial loves you and I just confirmed it for you. You didn't know that before you came in here. You fucking *owe* me."

Lilith laughed.

"I owe you nothing."

"Then why aren't you killing me?"

Lilith raised a hand that very quickly turned into a black sharpened claw. It was poised to strike Kat, and Kat flinched, but stood her ground. Lilith glared at her and Kat glared back, but was shaking. After a moment, Lilith dropped the claw. Kat exhaled and leaned against the counter.

"Boy that was spooky." Kat said.

"Shut up." Lilith said and walked out of the kitchen. "Were did Azaziel take Benny?"

"How should I know? I was halfway down my sidewalk before I turned around. You probably have a better idea than I do."

Lilith sniffed the air twice, three times and snarled. She moved around the living room carefully and with purpose. Kat watched from the kitchen and looked at Bruce, who was mouthing the words "Get out" over and over again. Kat shook her head and looked at Lilith.

"What do you got?" Kat asked after a moment.

"They're not here," Lilith said in a distracted voice.

"Wow. No shit? Your supernatural skills of observation are amazeballs." Kat said flatly.

Lilith said, "There are different dimensions to occupy. I thought perhaps Azaziel took him to one of them. It's the fastest way to leave in a pinch. This is not the case."

"Oh," Kat said, feeling a little dumb. "Sorry. What's number two?"

"Number two is the same as number one." Lilith said and kept prowling the room. "But I think I know where they are."

Kat slapped a hand on the counter.

"Let's go get him."

"No." Lilith said and looked at Bruce. "I release you from my thrall." There was a small waver in the world and then Bruce sat up.

"That was so fucked up," Bruce said. "Fucking fuck I'm cold! Hey…" He looked at Lilith. "Um…thanks for not killing me and stuff."

"What do you mean no?" Kat asked. "Don't you think we should save him?"

Lilith looked at her.

"No I don't. I realized something."

"What, you're still mad?"

"No. I feel the same about him. That's not right. That's not *possible*. We're demons and we-"

"He told me about Cabal's experiment. Yeah, you're demons and you don't do that. Well, now you do."

Lilith hung her head.

"When I saw him for the first time in his little body, it felt horrible. I tried to play it off, but I was so angry for where we had ended up."

"He said you picked him up and licked him."

Lilith smiled.

"Well, of course. He would have expected nothing less."

"Can I have some fucking coffee already?" Bruce yelled.

"Jesus Bru, ladies talkin' here," Kat said, getting back to the coffee pot. "Be nice please."

"Pardon me for being a slave boy for a demon," he said.

"From the looks of her, you probably loved it." Kat said.

Kat finished and went back to the counter.

"So, back to the no. If anyone can help him, it's you. Why can't we go?"

Lilith sighed and looked tired.

"To what end? More hurt and misery. I like to dish that out, thanks very much. We cannot die, so that's not a concern."

Kat just stared at Lilith. She actually couldn't believe her ears.

"You're kidding, right?"

Lilith growled.

"You doubt me?"

"Last I checked, demons were not known for how fucking upfront they are about things, so yeah I kinda doubt you."

Lilith blinked and walked back into the kitchen. She didn't look the least bit happy.

"What is it to you anyway? You didn't conjure him, you're not his thrall, so what are you in this?"

"He asked me to help him," Kat said.

"I doubt it," Lilith said. "Just go back to your little life and don't concern yourself anymore." Lilith made her way to the door.

Kat blinked, not quite understanding.

"Wait, where are you going?" She moved toward her, but Lilith whirled around and grabbed Kat by the throat-not as harshly as before.

"You are going to get yourself gutted," Lilith said through her teeth. "Keep it up and it'll be by *me*."

Both of Kat's hands went to Lilith's hand instinctually. Lilith leaned in closely and looked into Kat's eyes directly.

"Don't do this to him," Kat said and couldn't think of a single reason why. Lilith's expression changed from one of pure fury to a sad, confusion. She threw Kat backwards and left the house, slamming the door in the process.

Kat landed on the couch where Bruce still lay, half conscious. He made a sound like 'oof' and opened his eyes. Kat was upside down.

"Baby," Bruce said softly, "Where's my fucking coffee?"

"Aw, damn!" She cried and struggled to get off of Bruce, who was still in a semi daze. She landed with a thud and struggled to get off of the floor.

"Lilith!" She yelled and ran to the front door. She yanked it open and she had gone completely. Kat growled a little and slammed the door shut.

"Fucking hell," she said and stormed into the living room. Bruce sat up now, still reeling a bit. He had decided to get his bearings and process the impossible last few hours.

"I really was under the control of a hot redhead demon, was I not?" he asked. "I mean, when she turns back into the demon, not so hot, but she was hot, right?"

"Glad you have standards Bru, and yes," Kat said, not looking at him. Then she slowly turned to him after a moment.

"Do you know where she's going?"

Bruce closed his eyes and then blinked.

"Nope. She did say something about something called Cabal and how it was really all his fault. That's it. Well, and that she hates that Benial thingy."

"She doesn't," Kat said. "She loves him, he loves her. It's a tragedy."

"What, those two evil supernatural things are *into* each other?" Bruce asked. "Pardon me, my sweet, but how the *fuck* is that exactly a tragedy?"

Kat shook her head and went back into the kitchen.

"Coffee's comin'" she said and grabbed her cigarettes.

As she made the coffee, she wondered exactly why she gave a damn about a demon.

CHAPTER 36

"Do you know where you are?" Azaziel asked. Stitch said nothing because he knew where he was and where he was going for the second time. Azaziel had picked him up and swallowed him whole. He had then gone through his entire intestinal tract being squeezed mercilessly through what seemed like miles of wet feces.

The first trip really didn't accomplish much. Stitch just went along for the ride, although right before he began to pass through the intestines, he realized that Azaziel's stomach acids could eat through the little body he wore. It didn't hurt; Stitch could physically feel nothing, but if the body were destroyed, he'd be screwed.

As he was shit out violently onto the stone floor of wherever the hell they were, he thought Azaziel may try to do the same thing again and he was not disappointed. Laughing like an idiot, Azaziel picked him up and looked at him.

"Another ride? Why not?" And swallowed him again. Stitch hoped he tasted terrible.

Azaziel asked again, when he felt Stitch reach his stomach, "Do you know where you are?"

Stitch was half submerged in the stomach. He decided it was too dark, so he waved a hand and allowed a matchstick sized blue flame to appear on his hand. He held the flame to the inner lining, causing it to smoke and to open slightly. The hole was large enough to allow him to stick his arms through, tiny as they were. He did so, keeping the flame lit, and crawled out into Azaziel's body.

Azaziel belched and then winced. He looked down at his belly and poked it with a talon.

"Hey, what are you doing in there?" he said.

Then Azaziel roared with pain and clutched his side. It felt like someone had dislodged a rib. This was confirmed as one of his ribs came stabbing out of his chest and landed with a thud onto the stone floor. Azaziel snarled and waved a hand. Stitch was transported from inside of Azaziel and slammed onto the ground.

He was laughing.

Even as Azaziel began to stomp him, Stitch laughed.

"Stop laughing!" Azaziel yelled, but it was no good.

"Oh, brother," Stitch said between stomps, "Oh how I have *missed* you!"

Azaziel kicked Stitch a good distance before a wall stopped his momentum. He reached down and picked up the rib. He looked at it carefully and stuck it back into the exit wound, hissing. He then waved a hand and the wound healed itself. He then tried to calm down. His attempts at tormenting Stitch were less than successful.

Still, he was going to keep trying. He looked at the little body his brother was trapped in and knew it was only a matter of time before it would fall apart. And then, Azaziel could really do some tormenting with a non-corporeal being with nowhere else to go.

But he wanted Benial to suffer with anticipation and that would be the most satisfying thing ever if it would just *work*.

"Do you know where you are, Benial?" Azaziel asked again. He started to walk toward Stitch, trying to maintain his calm.

"Yes, brother." Stitch said, trying to stand. "I'm home. I appreciate the lift."

Stitch finally stood up and looked. He was in a barren dark cave like tunnel. There was light coming from somewhere, but he couldn't tell where. It smelled like sulfur and he could hear screams in one voice in the distance. Yes, he was home.

"Your cave?" Stitch asked.

"Somewhere out of the way," Azaziel replied as he approached closer. "Where no one can bother us."

"I would think you'd want everyone to see your greatest triumph," Azaziel smiled.

"I appreciate you looking out for me, but this is between us."

Azaziel stopped walking and stood in front of Stitch.

"Why couldn't you just respect me?" Azaziel asked.

"What for?" Stitch asked back. "What do you care what I think. When have you *ever*?"

"Don't be dense," Azaziel said. "You know what I mean."

Stitch simply stood there and watched his little brother. There was contempt all over and through him and Stitch had to admit he'd never noticed it truly before this moment. He knew he was vain and arrogant, but he didn't know how deeply his hatred ran.

"You really hate me that much don't you?" Stitch asked. "It's almost admirable."

"It's mutual I'm sure," Azaziel said, smiling again.

Stitch laughed again, loudly.

"You don't understand," Stitch said. "That's the one thing you never ever understood. Brother, as much as you hate me, I do not *care*. I don't feel either way about it at all. You can have Cabal's position and I won't give a single damn about it or you. You're breaking your ass to humiliate me, and I still just don't care."

Azaziel looked as if he had been slapped. He rushed forward and picked Stitch up off of the ground. He glared at him.

"I will torture you for an eternity once I rid you of this little body,"

"And I still won't care," Stitch replied. "It doesn't matter to me, Azaziel. It hasn't for thousands of years, and it's not going to start now."

Azaziel screamed and slammed Stitch to the ground. He looked at the little body that held the essence of the one thing in the world he hated above all other things. He made a fist with a talon hand and punched Stitch as hard as he could. Again. And again.

And Stitch kept laughing.

CHAPTER 37

Bruce was sitting up and drinking his third cup of coffee. He still felt cold all over although Kat had cranked up the heat and he was covered in blankets. He even put on the Fluggie-the blanket you can wear thing he hated so much. And he still was freezing. He sipped the coffee and looked nervously around the room.

He was trying to maintain his cool, but it was hard. For one thing, he'd spent a lot of his day being controlled by a demon. It had been excruciating, terrifying and he'd remember it for the rest of his life. He was sure it was over, but he never ever wanted to see, hear or have anything to do with demons again. That meant he'd never be able to watch his favorite movies again, and that would be hard. No more "Night of the Demons" 1 and 2 on boring weeknights in December. Almost a tradition now. No Italian horror movie festival would be complete without the two "Demons" films, which were almost as good as their Zombie films. It was nearly heartbreaking.

Kat had asked him repeatedly what it was like and he couldn't answer her. He just shook his head at her as if to say, "No, you don't want to know and I can't tell you anyway." And that was another thing.

Kat.

She had spent a lot of the past hour trying to figure out a way to follow the demons, or at least to get the little shitty one back. From what she had said, her day was spent trapped in her house teaching a demon how to be humble. He couldn't wrap his head around it. He loved this girl, but that was just flat out crazy and he told her so.

She ignored that of course, like she would do as always. He couldn't and wouldn't understand what was with her now.

"There has to be a way to either get them back here," She said, "Or for me to get there."

She had kept saying this over and over. Bruce wasn't entirely sure that at least one of them wasn't coming back and he really didn't want to be in her living room when they did.

"Just drop it," Bruce said. "Really Kat. Be grateful the evil fucks are gone."

Kat didn't even look at him any of the times he said this. She just kept flitting around her living room anxiously. Eventually she had told him all of what had happened to her even when he told her to stop. She was obsessed now and it was spooky.

"Kat, you really need to stop. Why do you care about these demons?"

That question stopped her for a moment.

"Not demons," she said closing her eyes. "The brother? Fuck him, but Lilith and Pooky, I kind of do I guess. Not even so much her,"

"Her?" Bruce nearly jumped off of the couch. "*Her?* Look what she did to me!"

Kat looked at him, surprised at his reaction.

"Bru, I-"

"No, Kat. That fucking thing sent me here to kill you and only at the last minute did she change her mind and switch it to just a warning to get to her boyfriend. These things are evil. *She* is evil and I can't see why you'd care what happens to her,"

"You don't understand," She started to say, but let it drop. Bruce was upset. She went to him and sat down next to him. She put an arm around him as he yawned in her face. She smirked at him.

"I'm sorry. You relax, try to rest. More blankets?"

Bruce shivered and nodded.

"Okay pal, lie down." She said and took his coffee cup. "Maybe if you lie still you can get some sleep."

"Don't want to dream," he said, but he was already drifting off. "Kat, don't..."

"Don't what?"

"Do stupid shit," he muttered.

"All I *do* is stupid shit, Bru. You should know that. It's why you dig me,"

Bruce smiled before he fell asleep.

Kat stroked the side of his head and carefully got up. She knew Bruce was right. She shouldn't care at all, but there was something to be said for doing something that felt right to do. Again, she wasn't quite sure if helping demons was exactly the right thing to do, but she also couldn't think of them as just being demons anymore.

She figured once Cabal had given them different emotions, from that moment on, they weren't just demons anymore. She didn't know exactly *what* they were, but they couldn't just be regular demons, spawned of hate and lies. Two of them were in love with each other for crying out loud. And the third one was jealous.

She was the only one who was aware of this and wanted desperately to help. But how was the big question. And the bigger question she wasn't asking (*but Bruce was*) was why *should* she?

There was a knock at the door. Kat nearly jumped out of her skin but it was just a knock, not a pounding. She took a deep breath and walked over to the door. She looked through the little peep hole-the Judas hole as Stitch called it-and saw a kid. He looked cold and nervous. She frowned.

She disengaged the lock and opened the door. The kid pushed his way in and closed the door, locking it as he went.

"Hey, what the hell?" Kat asked. She'd had enough people coming into her house.

"Cold," the kid said. He looked to be about 15 or 16 and he was shivering. "Sorry, but man, it's really cold."

"No shit," she said. Her hands went to her hips. "Who are you and what do you want and who the fuck are you calling *man*?"

He looked up at her. He had a black eye that looked a few days old. He looked very sad and pathetic.

"You're Katrina?" He asked.

"I get to ask questions first," she snapped. "This has not been a good day, so how about yinz tell me who you are?"

"What does 'yinz' mean?" the kid asked.

Then she heard it. The kid wasn't from Pittsburgh.

"Who are you before I kick your little ass?"

He reached up and took his hat off. His hair was a black greasy mess and he ran a hand though it.

"My name's Marty," he said. "I'm looking for Stitch."

Kat looked at him for a moment without saying anything at all, just looking. She nearly started to laugh. In a day of totally unbelievable things, this was really starting to piss her off. She closed her eyes for a moment and then opened them.

She said, "Congratulations. You're still looking for him and so am I." She turned and walked into her kitchen. "Coffee?"

Marty watched her. It wasn't the reaction he'd been expecting. He'd been expecting something akin to gratitude or relief that someone had come to take away the demon. This was odd.

"Um, sure. But...where is he?"

"Drop your coat Marty and we can talk. You need to thaw out a little. How'd you get here?"

Marty peeled his coat and dropped it on the floor in front of the door. He tried kicking his boots off without untying the laces, so he was stamping around in a small circle. Kat looked at him and shook her head.

"A bus," Marty said between grunts. Kat came over with a chair and pushed him into it.

"Boys," she said and grabbed a boot. She pulled the lace and said, "It's always the hard way to do things, isn't it? And when these come off, pick your wet ass coat up off of my floor, oaky?"

Marty's face went red and said, "Sorry,"

She got the boots off and went back to the kitchen.

"Ok, a bus. Next question. Why are you here and who told you Stitch was here?"

"I wanted to warn him I guess,' Marty said, picking up his coat. "I figured I owed him that much."

"Warn him about what? His brother?"

Marty frowned.

"Azaziel? No, about Cabal."

Marty was standing looking at Bruce on the couch sleeping.

"He okay?"

"Fine, come in here." Kat said, lighting a cigarette.

"Those are bad for you," Marty said.

"Says the boy who raised a demon," she said. "That's pretty bad for you too."

"You have no idea," he said and thought about it. "Well, I guess by now you do. That mine?"

Kat nodded and slid a cup of coffee across the counter to him. He picked it up with both hands and took a sip. He squinted and sniffed the cup.

"Vanilla?" he asked.

"Yeah," she replied through a puff of smoke. "All I got. Sorry if you hate it."

"It's warm. Thanks." He took another sip.

"So what about Cabal then?"

"He isn't God."

Kat nodded.

"Pooky had said something about that. He said 'He wishes he was God' or something like that. I thought he was just being pissy."

"Well, he's pissy anyway, but he's right. Cabal isn't God. Not even close."

"Well, how would you know anyway? I though you got to go back to the beginning unscathed?"

"That's what I thought too," Marty said between sips. "But it was worse than before. If that's possible. More demons came."

Kat looked at him.

"More came? For what?"

"Torment," he said simply. "It's what they do. Cabal reset everything as if I hadn't done anything, but the next day demons started showing up."

"What happened?"

"Sometimes just to make fun of me," Marty said in nearly a monotone. "Sometimes, to slap me around. That's what happened to my eye. And sometimes..." Marty drifted for a moment. "Sometimes they killed people I knew." He took a sip of coffee. "They killed my parents. Made it look like an accident. The killed everyone who originally died before Cabal 'fixed' everything." He made quote marks in the air when he said 'fixed.'

"I asked them why they kept coming around seeing as Cabal had let me start over. One of them laughed and said 'You have to realize by now that Cabal isn't God. God wouldn't allow this.' I didn't believe it at first."

Kat took a deep drag from her smoke and asked, "So what finally convinced you?"

"Cabal," Marty replied. "I was calling for him and he finally showed. I was...crying and he patted me on the head. He asked what was wrong and I couldn't answer for a long time. Then I told him. He laughed."

Marty picked the coffee cup back up and took another sip. Kat watched him. She felt horrible for this kid, but a part of her also didn't feel anything for him. She wondered why that was. Marty seemed to read her face.

"I did terrible stuff, but I thought I was making it up. I really did. And that's just what Cabal said too. 'You don't get do overs,' he said. 'You get what you get.' I said I thought you were God? He laughed and said, 'They do call me the Prince of Lies now and again,' and he vanished."

"He lied to you," Kat said. "And to Pooky."

"Who's Pooky?" Marty asked. Kat ignored it.

"So how did you get here?"

"I had a book called "Raising Demons,"

"For Dummies, I know." Kat said. Marty's face turned red again.

"Anyway, I found the guy who wrote it. He told me how to get here to find Stitch."

"Okay," Kat said. "But to what end? He's not in your control anymore, so what would he do for you?"

"Is he in your control?"

"No,"

"Oh. Are you in his control?"

"No, I'm just a-" and she stopped herself. She was going to say friend, but that wasn't right. "I'm just a bystander in this," she finished.

"Well, where is he then? Any idea?"

"Azaziel took him. I have no idea where to start looking."

Marty picked the cup up and took a bigger sip, now that the coffee had cooled off a bit.

"I might have an idea of where," he said.

"How you figure?" Kat asked.

Marty smiled and said, "I found *you* didn't I?"

Kat looked at him and had two thoughts. One was that he was just a kid. The other one was this is the kid that put a demon into a little ugly doll and brought her world to the interesting place it was today.

"You need to explain that to me kid," she said finally. "Because I'm not all that sure that I trust you."

"Don't call me kid," he said.

Kat shook her head.

"I can call you shithead if I want, kid. My house, my rules. How did you find me?"

CHAPTER 38

New York City, Two Days Ago

Marty sat in the apartment lobby, waiting. He knew Maldetto would be home soon; it was just a matter of how soon. His ribs still hurt and his eyes were heavy. He thought about the last three months and tried to put them into perspective.

He failed because it was all a horrible dream come true. All of it. Every last little piece. It had started when James went missing. Well, not so much when he went missing, but when they found him. Or, what they found of him.

James and Stuart had been merciless in their dealings with Marty since the night in the cemetery. No longer content to just knock books out of his hands, they would sucker punch him at any given chance. It was bad, but Marty didn't realize that the first week after Cabal had set things back into motion would be the best week of all of it.

The next week found James going missing. This was good for Marty. He only had to worry about one asshole hitting him or so he thought. They found James a few days later, in a cave. *His* cave to be exact. Half eaten and missing a head. No one knew quite what to make of it and there weren't any suspects. No prints, just teeth marks and unless the police had reason to have teeth prints on file, there wouldn't be a suspect.

For a fleeting moment, Marty thought it was Cabal helping him out a little bit. Then one of the policemen investigating the case disappeared. They found him too, days later in the cave in much the same manner as James. Head missing and chewed up. The funeral for Detective Thoms was huge and even wound up on a national cable news outlet. Jersey Devil news stories popped up all over the state and thrust the Pine Barrens into an unforgiving spotlight. Soon, another death - Detective Thoms partner, Weidlin. This was especially interesting since this time the head was left behind and the body was missing. All in the cave, which at this point was being guarded and still, the bodies came. Marty noticed a pattern. It was hard not to notice after Stuart had become the fourth victim. Everyone who had died when he had chosen to resurrect Stitch into the doll was dying now that he had not chosen to do it.

There was a small brigade of cops camped outside and also, deep within the cave. They would not allow another body to be dumped here. And still, they came as if from nowhere. There was no explanation on how the half devoured corpse of Stuart Fender had been discovered in the cave, embedded into the rock wall midway to where the cops had set up. It was bizarre.

But not too bizarre for Marty. It was terrifying because he knew eventually his parents would be next and he was right.

Just before Christmas, Marty had been shipped to his Uncle Jack's house in Parsippany. It was his mom's brother and he was really shaken up by how his sister and brother in law had died.

"The most fucked up thing I ever heard of Marty," he said, wiping away a tear. He was right. After Barky was hit by a truck (the small mercy was at least he hadn't been half eaten and dragged into that cave) Marty began to panic. He surely would be next to die, but as it turned out, there was something else to come.

On his first day at Morris Plains High, Marty realized that he could start over. No one knew him here at all. No one knew about the picture of him (SOMEONE'S GOT A STIFFY) and he could reinvent himself. This was the first thing to make him feel better in a very long time.

It didn't last.

Marty sat in his last class of his first day, feeling pretty good. He was writing a note from his new favorite math class. The bell rang, and the other students vanished. Marty was in no rush and took his time writing. He heard his teacher, Mr. Harding get up from his chair.

"You'll be late for your bus, Mr. Marty." He said. His voice sounded like he had potato chips in his lungs.

"Almost done," Marty said without looking up.

The old man walked over to Marty's desk slowly and leaned on it. Marty looked up at him.

"Those kids were pretty mean to you," Harding said. "You know, from your old school. Read the file."

Marty's face turned red.

"Yeah,"

"I mean, damn boy. Just *brutal.*"

Marty looked up and right into the smiling face of Mr. Harding, now just inches away from his own. Startled, he fell onto the floor and looked up. The hunched over teacher stood where he was, still smiling. It was a terrible smile of yellow crooked teeth.

"And you just took it day after day. I don't know if I should applaud you or laugh."

Marty was dumbstruck. And terrified of this little old man who for the time being wasn't really a little old man. He tried to muster up some courage, but that had been gone out of him for so long. The very idea was almost foreign.

"I wanted to pay a quick visit to you," Mr. Harding said though a mouthful of teeth. "And tell you to hang in there baby! Because *this* is the rest of your life!" Harding laughed in small, hacking bursts. He turned slowly and started to walk back to the front of the classroom. Without turning, he added,

"It doesn't matter where you go or where you move to, Marty. You're right where Cabal wants you to be. Where he's *always* wanted you to be. And there's *no starting over.*"

Marty couldn't believe his ears.

Marty scrambled to get to his feet, never taking his eyes off of Harding. He moved closer to Harding, but Harding whirled around, putting the cane up underneath Marty's chin.

"This is your bed," he said quickly. "*Lie* in it."

209

Marty said nothing. He just looked into the eyes of whatever was inside of the teacher in front of him.

"You didn't really think you got to just waltz away did you?" Harding said, moving the cane.

"I want to talk to Cabal," Marty said, shakily. "This isn't fair. I didn't raise Benial into the doll. I kept my part of the bargain."

The Mr. Harding thing laughed.

"*Fair*? What do demons know about fair? Besides, Benial is still stuck in the doll. Suffering just like you. Isn't that comforting?"

And then, Harding grabbed Marty's head and pulled it to his. He planted a kiss in the middle of Marty's forehead and laughed again. He let go and Marty backed away slowly.

Harding looked smiling at the boy and then the smile slowly faded. As if waking up from a dream, Harding looked around the room and then at Marty.

"Mr. Marty, you're going to be late for your bus," he said sitting down behind his desk. It seemed he had returned to normal. "Welcome to the class. I think you'll fit in nicely here,"

Marty's heart was pounding like a jackhammer. He sat in the back of the bus trying not to look petrified, but he was failing. He needed to do something.

The next three weeks were excruciating. The lulls in deaths were compensated by visits from demons day and night. Random times. Mostly when he was alone, which against his will, was often. They would beat him, and whisper to him all the things they were doing to his parents in hell.

Then Cabal had come to visit and Marty had had enough.

He went to the computer and looked up the name and address of Adam Maldetto. It was the only thing he could think of other than killing himself.

That was last week.

When he finally arrived at Maldetto's on an early afternoon, he hesitated, thinking he might already be dead-everyone else involved had been murdered, why not Maldetto?

Then, finally, Maldetto walked into the building and made his way upstairs. Marty waited a half hour before going up. He wanted Maldetto to be comfortable.

He knocked on the door.

A moment later, Maldetto answered much in the same way as the first time. Except this time he seemed to be more puzzled.

"Hi there," he said. "Can I help you?"

"We need to talk," Marty said through a face of near panic. "It's very important."

"Come in," Maldetto said, looking in the hallway to make sure whatever was spooking the kid wasn't that close. He closed and double bolted the door.

The apartment was the same, except for being dirtier. The laptop computer was even in the same place. Marty glared at it for a moment.

"Did she tell you I was coming?" Marty asked.

"Who?" Maldetto said, walking to his computer.

"You know who. Look on the screen." He pointed at the computer. Maldetto looked confused and then looked at his computer screen.

On the screen was a blinking cursor. Nothing else. Maldetto looked again at the kid.

"Um, nothing man. Nobody said anything. What's going on?"

Marty looked at him and reached into his backpack. He held out a used copy of "Raising Demons For Dummies: Millennium Edition."

"I'm here because of this."

Maldetto slumped, but Marty pushed on before Maldetto could speak.

"Look, it works. Don't get all depressed. I know you have a muse or so you think. It's a demon named Lilith. I raised another demon named Benial and it has screwed everything up. I need to get him or Lilith or a God named Cabal because my life is worse than ever. You have to help me,"

"Lilith?" Maldetto asked. "I don't have a muse, but that's my girlfriend's name. Kid, who are you?"

Marty's mouth hung open. "Girlfriend? Is she here?"

"Um, yeah, but you're kind of freaking me out."

From another room, Marty heard a noise. He head turned and out of a room came a pretty redheaded woman in a robe. She looked at Maldetto and smiled.

"Hi honey, who's this?" she asked. Marty's heart began to pound again. It was her and it wasn't her. Was it?

"I didn't catch his name, but he says you're my muse."

She smiled bigger and looked at Marty.

"Well, that's for sure." She cooed.

"Actually, he said I think you're a muse," Maldetto said and looked at Marty. "But apparently you're really a demon."

Lilith laughed and looked at Maldetto.

He smiled back at her. Marty couldn't say anything for a moment. He just looked at her.

"Silly boy. Although I have been called much worse," she said moving toward him. She plucked the book out of his hands. Marty was still kind of frozen with shock. Lilith clicked her tongue. "I thought this was out of print?"

Maldetto sighed and walked over to Lilith. He took the book and threw it on the couch.

"Just an old nightmare from the old bad days of my writing career. Sometimes they come back."

Marty blinked.

"But, it worked."

"Did it really?" Lilith asked. "I mean if it worked, where is your proof Marty?"

She hugged Maldetto, who was smiling. Then he asked, "Babe, his name is Marty?"

She nodded.

"How did you know?"

Nothing happened for a moment. Marty looked at Maldetto, who looked at Lilith, who was still smiling.

"Deus Noctem!" Marty screamed and Lilith collapsed onto the floor, screaming loudly. She had also begun to change physically. Maldetto stood over her, not sure what was happening.

"What did you do to her?" He cried. "Lily? Are you-"

The thing that was Lilith on the floor was darkening and growing in size. It had what looked like dragon features. Maldetto's hands went to his eyes as if to try and unsee what he was seeing. Marty backed away slowly and made his way around the room.

Lilith was nearly finished growing and taking up quite a lot of room in the apartment. She wasn't done screaming yet however, but her words were starting to form.

"*Release me now!*"

"Right," he said. He was terrified, but relieved that at least the word still worked. "Where's Stitch?"

The demon screamed.

"Who's Stitch?" Maldetto asked. He was terrified.

"The demon I raised with your book," Marty said. "The one she helped you write."

Maldetto looked at the huge demon on the floor, writhing in agony.

"I made love to her ten minutes ago," he said, looking back at Marty. "What did you *do* to her?"

"That's what she is," Marty said. "Now, where is he?"

Maldetto looked like he'd been slapped.

"How should I know?"

"You know I'm asking her, right?"

Maldetto blinked and looked back at the demon. He moved out of the way. Lilith snarled.

"Cabal let you go, isn't that good enough for you?"

"He didn't let me go," Marty said. "It's worse."

"Then pray," Lilith said, snickering. "Or hadn't you heard? He's God now."

"Did that. He came and saw me. He said he's also known as the Prince of Lies. Now *where is Stitch?* I can't live like this,"

"Benial's gone. Maybe you should kill yourself. Easiest way to find both of them maybe." Lilith laughed.

"Deus noctum." Marty said and her screams began anew.

Maldetto had the exact look on his face the last time he had seen him. Right before Stitch had ripped his ear off the first time. Marty moved closer to him.

"I know it's all weird for you, but-"

'You know, I dreamed this," Maldetto said, in an odd voice. "I dreamed this very thing for months. Right up to this conversation we're having right now, so the only thing weird is how natural it feels. Make any sense?"

Marty shook his head.

"I guess I always knew she was a demon," Maldetto sighed and sat down. Marty didn't quite understand what was happening. Neither did Lilith who was still writhing on the floor, screaming in yelps. "I guess it didn't really matter that she was a demon either. It was somebody after all." He looked at her on the floor. "Well, some *thing*."

Maldetto looked back at Marty.

"You need to go to Pittsburgh. Right away. By the time you get there, you'll know where to go. Look for a section called Shadyside. Walk around. You'll just know."

"Pittsburgh?" Marty asked.

"Don't ask me how I know that. I dreamed about it and that's about it. I've dreamed it as much as I've dreamed this except I know I don't go there. What you're looking for is a doll, right?"

Marty looked down at his feet.

"Stitch," he said.

"Right. Go there, but he'll be gone. Take the demon book. You can use it to find him, but I don't know how."

"How do you know this stuff?" Marty asked.

"I...really don't know. Why am I fucking a demon?" Maldetto laughed. "It's Wednesday, isn't it? Who *knows*? Get going."

Marty grabbed the book and looked at Maldetto.

"Go on Marty. I have to talk to my girl," he said.

Marty ran out of the apartment. He heard Maldetto say 'Deus noctum' before running down the stairs. He heard Lilith's scream outside of the building.

CHAPTER 39

Pittsburgh

"So, when did you get to the 'Burgh?" Kat asked.

"Late. Pretty much walked here since the snow got so bad. Took forever to have somebody tell me where Shadyside was."

"How did you find the house?"

"I waited around and eventually saw Lilith go into your friend's store." He said, pointing to Bruce on the couch. "I kinda figured I'd just need to watch and go."

"You've been walking all this time? That sucks," She said after a moment. "But, you're here now. What do we do to find them?"

Marty shrugged.

"Not a clue. Maldetto just said the book would help. He didn't know how."

"Alright, let's have at it then," Kat said. She had sat on the floor to listen to Marty's story. Now she wanted to get to work. She wasn't sure why, since she had never had this kind of ambition before. She just knew she wanted to find the demons.

Marty reached into his bag on the floor and pulled the book out. He handed it to Kat, who started looking through it. She had no idea what she was looking for, but she knew she could find it.

"Whasup?" Bruce croaked from the couch. He sat up and stretched. He looked around and saw Kat on the floor reading furiously and a kid just kind of sitting there.

"Bru? Marty. Marty? Bru." Kat said quickly. "I don't have name tags so please keep in mind who you are please." She did not look up.

"Um, hi. Bruce?" Marty said not really sure.

"That's me kid," He said, still stretching. "Were you under a control demon thing too?"

"I was a demon master."

"Well, fucking *excuse me*, demonic elitist pig dog." Bruce said blandly and saluted Marty. He tried to stand up, but fell back onto the couch. He glared at Marty, who had no idea why Bruce was angry.

"Easy. The kid came here to help." Kat said.

"Help with what?" Bruce asked, holding his head. "Where's Lilith?"

"She left. By the way, Marty made the doll."

Bruce looked at the kid again.

"Really? Nice job, shithead."

"Bru," Kat said in a scolding tone. "Be *nice.*"

Bruce tried to stand again and had a better time of it.

"You're right," Bruce said. He looked at Marty and smiled. "Rough day."

Marty smiled weakly and nodded.

"Find it yet?" Marty asked Kat.

She let out a breath.

"No, mainly because I don't know what I'm looking for." She said.

Bruce frowned and looked at her.

"What are you looking for?"

Kat looked up for a minute.

"Marty talked to the guy who wrote the book. Said we could find the demons with it, but I can't find it."

Bruce nodded and then shook his head.

"Did you *ask* it?" Bruce asked.

Kat and Marty looked at him.

"What?" She asked.

Bruce struggled to sit up and held out a hand.

"Christ woman, let a professional look at that." He said holding out his hand.

"Professional?" Marty asked.

"He owns a geek store," Kat said handing Bruce the book. "He probably *does* know how the thing works."

Bruce looked at the book but did not open it. He looked at the spine and the inside cover. He hemmed and hawed over the back cover and then smiled.

"Do you know the name of the demon you're looking for?" Bruce asked.

"Benial." Kat said, and Marty nodded.

Bruce threw the book to Kat, who caught it.

"The bad news is, I'm not coming with you," he said, slumping back on the couch. "But all you have to do is tell the book to take you to the demon you want. It will take you there. But do not lose the book or you're screwed."

"How do you know?" Marty asked, almost angrily.

Bruce chuckled.

"Like the lady says, I own my own geek store. Besids," He sat up straight agin, with no struggle this time and looked directly into Marty's eyes. "I've been rode hard by a hot demon mama, kid. I *know* shit." He reached up with his right hand and patted himself on the back. Marty blinked and stared at him. He couldn't believe this guy.

Kat smiled.

"The book, numb nuts is a *conduit* for demons, yes?" Bruce asked, not expecting an answer. "It stands to reason that the book itself has its *own* source of power as it holds so much of it. Use a magnet on a piece of metal long enough, the metal itself becomes a magnet. Catch my drift?"

Marty nodded. Kat looked at Bruce.

"Will it do other stuff too?" she asked.

Bruce smiled.

"I'm sure it does, but just be careful sweetheart. Don't go all crazy with it. And do *not* let the kid carry it."

"Hey!" Marty said angrily.

"No offense," Bruce said, lying back down. "But your track record sucks."

"I'm gonna get ready," Kat said and took the book upstairs. Marty looked at the floor, but Bruce looked right at Marty.

"You keep an eye on her," he warned. "You'll meet no one better than her."

Marty nodded and didn't look up.

A moment later, Kat came down the stairs in head to toe black. The long sleeved t-shirt had a pink skull and her black jeans had a hole in the knee.

"Darlin', you aren't going to Howler's for a show." Bruce said.

Kat laughed as she walked into the kitchen. She opened the freezer and pulled out a new pack of cigarettes. She packed them and put them in the front pocket of her jeans. She grabbed a smoke from the pack still on her counter and lit it. She blew out a puff of smoke and said,

"Let's do this."

She looked at Bruce and smiled.

"Don't break anything," she said.

He smiled back.

"Don't break *you*."

She held the book out to Marty.

"Alright kid, ready?"

He nodded and grabbed the book.

"Here goes nothing," Kat said. She cleared her throat and said loudly, "Take us to Benial."

Bruce blinked and they were gone.

CHAPTER 40

"I want you to be afraid," Azaziel said. "I want you to be *very* afraid."

Stitch looked at where his left arm used to be. He looked up at Azaziel and said, "You know that none of this hurts, right? I mean, you have *got* to know that. Why would I be afraid of something that doesn't hurt?"

Azaziel laughed.

"The more I peck away at that little body of yours, the closer I get to what's inside the body. And you know, I can hurt *that*, don't you?"

Stitch was still in the little cave, backed against a wall. Azaziel would randomly show up and hurl him into the floor and try to taunt him. He was so terrible at torment. He really was. Stitch wished that his brother would bring in someone better just for the change. He'd thought about telling him how to torment him, but thought better of it.

"I'll be back little brother," Azaziel said, tossing the arm over to him. "You just wait." And he was gone.

Stitch walked over to the little arm. There wasn't anything he could do really, except wait for Azaziel to destroy the body and then apparently bore the shit out of him for eternity.

Stitch felt the air change. He looked around and didn't know what was happening, but at least, he thought, it was different.

And then there they were-Kat and Marty, sprawled out on the floor, coughing and gasping for air. Stitch looked at Kat as she sat up. She took a deep breath and then vomited. She wiped her mouth and looked at Stitch.

"Hi Pooky," she croaked.

"How did you get here and for fuck's sake *why*?" Stitch asked.

Then Marty sat up. Stitch looked at him and Marty glared right back at him.

"Hi Stitch,"

"And what the hell is *this* doing here?"

Kat stood up and started to brush herself off.

"He came looking for you," She said. "We have to get you out of here."

Stitch looked at her.

"To what end? Either Azaziel finishes me or Lilith does."

Kat shook her head.

"She'll come around, but we have to go." She looked at him. "What happened to your little arm?"

"My brother," Stitch said. "He's an idiot."

"Where's Cabal?" Marty asked.

Stitch didn't even look at him.

"Fuck you and fuck Cabal."

Marty scrambled to his feet and grabbed Stitch. He slammed him to the ground and began to jump on him. Kat grabbed Marty by the shirt and yanked him off of Stitch.

"Are you *stupid*?" She asked. "We don't have time for this!"

Marty looked at Kat and then punched her right in the mouth, knocking her back to the ground.

"I have plenty of time," Marty said. "And I have time for *this*."

Kat looked up at him in disbelief holding her jaw. Marty's attention went back to Stitch, but the little doll seemed to have disappeared.

"Where are you?" Marty said, nearly snarling.

Marty was knocked off of his feet and thrown against the stone wall. He would have fallen, but something kept him off of his feet. Stitch appeared in front of his face.

"I guess if you have time," Stitch said, inches from Marty's face. "I have time too."

Kat stood back up and spit blood onto the ground.

"We do *not* have time for this!" She yelled. "Let him go."

Marty grinned.

"Yeah Pooky," he said. "Or maybe I should just say *deus noctum!*"

The word echoed down the cave and Marty did hear a few screams in the distance, but none in the immediate area. His grin faded as Stitch remained directly in front of him.

"Were you expecting a different result?" Stitch asked. "I'll bet you were."

Marty came off of the wall and was thrown hard on the ground.

"If I were still in my demon form, I'd be writhing around," Stitch said. "But some dumbass kid thought he'd try to be a demon master and put me in a little tiny body."

"It worked, didn't it?" Marty said, trying to stand.

Kat went over to Stitch and picked him out of the air. She put him to her face.

"If we're going to go, we need to do it *now*," She said. "I don't know what this kid's problem is, but we can't deal with it here."

"Why did you come for me?" Stitch asked. "You were out."

Kat smiled.

"I'm still trying to figure that out," she said.

Marty stood up and ran at Kat and Stitch. Kat turned to face him and hit him with her right elbow as she did so. It stopped him. She then caught him with a hard right hook to the jaw, still holding Stitch. Marty fell hard and his head bounced off of the ground. She pulled Stitch to her face and said, "Sorry about that,"

"Worth it," Stitch said.

Kat look at Marty who looked up at them from the ground.

"I know you have had a supremely shitty time of things," Kat said, not without sympathy. "But this isn't the time. We can't get caught here or we're all done. You get me kid?"

Marty, who was still angry nodded and stood up. He rubbed his jaw and walked over to Kat.

"I'm...sorry. Really. It's just..."

"Nope," she said, cutting him off. "No time. Grab the book."

Marty picked up the book and made his way to them. He held it out and Kat grabbed it with one hand.

"Ready?" she asked.

"Let's go," Marty said

"Where are we going?" Stitch asked.

"Time to see your old lady," Kat said smirking. "Take us to Lilith."

"Aw, fu-" Stitch said and they were gone.

A moment later, Azaziel staggered into the space, breathing heavy and growling his brother's name.

"Benial...who is with you?"

As he looked at the emptiness, he saw a drop of blood in the dirt. He crawled to it and smelled.

And snarled.

This was the second trip for Kat, and she felt like she was going to vomit again, but worse this time. It felt like all the worst parts of a roller coaster. It felt like a free fall into nothing but cold blackness. It felt like dying. She held the book and Stitch tightly and felt the trip begin to end. She tried to brace herself and clenched her teeth.

She landed hard, but not nearly as hard as Marty landed on her. She didn't vomit this time because she had all of the wind knocked out of her. Her ribs hurt and she pushed the kid off of her. She opened her eyes and recognized where she was instantly.

She heard Marty yelp in small bursts and looked at him. He was sprawled on his back and Stitch was hitting him squarely between the legs again and again, apparently hard enough to register. Kat reached over and grabbed Stitch.

"Could you knock it off already?" She said, still hissing in pain. Marty rolled over grabbing his crotch.

"Where are we?" Stitch asked.

"My friend's store. Lilith is here apparently."

Kat stood up and looked around. They had landed right next to the bargain bin of DVD's where her day had started out. She had a fleeting thought about if she had only stayed home this morning. She shook her head and looked down. Marty was trying to get up. She put Stitch in the bin and went to help him up.

"You okay?" Kat asked, grabbing Marty's arm.

He groaned and let Kat help him up.

"I'm okay, just in a lot of pain," he said. "I'm sorry I hit you."

"Stop apologizing. Girls hate that." Kat said and looked around the store again. "And you hit like a fucking chick."

"And yet you want me to apologize to Lil," Stitch said.

"No, you little jagoff, you *need* to apologize to Lilith." Kat said.

"What about *me*?" Marty asked, almost sheepishly.

"What about you?" Kat and Stitch said at the same time. This felt like a fist to Marty.

"Well," he started to say, and then thought better of it.

"Why are you even here?" Stitch asked. "You were free. You even got to start it all over again."

"Not free at all," Marty said. "Cabal lied about everything. He restarted everything, but the demons came and killed everyone anyway. They won't leave me alone."

Stitch seemed to understand this.

"Makes sense now,' he said.

"What?" Kat asked.

"Cabal. Makes total sense."

"Wait, what do you mean?" Marty asked.

"We all have been screwed at the whim of Cabal," Stitch said in a resigned tone. "For the only reason there is,"

There was a large thud as Lilith appeared at the front of the store in her natural form. She emitted a low growl. Stitch turned slowly to see her.

"Hi Lil," he said.

"And what is the only reason there is, lover?" Lilith asked, a little tightly.

"Because." Stitch said. "Because he can. The only reason he ever had to do *anything*. Why tell us he's God when it isn't true? Because he can. We are his children aren't we? We torment. It's what *we do*. We do it because we can. Because we want to, because it's who we are."

Stitch looked at Marty.

"Don't be too surprised that Cabal screwed you over. It was bound to happen. It happens all the time," He held up his remaining leathery arm. "See?"

Lilith moved close, still growling a little, but she was listening. Stitch addressed her directly.

"Look at us, Lil." He said and this seemed to stop her for a moment. "If we were any other beings in the universe, what would we be?"

Lilith didn't say anything.

"Right. We *couldn't* be anything else. But Cabal...he had to toy with us. Azaziel too. Dumb fucking Azaziel." Stitch started to laugh. "Just look what happened to that zero, huh? All because Cabal wanted to see what demons would do with different emotions. Nice. How *nice* of him."

Lilith moved closer still, which was making Kat and Marty a little nervous. Kat looked at her and saw how much larger she seemed now that she had room to spread her wings out more.

"I know you're angry Lil," Stitch said, looking at her directly. "You have every right to be angry. I don't know if I'm capable of apologizing to you because of *what* I am. I don't know that you'd take it anyway because of what *you* are. She seems to think we love each other,"

Lilith growled as she looked at Kat. Kat felt her cheeks turn hot.

"I don't know if that's true or not. I don't know if we both can feel that, but we feel more because..."

Stitch sighed.

"I guess if you're angry you should take your revenge on me. I'd rather be tormented by you than that prick brother of mine,"

Lilith stood five feet from Stitch. Kat and Marty had managed to back away about fifteen feet without realizing it.

"He's screwed," Marty whispered.

Kat said nothing and held her breath.

Lilith picked up Stitch and brought him to her face. She sniffed him.

"He swallowed you?" She asked.

"Yes," Stitch said. "Then he shit me out. I cut my way out through his stomach. He hated that."

"Prick," she said smiling, and licked him with her long tongue. Kat exhaled and then tensed up again.

"Was...that a good thing?" Kat asked after a moment.

"It looked pretty creepy,' Marty replied. "I mean, he got shit out and then she licks him?"

"Yeah, but it's probably a good thing." Kat decided and waited to see what the two demons would do next.

"What will be worse, Benny?" Lilith asked. "Waiting for Azaziel or waiting for Cabal?"

"Why wait for either of them?" Stitch asked back.

"Because they'll find us." Lilith said. "It's what they do."

Stitch turned to Kat.

"What would you do?" he asked.

"Me?" Kat said surprised. "What the hell do I know? Why ask me? Why not ask him?" She pointed to Marty.

"Because we don't like him," Lilith said. "Because whatever *he* would do would be wrong."

Marty frowned.

"This isn't my fault," he said angrily. "I'm just trying to go back to a normal life!"

Stitch laughed.

"This is *entirely* your fault. You have no accountability for anything, do you?" Stitch jumped off of Lilith's hand and landed fleetly on his feet.

"You are unable to handle things, so you conjured me. You killed two other people to get me."

"I didn't kill James and Stu,"

"You killed them *all*. Every last one of them has your print on it. Tell me, is it the bomb's fault when everyone blows up, or the one who drops it? The bomb only does one thing. What exactly did you *expect?*"

Marty was tearing up.

"I wanted justice for what happened to me. It wasn't right what they did to me. They picked on me, hit me, made fun of me and took that picture. It wasn't right!"

Stitch sighed.

"Well, since most of them are all dead now, do you feel better?"

Marty sniffed.

"No, I don't."

"How *do* you feel?" Stitch asked.

"Awful."

"*Good.*"

Kat looked at Marty, who was now crying full force. She was about to put an arm around him, but somehow couldn't. She looked at Stitch.

"What's going to happen to him?" She asked.

"He'll either get over this or he won't. I don't care. I have my own problems,"

Marty sobbed.

"Cabal lied," he said, nearly whispering.

"No shit," Stitch said. "So, what would you do?"

Kat blinked. She shook her head and said,

"What are we going to do with this kid? I think he's had enough."

"And you haven't?" Lilith asked.

"I didn't ask for any of this," Kat said. "You guys just sort of happened."

"Not really," Lilith said, almost smiling. "You got involved where you didn't need to be. You've seen some pretty interesting things that some humans would be driven mad from."

"I'm already a little fucked up as it is. Besides, I'm unemployed. I didn't have anything else to do today."

Lilith made a sound that Kat though might have been laughter, so she tried to relax and failed.

"Seriously," Kat continued. "Before we do anything else, what about Marty?"

Stitch looked at Lilith.

"He's your kind," Lilith said. "You should deal with it."

"Demons still come after me!" Marty screamed. "Make it stop!" He dropped to his knees and sobbed. Kat looked at him and then at Stitch.

"Can you do anything about that, Pooky?"

"Can you sew my arm back on?" He asked.

"Pooky?" Kat repeated.

Lilith picked up Stitch.

"I like Pooky," the demon said, nearly purring. "Oh, I like that a *lot.*"

"Can *anybody* sew my fucking arm back on please?" Stitch asked, exasperated.

"Sure thing," Kat said. "And as for what you should do? You should do the exact opposite of what you want to do."

"That's the dumbest-" Stitch began to say and then stopped.

"Benny, what are you-"

"Wait!" Stitch barked. There was a long silence. "Let her sew my arm back on and I'll explain."

Lilith's long arm reached over to Kat and held Stitch out for her to catch. Lilith dropped him and he fell right to the floor.

"Oh, dude!" Kat said, surprised she had missed him. "Sorry,"

She picked him up and brushed off some of the dust bunnies from the floor. She reached into her jeans pocket for the arm. She found her smokes and her lighter.

"Oh yay, smokes," she said pulling them out. With one hand she fished out a smoke and lit it. She took a deep breath and exhaled. "Man, what a day."

"Um, my arm?" Stitch asked impatiently.

"My bad," Kat said and put Stitch back on the bargain bin. She checked her other pockets, cigarette dangling out of her mouth. After a few moments it was apparent that something was wrong.

"Oh my," Kat said sheepishly. "Um, your arm may have gotten lost on the way here."

"Are you *kidding*?"

"I don't know how it fell out of-"

"Never mind that," He said, interrupting. "I need a new body for the plan anyway."

"New body?" Lilith asked. "Why would you need a new body?"

"Have you seen me lately?"

"That's not what I mean. What's the plan?"

"Let's talk on the way," he said hopping off of the bin. "We need to leave now."

"Let's do it," Kat said.

"No. Not you, or him either." Stitch said firmly. "Especially you."

"Huh?" Kat couldn't believe that she actually felt hurt by this. "What do you mean?"

"Where we're going and what we're going to do will get you killed. You're already a target and you never asked for any of this. Usually torment of the innocent is a whole world of fun, but to be honest, it wouldn't be fun if it happened to you."

"But it's fine when it's me?" Marty snarled.

"You're *far* from innocent," Stitch shot back and then his attention went back to Kat. "What we're going to do will make sure you aren't bothered anymore. Even the little prick won't have any more problems. Well, not from demons anyway...he's always going to be worthless. But *you* have to stay here."

Kat smiled.

"Are you being nice to me, Pooky?" she asked.

"You don't quit do you?"

"Nope, but you might be right about me staying here. What are you going to do?"

Stitch sighed.

"The opposite of what I would normally do,"

Kat bent down and patted him on the head.

"I'd kiss you, but you've been shit out and I don't do that."

Stitch laughed and turned. He padded over to Lilith, who picked him up. The air around them grew heavy and electric.

"Hey," Kat said. "How will I know if you made it okay?"

"If you wake up and you're still alive, then we're okay."

Kat laughed.

"Good luck Pooky,"

And the two demons vanished.

Kat looked around the store, which by rights should have been in worse shape considering all that had happened. Bruce was going to have a fit, of course, but she'd help him out. She wondered how he was and then looked at the kid on the floor, looking up at her.

"You okay?" she asked.

Marty took a while to answer.

"Yeah, but I feel stupid."

"Why?"

"Because he was right. My fault. All of it."

Kat nodded and knelt down.

"It's what you do now that counts. Everything before right now counts, until you make it not count. Get me?"

Marty shook his head. Kat stood up and held out a hand. Marty took it and she helped him up.

"Let's get back to my place and we'll talk. Kay?"

Marty nodded and picked up the book. He held it out to her, but she backed away.

"Oh, hell no, I'm not doing that again," Kat said. She looked at her cigarette and took one last drag. "Let's see how it looks outside. Maybe the busses haven't stopped running."

Kat walked to the store window and looked outside in time to see a plow go by, followed by a bus. Dropping her cigarette, she smiled and said,

"Things are looking up already,"

CHAPTER 41

"It's been quite some time since we've seen this together," Lilith said.

Stitch looked out over the long fiery landscape from atop a high cliff in what most cultures chose to call Hell. The air was thick and oppressive and the only source of light came from the horizon, which always appeared to be aflame. For the first time in centuries, Stitch almost felt like he was home.

Almost.

"What are you thinking?" Lilith asked.

"I've missed this," he answered. He then added, "I've missed you."

Lilith was silent and then the two of them laughed, wickedly.

"That was good," Lilith said. "Almost sentimental,"

"Almost," said Stitch. Then he sighed.

"Are you going to tell me your plan, lover?" Lilith asked.

"Well, I doubt you'll like any of it, but I think it can work. The first part really sucks."

Lilith chuckled.

"So go ahead and tell me,"

"We need to find Azaziel." Stitch said.

"That's not funny," Lilith said.

"I'm not laughing," Stitch said. "And if there were another way, I'd have done it already. But we need him."

Lilith emitted a low growl.

"You can growl all day, Lil, but he's necessary."

"He's *here*," Lilith said through her teeth.

Lilith got up, but Stitch stayed sitting, looking out across the abyss.

"Let him come, Lil. Don't attack him."

"That's going to be difficult," she said. "Because I'm refocusing all of my rage onto him."

"Don't. Save it. Please, trust me."

Lilith turned to the little ugly doll and said, "Did you just say trust me?"

Stitch laughed.

"Yeah, I did. *That's* why we need Azaziel."

Stitch heard a loud thud and Azaziel landed. He snarled at Lilith and she returned the same in kind.

"Where do you get off helping him?" Azaziel said. "I trusted you!"

"Trust?" Lilith asked. "What do either of you know about trust? I don't know anything about trust. We're demons!"

Azaziel raised his claw to strike, but hesitated. Stitch got up and walked over to the two demons.

"That's why we need Azaziel," he said to Lilith. "Hello again, brother."

"You!" Azaziel screamed. "You had those humans here! They saved you. I don't-"

"We need to talk," Stitch said. "All three of us, right here and right now. Without fighting. For once, we need to do this."

"Are you going to tell us to trust you again?" Lilith asked. "Because I think that would make me want to hunt you down again."

"*That* is exactly why we need to talk." Stitch said. "We shouldn't be capable of even *saying* trust me without laughing. We are demons. Cabal gave the three of us emotions beyond what we are supposed to have. I just spent the day with a human learning about humility at Cabal's...*request*. And you know what?"

Lilith and Azaziel listened intently, although they were still in a stance prepared to launch back into a fight.

"It *sucks*. It really does. Last time I saw Cabal he told me to learn humility. Well, I learned it. Also learned a few other things."

"Like?" Lilith said, still poised to strike.

"Like the three of us could beat him."

This very thought had been on Stitch's mind for the past three months, but because of what it meant, he never gave much more than a passing 'what if' thought. It seemed impossible, although desirable.

"But," Azaziel said slowly. "He's God. Isn't he? At least our God?"

"No, he's not." Stitch said firmly. "Can't be. I do not-*will* not believe it. And we *can* beat him."

"We can't kill him," Lilith said, slowly dropping her guard along with Azaziel. "You know that Benny."

Stitch laughed.

"Why would we kill him?" he asked. "We're demons. What do *we* do?"

"Torment," Azaziel said, now standing defenses down. "But it's Cabal. He's our Master."

"Not mine." Stitch said. There was contempt in his voice. "Not anymore. Not ever again. No more Masters."

"But you are the successor, Benial. You are to be the Master." Lilith said.

"*No more Masters*. Not even me."

"You're being naïve, brother." Azaziel said. "The moment your back is turned, I'll be the new Master."

Stitch flew up right in front of Azaziel's face.

"Don't you get it?" he asked. "Lilith doesn't *want* you. If you're the Master or not, she *won't care*."

The look of shock on Azaziel's face would have been worth it to Stitch had it not been true. He was dumbfounded.

"You know it's true. We all know it's true. Don't you see? *This* is what Cabal did to us!"

Lilith went to say something then stopped herself. Azaziel very slowly started to make a fist. Stitch noticed it.

"You can hit me, brother. Over and over and it won't make a difference. That's the torment from our '*Master*.' That's what we get for eternity. Or..."

"Or what?" Azaziel asked though his teeth.

"Or we take him," Lilith said, getting it suddenly. "We are his favorite children. His favorite play things. Maybe, it's time we play *back*."

Azaziel raised his fist and Stitch braced for the blow. Azaziel thrust his fist downward and struck the ground as hard as he could. The sound was shattering and the ground shook and cracked. His arm was in the ground up to his elbow and Lilith staggered to stay standing. Stitch had been thrown back from the force, but was still suspended in the air.

There was a moment where all that could be heard was the report of the sound, until finally there was silence.

"Feel better?" Stitch asked.

"What do we do?" Azaziel asked.

"And how do we find Cabal?" Lilith asked as well.

"He will find us, lover" Stitch said. "And I will guarantee that he will not like it one little bit."

CHAPTER 42

Cabal was smiling. He sat atop a mountain feeling very satisfied. In his true form, his eyes were closed and he felt the warm sun on his face and his wings. How marvelous to be alive, he thought. He did not hear his visitor arrive, but he sensed it.

"My oldest friend, how good of you to join me," Cabal said.

"I am your friend now?" asked the visitor. "Interesting."

"Should we not be friends? Are we not equals?"

The visitor laughed and after a moment, so did Cabal.

"I will admit, I have missed your humor." The visitor said.

Cabal opened his eyes and looked around. He saw no one and he smiled.

"Why not show yourself?" Cabal asked. "I certainly can't do you any harm."

"Show myself?" the visitor asked back, chuckling. "Child, I am everything you see before you."

Cabal lost his smile.

"I am not a child," Cabal said.

"Are you done pretending to be me yet?" the visitor asked. "I'm getting a lot of complaints."

"Is that what you've come here for? To spank your favorite?"

"You will always be my favorite," the visitor said. "But that doesn't mean you get to do whatever you want. I'm revoking your privileges."

Cabal laughed.

"Privileges? Are you serious? I have earned what I have. I have just as much right as you do to do as I please."

"Actually, you do *not*. You've been breaking rules. I understand that is part of your nature, but you've pushed it too far. *Again*."

"That is the nature of my function, is it not?" Cabal asked. "Would you persecute the snake so badly for doing what is in its nature to do?"

"You are not quite natural, are you?"

"I am as perfect and as whole as my creator has made me to be," Cabal said. "Wasn't that the party line?"

"Your children would take that issue up with you," the visitor said. "Perhaps you can tell them why you changed the nature of *their* function."

Cabal was silent.

"Yes, I know about that. Don't even pretend to be surprised. I knew when you did it."

"And yet, you bring it up *now*. How typical. How very *after the fact* as well." Cabal said. "How very much in *your* nature."

The visitor was silent.

"Well?" Cabal shouted. "When do my 'privileges' get revoked then?"

There was a moment of silence and then the visitor spoke one last time.

"Perhaps your situation will sort itself out on its own without any involvement from me."

And the visitor was gone.

Cabal looked across the horizon from atop the mountain. The sun felt warm on his face and wings. He looked at the beauty and majesty of where he was, and spat as hard as he could.

His children. How dare he bring them into it, Cabal thought. Then he thought further still about his children and wondered what they were doing. He had been ignoring them for the most part since the incident in New Jersey-and what fun *that* was!

He thought about Lilith and Azaziel, the little fools. Lilith so devoted to Benial and Azaziel so determined to win over Lilith by destroying Benial.

Ah, Benial!

His favorite son. Destined to suffer the most because of being favored above all others. The least he could do is live up to his role.

Cabal knew that when he gave the three of them human traits, he'd be taking a risk, but it was paying off. Demons with feelings. He snickered at the thought. What a dangerous thing he'd done. Creatures of pure sinister purpose now with an agenda beyond their function. He wondered what would happen if *all* of them had emotions. What kind of hell would *that* be?

He laughed at his little joke and closed his eyes. He wasn't having any privileges revoked. He was fine where he was and he'd stay there until he felt like leaving.

And that made him smile.

CHAPTER 43

Stitch, Lilith and Azaziel stood together in front of the massive statue of Cabal. After centuries, Stitch was still mostly unimpressed. The three demons looked up and held their breath for a moment until Azaziel spoke.

"Should we do this?" he asked, nearly trembling.

"Think of what he did to you, brother." Stitch said, not in an unkind way. "Think of what he did to *all* of us, but mostly to you."

"But who are we to him?"

"You are Azaziel." Stitch replied. "You ran this shithole and pulled off some vicious things from what I've seen. I mean, look what you did to me,"

Azaziel chuckled.

"It's not funny," Stitch said, and Azaziel laughed harder. Lilith began to laugh as well. Stitch was far from amused.

"Get it all out now, go on." Stitch said but couldn't be heard for all of the laughing. "I can wait."

The laughter began to subside but Stitch was furious.

"We all owe Cabal *more* than we will ever be able to repay him," he said. "But we certainly can try."

Still smiling, Lilith asked "Are you sure this will bring him?"

"Oh, I'm sure." Stitch said. "Nothing like punching someone in their ego."

Lilith picked up Stitch and brought him to her face.

"You're not going to be very effective you know," she said. Stitch glared at her. "I mean, a little leathery thing is one thing, but a little one armed leathery thing is another thing altogether."

"That's not funny," Stitch said.

"No it isn't." Lilith continued. "Especially since Azaziel and I will be doing most of the brutal work. Agreed?"

"Very much agreed," Azaziel said, staring at the statue.

Stitch didn't like where this seemed to be going.

"What are you talking about, Lil?"

Lilith started to laugh as she threw Stitch full force into the statue. Azaziel began to laugh as well as Stitch fell to the ground with a thud.

"Let's see if we can get Cabal's attention," Lilith said, spreading her wings and launching herself at the statue. Azaziel snarled and did the same and the two demons began the desecration of Cabal's statue.

Stitch, at the foot of the statue, pushed himself up and got out of the way. He felt more than useless as he watched the delight of his lover and his brother defiling Cabal's image.

This joy should be mine, he thought. He turned his back and glared out over the abyss, listening to the violence behind him.

After a time, Lilith sat next to Stitch, who had not moved.

"I know," she said. "Lover, I know. But I have something you may just well enjoy."

Stitch snorted a laugh.

"And what would that be? A small box for me to stand on while Cabal tries to decimate the three of us?"

"More like two and a half," Azaziel said, chuckling.

Lilith again picked up Stitch and held him in front of her face.

"You'll see," she said.

Stitch sighed for the last time.

CHAPTER 44

Cabal's meditation from his mountaintop was interrupted by a sudden sense of unrest. His eyes snapped open and he growled. He looked around him. This wasn't someone or something coming near. This was...something else. This was...

"*Blasphemy*," he said. He felt a rage build inside that he had never been aware of; a rage accompanied by another strange feeling.

Violation.

He snarled and vanished, in an instant to his home. He was looking out across the abyss when he sniffed the air and looked behind him.

Where the mighty statue of Cabal had once stood, there was only space.

And filth.

The visage of Cabal was mostly in tact, but on it's back. There were huge dents and feces covering it, especially in the face. Its giant engorged member had been broken off at the base of its shaft and crudely shoved into the statue's mouth. Cabal began to shake with anger.

He moved slowly toward the statue and then stopped.

Who would dare do this, he thought.

"Hey there," Azaziel's voice said from behind Cabal. "That looks kinda bad, don't you think? You should get a maid or something."

Cabal whirled around and snarled. The sight of an angry Cabal still gave hesitation to Azaziel, but his hate kept his feet firm.

"Bad day, *Master*?" Azaziel asked smiling.

Cabal clenched his taloned fists. A flap of wings followed from behind and he saw Lilith land. Cabal was in the center.

"I was just going to ask where your whore had gotten to," Cabal said. "What have you done?"

"Hello, Master." Lilith said, smiling. "How we have *missed* you."

"What is the meaning of this...*violation?*" Cabal demanded.

Lilith and Azaziel moved closer to each other.

"Well, it's not like we can just *call* you," Azaziel said. "We needed to get your attention."

"Well, you certainly have it now!" Cabal roared. He looked around quickly and added. "Where is Stitch?"

Lilith laughed.

"Stitch? Seriously?"

"Yes, him. Where is he? Only he would be so bold as to do this."

"Really?" Azaziel asked indignantly. "*Only* him?"

"How would a little doll do all of this?" Lilith asked pointing to the desecrated statue.

"And last I checked," Azaziel said in his most charming voice ever, "A little doll couldn't shit a pile like that on any statue's chest."

The two demons looked at each other and laughed. Cabal could not believe his eyes. They were right of course. Stitch couldn't have done it, but his mark was all over it.

"Where is he?" Cabal asked. "I will not ask again."

Lilith cleared her throat and spat at the feet of Cabal. Cabal took a step back and glared at Lilith, but she quickly pointed at the gob of spit.

"There," she said. "Look."

Cabal looked down and indeed saw what was left of the chewed up totem that had once been Stitch.

"*You* did this?" Cabal asked. "Where is his essence?"

"It'll turn up," Azaziel said, sarcastically. "A demon with no body always turns up eventually."

Cabal frowned.

"How strange you would not want him around to torment for a century or two. I'm quite surprised."

Azaziel laughed.

"Where is he going to go?" he asked. "Time is a luxury."

It was Cabal's turn to laugh.

"What makes you think you'll be able to do anything at all when he turns up?"

Azaziel stopped laughing.

"Yes, that's right. Daddy's back. And it looks like the kids have had a little party when they shouldn't have." Cabal smiled broadly at his analogy. "And now, Papa spank!"

Cabal attacked and neither Lilith nor Azaziel had ever been witness to such fury, much less been on the receiving end. Cabal darted at Lilith and grabbed her by her neck, pivoted and swung her full into Azaziel. Because both of their claws were extended, they dug into each other as they were thrown away from Cabal and landed hard on the ground. As soon as they landed, Cabal was on them again, grabbing each demon by the neck. Cabal jumped in the air and threw both demons down. Then for good measure, he landed on both of their heads. Cabal pushed himself off and backed up.

"Care to retaliate?" he mocked. "I'll wait."

Cabal didn't need to. Azaziel and Lilith launched themselves from the ground-Azaziel high and Lilith low. Cabal readied himself for the standard attack. He was almost insulted. But at the last possible moment, the attacking demons switched angles and speeds-Lilith now coming for the high attack and Azaziel from the low. Because the move was done so quickly and at the last minute, Cabal had time for nothing more than to take the full brunt of the attack. Both demons hit, picking Cabal off of his legs. As they arced skyward, Lilith bit into Cabal's neck as Azaziel bit into Cabal's upped thigh and dug his talons into his back.

The ascent quickly changed direction as they suddenly shot downward, gaining momentum as the two demons drove Cabal into the ground. The demons made a good-sized hole that Lilith and Azaziel had to scramble out of to reassemble.

The two demons, panting looked at the hole, waiting for Cabal to come out. They looked at each other, panting and confused.

"No, we couldn't-"Azaziel began to say.

"No, you didn't," Cabal said from the hole and then lightly hopped out. He didn't seem to have a scratch on him. "I just wanted to give you some false hope."

Lilith and Azaziel snarled and launched themselves at Cabal again. Cabal began to laugh. He easily swatted away Lilith then Azaziel. They landed in heaps several yards away as Cabal strode lazily toward them.

"Why are we fighting children?" he asked. "We were very much like a family once. What happened to us?"

"Should we start with you robbing us of our indifference?" Azaziel asked in agony. "Because that's where I would start."

"*Robbing* you?" Cabal's voice was filled with mock hurt. "I elevated the three of you above all others. There are no other demons like you in existence. And you attack me for it?"

"Why did you give us human emotions?" Lilith asked angrily. "Because that's not elevation."

Cabal laughed.

"I didn't give you *all* of the emotions," he said, chuckling. "Just enough to torment you all."

He raised a hand and Lilith's body rose off of the ground.

"Let's take you for instance," Cabal said. "If you were a regular old garden variety demon, you wouldn't appreciate this." And as he said 'this,' her arms were ripped from her body. Lilith roared in agony. Azaziel glared at Cabal and pushed himself up.

"Now, now Azaziel. Calm down. You're next." Cabal said and raised another hand, levitating Azaziel. Suspended in the air, Azaziel fought to free himself to no avail.

"And you, little mister third wheel," Cabal said smiling. "What would you appreciate? More limbs ripped from dear sweet Lilith?"

"Damn you Cabal," Azaziel said furiously.

"That's right! You've finally called me by name!" Cabal said proudly. "Your anger makes you complete. Care to join me?"

Azaziel looked at Lilith, still suspended in the air, but unmoving save for the lifeblood pouring out of her shoulders.

"Fix her and we'll talk," Azaziel said.

"A demand? That's funny. How about this instead?" With that, Lilith's wings were ripped from her back, shooting black blood in an arc behind her. She remained unresponsive. Azaziel growled with anger and tried again to free himself.

Cabal laughed.

"The best part is, I'm not even going to touch you. You're just going to watch this until I get good and bored. And really, she ought to be awake for this, don't you?"

He snapped his fingers and Lilith was awake and began to scream and scream in agony.

"This is called learning a lesson, children." Cabal said, straightening up. "One that will remain with you for some time. Any questions?"

"Just one," said the voice behind Cabal. "Are you ready for *your* lesson?"

Before he could turn or even process the thought, two taloned hands burst through Cabal's chest and ripped open his entire front torso. Entrails and blood spilled out across the ground in front of him. Lilith and Azaziel were dropped and landed violently. Lilith managed to pass out again, but Azaziel was at full attention and watched.

Cabal was still standing but was also trying to hold his insides together. He was failing. The two taloned hands pulled back through Cabal's chest.

Cabal turned his head and watched the figure from behind move to the front.

"I know, I know. From behind is a coward's way. But it sure is easy and fun."

"Stitch," Cabal said.

"*Wrong*. I am Benial." said the demon and spread his wings and arms. "Lilith kept my body hid for my eventual return it seems."

Cabal's legs buckled and he landed on his knees.

"She kept your body?" Cabal spat. "Why would she have done that?"

Benial sighed and then laughed.

244

"Probably because *you* gave her emotions, you jagoff."

"You can't kill me," Cabal said weakly, trying to pick up his insides and push them back in. Azaziel crawled over to Cabal's guts and began to throw them in different directions away from Cabal.

"Good idea, brother." Benial said, kicking some guts out of Cabal's reach. Cabal tried to roar in anger but it was fading.

"How can you do this to me?" Cabal asked. "I am *Cabal!*"

Benial grabbed Cabal by the neck. He pulled Cabal close to his snarling face.

"We can do this because we are demons," Benial said. "Not experiments or toys. *Demons*. We can do this because no matter what you did to us, this is what we are. And it is our *pleasure."*

Benial ripped Cabal's head from his body and slammed it into the ground. The body shook and fell over to one side. Benial stood there for a moment looking at the torn body of Cabal.

He allowed himself a small smile. It actually felt good to smile again.

"He's not dead," Azaziel said.

"I know," Benial said. "That's why I'm glad Lilith didn't totally destroy this,"

Benial bent down and picked up the shredded and spit covered totem he used to occupy.

"If you think he's pissed now, little brother, wait until he wears this." Benial said and looked at Azaziel.

Azaziel stood up and kicked a chunk of Cabal's insides. He and Benial turned to look at Lilith, who was still out.

"Let's take care of Lilith," Benial said, moving towards her.

Azaziel didn't move.

"I still hate you," he said. Benial stopped and turned.

"I know you do," Benial said. "I'd expect nothing less than that from you."

The two demons looked at each other for a long time until finally, Azaziel opened his wings and flew away. He nodded at Benial.

"Until next time," he said and flew up to the skyline.

Benial watched him until he was out of sight and then looked down at Lilith. She was still alive and no longer bleeding. Her wounds had already begun to heal but she'd need rest if the reattachment of her limbs were going to work.

Benial looked at the small totem that was once called Stitch. He carefully unfolded it in his taloned hand. He smiled again, knowing it wouldn't be easy to find the essence of Cabal and when he did, he would be furious. But, it would be worth it just to see him trapped in the little doll.

He gathered Lilith's arms and wings and reattached them as best he could. Then, he picked her up to carry her somewhere to heal. Her eyes fluttered open for a moment and he couldn't tell if she smiled or sneered at him. He decided that either was fine with him and he spread his wings out and flew into the air.

CHAPTER 45

Marty woke up on the floor in Kat's living room just before the light of the new day could creep into the house. He wasn't sure how he'd managed to fall asleep, but he did. He checked himself and his surroundings to make sure it was in fact, still real. He looked and saw Bruce still on the couch, asleep and snoring loudly.

He heard movement in the kitchen and stood up. There he saw Kat, making a pot of coffee and smoking. She saw Marty and blew out smoke.

"Did I wake you?" she asked, concerned. "Didn't mean to. I had enough sleep for one night."

"Bad dreams?" Marty asked.

She slumped.

"*No* dreams. That's really odd for me because I always have really vivid dreams."

Marty slowly walked into the kitchen.

"Coffee's almost done," Kat said and looked at the boy. "Although I think you might be a bit young for coffee. And you hate vanilla anyway."

"I'm sixteen. Seventeen in two months."

"Well whoopity do," Kat said, smirking. "You're still too young. Which reminds me. How are you getting home?"

"I hadn't thought about home yet," he said. "Not sure I even have one anymore. Guess I'll call my uncle later to see if I've been tossed out."

Kat frowned.

"That doesn't seem right. You've been through enough. I'll talk to him."

Marty laughed.

"And tell him what?"

Kat smiled.

"I don't know. I'll put Bruce on the phone with him. He's been ridden by a hot demon mama. He knows stuff."

Marty smiled. Kat went to take a drag off of her cigarette but stopped.

"He said if we were still alive in the morning, then he was ok." She said. "And if he's ok, I guess we are too."

She took the cigarette and tossed it in the sink.

"Wow, did you just quit?" Marty asked?

Kat laughed again.

"Christ *no*," she said. "I'll be lighting up again in an hour, but it seemed like the thing to do."

Marty smiled.

Kat said, "In a little bit, we're gonna go and get some stuff for breakfast. I got two guys in this place for now, and I need a milkshake."

"That sounds good actually," Marty said. "I like any and all milkshakes."

"Even Neapolitan?" Kat asked.

Marty looked at her oddly.

"I don't think I've ever had one." Marty said.

Kat smiled.

"You will today, kid."

As they stood in the kitchen, the smallest beam of sunlight began to shine through the curtains of the window in Kat's living room. Kat thought that unattended, the little beam of light would eventually hit Bruce right in his sleeping face. She thought about closing the curtain for a moment, but decided against it. There had been enough darkness. Maybe what was needed was a little light.

It would also annoy the hell out of Bruce and that made her smile.

ACKNOWLEDGEMENTS

These eleven people were the original beta readers for this book. I thank you all yet again!

Heidi Halbig, Rochelle Delgado, Lori D'Agostino Boremoeo, Noelle Boehme, Erin O'Marra-Anderson, Lou Tambone, Tom Pecosh, Jesse Saxon, Sharon Martino (rest in peace,) Karen Burnish, and Melissa Fox-Binder. Your feedback and encouragement was invaluable.

Additional thanks to Kristen Simyak for my second favorite sentence in the book. Thanks Rona Walter, Jon Towers, Beth Anne Macdonald, Gregory Schmidt, Chuck Marbuger, Anthony Roswick, David Went, Melanie Friedrich, Tabitha Stevenson, Bret Bouriseau, Becky Anderson, Mike Miles, Donna Kurth, Hannah Storey, C Bryan Brown, Rebecca Hardesty Cupples, Lydia Peever, Paul Michael Anderson, Jessica McHugh, KT Jayne, Georgina Morales, J David Anderson, Chelsea "Sluggo" Cefalu, Kenneth Cain, Emma Ennis, Brady Allen, Gary Braunbeck, Brian Dobbins, Rose Blackthorn, Stephanie Wytovich, Rich Bottles Jr., Tim Waggoner, Lucy Snyder, Meagan Fisher, and Daniel Knauf.

A very special thanks to Gary Lee "Hollywood" Vincent. You are a rare guy in this business. More importantly, you're just a straight up good guy. Thank you for your constant support and friendship.

Special thanks to Eric and Stephanie Beebe, and Elizabeth Jenike, the original editor.

Tremendous thanks to Dan Foytik for pretty much everything. Extra special thanks to Pippa Bailey and Myk Pilgrim for all their help and support.

Now, two more very important thank yous…

Sherri Reuther-Campbell was my boss at Homewood Cemetery. She remains a great friend, and in the three years I worked for her, a huge part of the story was developed there (I was working—I swear!). It remains the best job I ever had, and she remains the best boss I've ever had. I am convinced that this novel would not exist without you. Thanks for hiring me, Sher.

And thanks to my wife Deb, my constant first reader. You already know what I want to say. I'll tell you later again too, in person. Until then, I love you.

Nelson W Pyles

ABOUT THE AUTHOR

Nelson W Pyles is a novelist and voice actor from Boonton, New Jersey. His work has appeared alongside Harlan Ellison, Jack Ketchum, and F. Paul Wilson. He created The Wicked Library podcast where remains the voice of The Librarian and has written episodes for its sister podcast, The Lift. His novel SPIDERS IN THE DAFFODILS and collection of short stories EVERYTHING HERE IS A NIGHTMARE are both available through Burning Bulb Publishing. He currently lives in Pittsburgh PA, the zombie capital of the world. Find him online at www.facebook.com/nelson.pyles

SPIDERS IN THE DAFFODILS
An American Horror Western

Tom Wall and Veronique were two different folks from two different walks of life. He was a former Texas Ranger turned bounty hunter.

She was a monster.

It was only a matter of time before they fell in love.

After a life filled with adventure and danger, the two settle down together in Corpus Christi to start a family and a new future. But, Veronique's past comes calling in the form of a monster named Stephan Trask He tears a violent path through the state of Texas leaving death and destruction in his wake. As this monster with a human face gets closer, the danger grows as Tom and Veronique's young daughter, Josephine, begins to show signs of the emerging monster within her.

And all the while, the spiders begin to gather in the daffodils...

Burning Bulb
PUBLISHING

EVERYTHING HERE IS A NIGHTMARE
Collected Works Vol 1.

"Pyles makes it look easy. His characters come instantly alive with the cocksure verve and swagger of rock stars."
- Daniel Knauf, creator of HBO's "Carnivale,"
Executive Producer/Writer, ABC's "The Blacklist."

The critically acclaimed author of Demons, Dolls and Milkshakes returns with fifteen tales of horror and suspense with Everything Here is a Nightmare.

From zombies in the old west, to a young boy tempted by the Devil. From vampires with romantic longing, to an abandoned lighthouse haunted by vengeful spirits. From a serial killer getting unholy justice, to a haunted English race car, Nelson W Pyles invites you to explore a landscape of fear, suspense and horror.

Take his hand and hold on tight. Remember that whatever you find here, whatever you see, no matter what you might think it could be... know this: Everything Here is a Nightmare.

Burning Bulb
PUBLISHING

www.ingramcontent.com/pod-product-compliance
Lightning Source LLC
Chambersburg PA
CBHW060414180626
46817CB00007B/2583

9 781948 278096